Silver Moon Readers Service
c/o DS Sales Ltd.
PO Box 1100 London N21 2WQ

Silver Moon Books Inc
PO Box 1614 New York NY 10156

Distributed to the trade throughout North America by
LPC Group, 1436 West Randolph Street, Chicago, IL 60607
(800) 826-4330

SLAVEGIRL FROM SUBURBIA

by

MARK STEWART

This is fiction - In real life always practise safe sex!

SLAVEGIRL FROM SUBURBIA by Mark Slade

1 Rachel's Awakening

Lying naked on her bed, Rachel Saunders relished the burning soreness around her waist and wrists, and the feel of the soft dressing gown cord pressing into the slight swell of her trim belly. Suddenly she blushed; and forced aside a moment of guilt. As her mother would have said, Rachel had been naughty; although that had been when she was a girl and her mother had caught her in the act of masturbating.

And now? Well, yes, Rachel had been masturbating, but living alone as she did, she could carry her fantasies a bit further. And had she progressed some! For months now Rachel had been livening up her lonely sex-life with ever increasing bouts of wild masturbation, and delicious sessions of experimental DIY bondage; imagining that she was a captive, a slavegirl subject to the will and demands of her imaginary, sadistic potentate.

The very first time she had tried it she had found it awkward; difficult even, to tie herself up, but definitely exhilarating. Over the weeks though, she had got used to the contortions she needed to perform to bind herself, and had worked out how best to weave the silken cord about her naked body; to simulate being bound. She had to be naked. That had soon become apparent to her. It was the best way to enjoy her make-believe world of torture, masochism and slavery.

She had discovered that the best way, for her, was to secure a noose around her waist, with the slip-knot in the small of her back. Once the knot was in position, she could pull the free end forwards, between her shapely buttocks, to slip it underneath the bight, across her stomach. Then, simply by pulling downwards towards her thrusting love-mound, the cord would dig into her sex-lips, starting her juices flowing. Once aroused, she could begin her masturbation, forcing her fingers deep into her sex, thrusting aside the cord, causing an even deeper thrill as she virtually assaulted herself, imagining she had been stripped and tied against her will, to be used as a plaything by a masterful man. So the thoughts ran, wild, sensual and erotic, as she heightened the pleasure, of her masturbation.

Now, the bight of the cord was still between her thighs; looser, but still gripped into her warm, swollen labia. Her mind was still full of the erotic images she had conjured up over the last few minutes. She was still breathing heavily, and the final throes of her self-induced orgasm were tingling through her body. She had only just let go the cord, allowing it to slacken, but with a deep contented sigh she took the loose end once more and pulled it tight, so it slid back between her sex-lips. She lifted her hips clear of the bed; pulled the cord even tighter, gasping as she relished the burn around her waist; relished the shivers of delight running through her body as the cord dug into her hot throbbing sex cleavage.

Rachel moaned and pulled the cord back down, alongside her fingers, now coated with her warm, wet, sticky juices. She ground her silken, thighs together, letting out a gasp of ecstasy as she felt the cord dig even deeper into her bulging, eager sex-lips. All the while, she was wriggling her pelvis against the harsh stricture of the cord, and with another gasp of pleasure she pushed her fingers past the binding, delving ever deeper into herself. She let out another sigh as the familiar tingling spread through her crotch and her stomach. She wanted more of it, but there wasn't really time. Regretfully, she let go the cord and lay back for a moment, still allowing her hands to flutter about her genitals, playing gently with her swollen clitoris, her palm rubbing hard into her frizz of velvety blonde pubic hairs.

Then more guilt flooded over her, causing her to pause. She loosed the cord then frowned, allowing her lustful feelings to subside. As always after a session, she tried to work out why she had become so preoccupied with it all. It had started a few months before. She had overheard two men talking in the restaurant of the private health-club where she worked as a Personal Fitness Instructor. She knew the one man, Charles Stone, fairly well. In fact, when he had joined the club, Rachel had been allocated to give him his fitness assessment, and subsequently, he had specifically paid for her to give him a course of personal supervision.

Stone was a good bit older than Rachel, but he was a decidedly attractive man. The attraction had grown, as she had got used to hearing his deep, rumbling voice and surprisingly she had begun to relish his slightly demanding manner. Right from the start, though, Rachel had been obliged to suppress nervous tremors of desire as she had savoured the delightful sight of his surprisingly supple muscles, rippling beneath his deep even sun-tan.

Even so, on the day Rachel had been eavesdropping, Stone had managed to cause a flutter of nervous apprehension in her stomach, as she'd realised what he'd been saying. Perhaps he hadn't realised how far his voice carried. Or had he meant her to hear? That didn't matter. The topic of conversation had frightened her a little, but it had also aroused her curiosity.

The only customers in the restaurant that morning, the two men had been talking about sex.

There was nothing unusual in that; except they had been discussing kinky sex. Sadism and Masochism. S&M, they called it didn't they? Then, as the conversation went on, she had realised she wasn't as shocked as she ought to have been.

In fact their talk of men dominating females; of women kneeling before them and even, God forbid, being whipped and chained, had gradually fired her curiosity. After all, she supposed, there had to be a certain amount of Masochism in anyone who suffered, as she did, merely to keep fit, even if they didn't acknowledge it. As for herself, she had often wondered if there was anything for her in the S&M scene...

It was just a few days later that she saw Charles Stone again, in the local bookstore. He was been standing near to the adult section, flicking through a paper-back. Rachel was a few yards away, but she could see the title - 'The Master's Whip.' Strangely, her pulse quickened as she could also make out the picture of the undraped, collared blonde on the front cover.

A little flustered, she moved away to walk around the store. Casually she examined other shelves, but kept one eye on Stone. Finally, he made his purchase. Once he had gone, Rachel went over to the shelf, with her heart thumping in anticipation. There were a number of copies of 'The Master's Whip.' She felt the embarrassed guilt stealing over her as she took one of the slim volumes down and scanned the first few paragraphs. It was immediately clear, the book was written with men in mind; a certain type of man. The theme was quite explicit. Male domination of young, attractive women.

The words leapt off the page almost and she actually felt herself getting wet; sucked in a gasp of surprise as her labia began to swell. God! She could almost smell herself! She swallowed nervously, realising how much she was fascinated. Even by the first few paragraphs. They neatly foreshadowed the titillation to follow and Rachel wondered if she dare actually buy the book. She certainly wanted to know what was to happen to Natalie, the slavegirl heroine. The character was naked within the first few sentences and if the first chapter was anything to go by, she was going to endure a lot more suffering. Resisting the temptation to read Chapter two, Rachel decided. She would buy the book. Still nervous, with her pulses thumping, she went across to the pay point.

Of course, it had to be a young man at the till. He hadn't taken much notice as he'd collected her money, rung up the purchase and wrapped the book. There was just the slightest hint of a knowing smile as he pressed the receipt into her hand. "Thank you for your custom Miss. Come again."

Had he put an inflexion in the word 'come'?

Rachel thought he had.

Cheek! Should she complain?

But she couldn't. Not without increasing her discomfiture. Besides, the man might well have been genuine, thinking of her future custom.

Cheeks burning, her mind in a flurry of embarrassment, she virtually fled from the shop, the book clutched to her chest as she tried to slow her pulse and lose herself in the crowds.

Then, strangely, she realised that she had enjoyed the stress of the situation. Not so much the thrill of 'danger', but more the slight sense of suffering; of being at the mercy of that young man, should he have chosen to tease her openly. The suffering was mental of course, but she knew she had not objected to that. She had even wondered what it would be like to be alone with the man and what it would feel like if he had spanked her. Then the young man's image was pushed aside by the thought of Charles Stone. Now there was a man who would really know... Wouldn't he?

After reading the book, Rachel couldn't resist buying more, not from the shop, but by mail order, from the address that had been in the back of the book. In fact, by now, she was becoming deeply interested in the subject of Sado-Masochism. She soon found herself gazing at a long length of dressing-gown cord she had in her workbox. There was also a leather belt hanging in her wardrobe, and she had taken to caressing the thin strip of leather, smelling it even, wondering what it would feel like, on her flesh. It had been but a short step to actually experimenting and one sunny afternoon, she had gone to her bedroom, determined to enjoy the thrill of the sort of thing she had read about, in those books.

She still recalled that first time.

Awkwardly, she had wrapped the cord about her naked hips, threading it between her thighs, pulling it tight, so it was cutting into her labia. It had really turned her on. In moments she had abandoned herself to the insistent massage of her hand as, with the other hand, she lashed the belt around her hips, so it curled into her soft rounded buttocks, stinging as it landed. The pain increased her enjoyment beyond imagining; the burning friction of the cord stimulated her arousal. Then, swinging wildly with the belt, she had begun to whip herself with increasing vigour, gasping as her skin shivered into goose-bumps in response to the strangely erotic sensation of the leather cutting into her skin. Soon she was gasping out loudly each time the leather stung her buttocks and thighs as the free end curled itself around her body and with her other hand, she invaded herself, her fingers thrusting deeply into her sex-hole.

Now, Rachel breathed a contented sigh as she recalled that first time. It had been wonderful, but it wasn't easy, trying to whip yourself with a leather belt. Every now and then, the end of the belt had caught her out when, in her frenzy, she had given herself a wilder blow and the flying tip flicked right around her hips, to sting into her groin, causing her to yelp as it cut into her moist swollen sex, aggravating her throbbing clitoris. But that had made her enjoy the experience even more, Yes, it had hurt, but there was a definite sense of satisfaction from the pain, even after her orgasms had abated.

The only disappointing part of the whole procedure was

the fact that she couldn't tie herself properly. Only someone else could do that. Only then, could she know the full thrill of bondage; really experience what it would be like to be under the control of a dominating man; which she knew was what she really wanted.

Lately, she had been thinking of Charles Stone. A lot. Probably more than was really good for her? That didn't matter. It was nice to fantasise in her sessions that it was Charles who was her imagined Master.

Yes!

Her Master!

That was how all the girls in the books referred to their tormentors, and now she savoured the word, conjuring up a picture of him. 'Oh! Master Charles!' She breathed to herself, savouring the thought of him for a moment. Then, she sighed and pulled the cord aside to get up off the bed. She couldn't indulge any more today. She was due at work the day after tomorrow and, whilst she hadn't used the belt on herself today, the rope burns would be imprinted in her skin for a day or so and she dared not go into work with the evidence still showing.

A little sad that she couldn't indulge herself until the weekend, she sauntered into the bathroom and filled the bath. As she waited, she began to wonder. Should she make a suggestion to Charles Stone? No. Perhaps not. Better to start with just giving him a normal come on. She knew him well enough to know he would respond favourably. She had caught him looking at her legs before.

She didn't mind that of course and she knew he would be keen for sex.

But when she got around to the subject of S&M, would he run away?

She didn't think so.

There was a satisfied smile on her face, as she tested the

bath-water.

2 - Abducted

Rachel knew she was breaking 'Toners' Health Club rules. For safety reasons, she shouldn't be swimming in the pool, whilst alone in the place.

But what the Hell!

If anything happened, that would be it. Who would be able to punish her then?

So she was swimming. Alone.

Tonight she was duty attendant and she had seen the last of the club members off the premises ten minutes ago. Besides which, every one of the staff knew it went on; they all did it. It was just that no one ever mentioned it. So now was a chance for a 'skinny-dip'; a nice, long, nude swim before she covered the pool and locked up for the night.

For some strange reason, nude swimming was always far more sensuous than swimming in a costume. So Rachel was enjoying herself; relishing the feel of the warm water flowing past her nakedness, brushing her like a satin cloak as she slipped quietly and expertly along the length of the pool. Nude swimming? Sensuous did she say? She rolled over languorously a couple of times, and let out a groan of pleasure. No! Sensuous was the wrong word. It was sexy! And it turned her on. Almost automatically, her thoughts turned to Charles Stone and she paused, treading water for a moment. Then she hugged herself, allowed her hands to wander over her delicious form before rolling onto her back to start a slow, backstroke.

High above her, the security video camera silently tracked

her as she swam.

In the stuffy quiet of the security control room, Elizabeth Stone stared into the light from the fourteen inch monitor screen as she watched the image of the naked girl scything through the water. Her mouth turned down in a distasteful grimace, then she turned to the tall hugely obese man standing just beside her swivel-chair, "Well Ernst, Charles and I were right. Yes?"

Deep in his fleshy cheeks, Ernst Hartman's narrow eyes glittered and his pudgy features worked into the grimace he used for a smile. He ran a hand over his bald head and wiped sweat from where it trickled over his brow. "She's good meat, Mrs. Stone. Definitely the type, Sheik Abbas likes. You and Mr. Stone should make some serious cash from her hide."

The woman shrugged. "Well this time, I have to act independently." Her lips tightened. "My precious bloody husband is getting to be a little too fond of her." She looked at the monitor, just as Rachel was climbing out of the water, and walking out of the field of view. She changed over cameras, in time to see Rachel slipping into the Jacuzzi. Elizabeth Stone gave a sarcastic smile. "Although, as you pointed out Ernst, I can see what attracts him so."

Hartman nodded his agreement, then shrugged. "Yeah, well. A slavegirl's looks don't cut any slack with Sheik Abbas. He uses the sluts as he sees fit." He nodded towards the screen. "This little mare will be in the stables, almost before she knows what's going on." His smile became colder and he licked his lips. "She's going to look great, harnessed to a trotting-gig." He stroked his jaw. "Or maybe the Sheik will have her saddled." He chuckled then. "And with long hair like that, who'd need reins?"

"Personally, I couldn't care less." Elizabeth Stone shrugged her elegant shoulders. "I just want her out of the way." She looked up at Hartman. "I'm getting a little tired of waiting for Charles to decide the girl is ready for trade."

Hartman chuckled. "This time, Mrs. Stone, it's just you getting paid." He tapped the monitor screen with his fingernail, indicating the image of Rachel, who was now stretched out in the bubbling water. "Money on the hoof."

"Exactly Ernst. Money on the Hoof!" Elizabeth Stone's smile glittered as she looked at him again. "The girl will really be out of the picture Ernst?"

Hartman nodded and snapping his fingers said. "Just like that!"

Elizabeth Stone smiled icily. "The lady vanishes, eh?"

"Poof! Gone!" He laughed.

Another cold smile from the woman. "Next time, perhaps Charles will keep in mind why we acquire these girls in the first place."

Hartman grinned lazily, and nodded towards the screen again. "If your husband's taste in women doesn't alter, we can accommodate all the girls you can find." His ugly features twisted into a grimace of a smile. "Seems we got a regular source of supply." He paused. "So long as you don't give up." He grinned slightly.

"Give up?" The woman shook her head. "Why should we? The white-slave trade is lucrative, Charles enjoys money." She glanced up, grinning. "Although, I shall have to dissuade him from hanging onto them for longer than necessary."

Hartman chuckled, then pointed to the monitor again. "So we take her now Mrs. Stone?"

She nodded. "Right now Ernst."

Hartman leaned closer to the monitor as the girl rolled over onto her front, ducking her head under the bubbling water. "You're the boss Mrs. Stone."

"Sheik Abbas is the real boss, Ernst." She pursed her lips.

"But I see what you mean." She stood up and pointed to the security recording apparatus. "We had better switch this thing off. No sense in leaving any evidence of what we are about to do."

Hartman, grinned. "Too true!" Leaning over towards the control panel, he switched off the video recorder.

Hartman and the woman soft-footed into the pool area, to stand at each side of the Jacuzzi.

Rachel was completely unaware of their presence. Her eyes were closed and she was laying right back in the bubbling foam. Still with her eyes closed, she raised her arms and rested them on the tiled surround of the bath. She half-lifted herself from the water, her lithe body rising easily, bending backwards as she stretched, luxuriously, still completely unaware of the watchers. Her ample, well-formed breasts were pushed upwards and outwards, her nipples standing proud and hard against the soft flesh as she stretched her arms upwards and outwards. She gave out a relaxed sigh, opened her eyes, and saw them.

Rachel's heart missed and she drew in a shocked breath.

Elizabeth Stone was standing right in front of her, as large as truth, her hands hidden behind her shapely hips, her tight fitting, black-satin dress gleaming in the soft glow of the pool lights. She looked imperious, as she rocked back and forth slightly on her heels.

Rachel felt her mind lurch. Elizabeth Stone! What was she doing here? Common sense returned briefly. Clearly the woman wasn't here on a social visit. Rachel groaned to herself. She must have found out about her and Charles. And now, she was here; looking as if she owned the whole place and there would be a scene. Rachel's hands raised to cover her breasts and with an embarrassed "Damn!" she dropped back into the water, sinking to her chin. "What are you doing here?" She asked, staring up at Elizabeth Stone. Rachel noticed the hard gleam in the woman's eyes and suddenly her mind filled with apprehension.

The woman shrugged. "I think it's you who should be answering that question." She gave Rachel a sly smile. "You're breaking Club Rules. You could lose your job."

Rachel frowned, and moved back from the pool edge. Her heart was beginning to race as she tried to sort her confused thoughts. "It isn't really any of your business," she said. "Now, if you want to speak to me, we can do it in the dressing rooms. So, I'd like to get out and dress, if you don't mind."

Contemptuously, Elizabeth Stone looked down at Rachel. "You can get out of the water, but as for clothes -" She paused and sneer temporarily deformed her lovely mouth. "You won't need clothes where you are going." She chuckled slightly, then gave Rachel another withering glance. "Although, I don't relish seeing your naked body, knowing my husband has been pawing your oh so silky young flesh."

Anger glowed in Rachel's face, but it was mixed with not a little fear. But to hell with the Stone woman. Rachel knew she didn't have to stand for this. She stared defiantly at the woman. "I'm not going to row with you, like some common tart!"

"Why not! That's precisely what you are!"

Rachel ignored the jibe. "Will you please leave!" Rachel tried to sound authoritative. "You have no right to be here at all."

"Oh I have every right. As one of the Board of Directors, I can come and go more or less as I please."

That stopped Rachel for a moment and she frowned. "You're on the Board of Directors?"

"Very much so. I am also a major shareholder and a good friend of the owner of 'Toners Health Clubs.' Her voice hardened. "Now! Out of the water and come here. AT ONCE!"

Rachel blinked, as indignation rose again. Who the hell did

woman think she was? Director she might be, but she wasn't going to get away with talking to her like that. She glared at the woman. "When you move aside, I'll get out!"

Elizabeth Stone sighed, then brought her hands from, behind her back.

Rachel's eyes widened in fear, as she saw the vicious looking quirt that Elizabeth Stone was holding in her hands. Rachel could see this instrument was no toy. It was the real thing; and real in its threat of the terrible pain it would inflict. The quirt was made of made of plaited leather and its thin end was split into four short tails, each fitted with a shining metal tip. Rachel flinched as the woman snapped the quirt in the air.

That was when Rachel became aware of the ugly, grossly overweight man, who had appeared quietly from the concealment of the alcove leading to the dressing rooms. He was dressed in training trousers and a tank-top. In his hand he held a long pole, with a loop at the end. Rather like an extended, dog-catcher's lead. Suddenly, Rachel's heart was hammering as she felt threatened again. What the hell was gong on?

The grotesque man stood at the edge of the Jacuzzi with a confident smile twisting his already ugly face into an impression of a gargoyle.

Elizabeth Stone ran the quirt slowly through her fingers and spoke slowly. "If you really insist on staying in the water, then, that's all right by us." She nodded towards the man. "This is Ernst Hartman. Allow him to introduce you to a friend of his."

The man's smile suddenly became colder and his eyes gleamed cruelly. He dipped the long rod into the water.

Rachel saw the rubber handle in the man's hand and noticed his finger curling around a switch. Suddenly she knew! The pole was an electric cattle-prod. Panicking now, oblivious of her nakedness, she made to get out of the water. She was far too late. Suddenly she was in the grip of a cramping, burning embrace as the water became live. She screamed out, the pain causing her to arch out of the water, her eyes popping and the cords in her neck standing out like thick string She flopped back into the hot, foaming water, gasping and spluttering. A moment's respite then another jolt hit her, shredding her nerve ends, slamming her from all sides, again forcing her to arch backwards, almost clear of the surface.

"Now bitch!" Hartman growled, pointing to the swimming pool. "Back into the water and swim." He gave her another brief jolt from the goad. "And move your arse!"

Still spluttering, trying to get her breath Rachel climbed out of the Jacuzzi. She didn't know exactly what was going on, but she knew what would happen if she didn't do as this slug told her. Trembling with fright she made to stand up, but suddenly she was on fire again, as another jolt of electricity shredded her nerve ends. The man ignored Rachel's wail of agony and grabbed her hair, pulling her head backwards. He bawled into her frightened face. "On your knees bitch!" He shook her head until she thought it would fall off. "Slaves don't stand unless they are told to!"

Rachel didn't understand. What did he mean? Slaves? The man must be mad; who did he think he was? She shook her head and made to speak, but all she did was scream as she heard a whooshing noise, followed instantly by a line of red-hot pain across her buttocks, as the quirt landed on her unprotected flesh. Her scream echoed around the pool area and she dropped to the floor, cowering, knowing she had just been whipped by Elizabeth Stone.

Hartman merely grunted, fisted Rachel's hair again and dragged her back to her knees. "Crawl to the pool, slut, or it's more pain!"

Clenching and unclenching her buttocks, trying to ease the

agony from the red-hot wheat across her bottom, Rachel nodded; knowing she should obey them, or be badly injured. Glancing fearfully upwards at the awful creature, she crawled towards the edge of the pool, her body shaking with terror.

Elizabeth Stone screamed out: "Move your dirty little arse!" The quirt landed again, this time across Rachel's shoulders.

Frantic now, Rachel scrabbled toward the edge of the pool and jumped in, almost sighing with the relief as the cool water soothed her shoulders and buttocks. Immediately she started a crawl to the far end, noticing that Hartman, was walking up the pool edge, keeping pace with her. She had just one chance. If she could reach the steps, she might get clear of the water before he gave her another jolt of that thing! Then she could run.

Run? Run where?

That didn't matter. She had to get away from this mad pair. Elizabeth Stone was clearly in control and had every reason to torment her; kill her even. If not that, maybe even help the man rape her. And who would hear her scream? No one, that's who! Still in panic, Rachel fairly ripped through the water. Almost before she realised it, she was on the far steps and climbing out. On the top step, with the water just up to her ankles, she stepped towards the tiled surround. That was when another jolt of power hit her and screaming in agony she dropped backwards into the water.

Hartman glowered at her as she floundered, looking up at him. He snarled. "I said for you to swim, slut!" He pointed towards the other end again. "Now get back in. Swim down there, climb out and kneel in front of Mrs. Stone!"

Rachel filled with indignant anger. "What did you say!" Then, suddenly, another savage jolt of current ripped through her body and she screamed, arching out of the water again. Arms flailing, thrashing about, Rachel struggled to stay afloat.

"You heard me slut!" Hartman said. "Now, do it!"

"I'll do no such thing -"

Another jolt from the goad, and she threshed about in the water, gasping, spluttering, trying to hold onto consciousness. Then, recovering, she shouted at him. "Who the hell do you think you are!"

"The one with the goad!" He laughed and dipped the thing into the water again.

Another surge of power gripped her body, not so strong this time. But finally Rachel accepted that she had to swim.

She swam, more awkwardly now. She was aware of a burning soreness all over her body, as her nerve ends protested at the treatment they had received from Hartman's goad. She started to swim towards the waiting Elizabeth Stone. She suddenly realised she was sobbing, as fear began to take hold of her. What were they going to do to her?

Hartman gave her no more of the goad, being content to walk along, keeping pace with her, gazing down with an arrogant sneer on his face; as though knowing she would obey him.

They had reached the shallow end again and Hartman grinned as Rachel, trembling, and sobbing, made her painful way up the steps. Then Hartman gave a whistle of admiration, as he took in the delightful view of Rachel's shapely form, as she emerged; her hips and buttocks moving in a natural wiggle as she gained the tiled surround and walked towards Elizabeth Stone.

Hartman's smile became cold as he stepped towards Rachel. His manner changed, abruptly. "I just told you slut! Now, on your knees and crawl!"

Rachel stopped and fury coloured her cheeks, staring at Hartman. "I will NOT! Damn you!" She turned her fury on Elizabeth Stone. "Now get out of my way!"

Then she was suddenly choking as Hartman lifted the goad

and dropped the noose around her neck. "You heard what I said, slut!" Hartman snapped at her, giving Rachel yet another jolt of the goad, for good measure and slamming her to the floor.

Rolling on the wet tiles in agony, fighting for her breath, Rachel tried to get her fingers beneath the ligature, but she was wasting her time. Then to settle the issue, there was another jolt from the goad, which made her think her head would fall off. Screaming out, she scrabbled about the wet slippery surface, until finally she was able to get to her knees. Gasping, head down, held there by Hartman's dog-noose, she stilled herself. Her long, blonde hair was hanging down; her energy leaking away, as though she was a squeezed sponge. As the pain subsided, she placed her palms flat on the tiled floor, then jumped slightly as she felt a tiny needle-jab in her bottom. Immediately, she felt slightly woozy and she shook her head, trying to clear her mind.

Then Hartman's voice again. "Crawl over to Mrs. Stone, like you were told." He pushed down on the pole again, forcing Rachel's head lower still.

Rachel tried to turn her head to look at Hartman. She would be damned if she would do this. They couldn't get away with treating her this way. The light-headed feeling increased, and Rachel knew, much as she might want to resist, she wouldn't be able to do so.

"You should learn to move your arse, slut!" Hartman snarled again, pushing her head right down to the floor.

Rachel's heart was racing now as she realised that the demanding tone in his voice brooked no argument. He seemed as if he was talking to an animal, and not expecting to be disobeyed. Who the hell did he think he was? She felt her heart miss, and, in bewilderment, she found herself experiencing a nervous tremor in her belly. Not unpleasant; something like the feeling she had when she was at home, amusing herself with her make-believe world of bondage; or when she was with Charles, in his sumptuous bedroom, allowing him to whip her; gently with the soft curtain cord, they used to liven up their sexy, bondage sessions. Then she groaned to herself. That had been play. This was real; so was the goad and the terrible quirt that Elizabeth Stone still held.

Rachel was suddenly in a strange, trance-like state. She knew she wanted to laugh at this huge bully, yet she was completely unable to find the strength of will to resist. Unbelievably, Rachel found herself obeying and, submissively, she began to crawl towards Elizabeth Stone, to stop at her feet, looking up at the woman.

Hartman had started to undress himself, and was dropping his trousers to one side.

Knowing, she had been drugged, Rachel began to feel her mind detaching itself from reality. She knew what was coming, yet whilst able to move, otherwise she felt powerless to resist them.

Hartman kicked off his shoes and pulled off his socks. Standing feet apart, he went on. "Now, come to me! Kiss my feet!"

Even in her drugged state Rachel found some rebellion. "I'll be damned -" She broke off and screeched out with agony as the leather burned into the backs of her thighs and she tried to clasp the hurt. Again the leather cut into her, across the top of her buttocks this time. With a tortured wail, Rachel crouched to the floor. She needed no further bidding. She couldn't stand any more of the lash. With the noose still tight about her neck, she moved as quickly as she could, scratching her way across the tiles, reaching for Hartman's feet. Regardless of the degradation, she felt, she began to paw and kiss at the man's feet.

Hartman then released the noose from Rachel's neck, cast the fearsome instrument aside and took the quirt from Elizabeth Stone. He pushed Rachel away, whilst he slipped his underpants down and stepped out of them. The wintry gleam was still on his face, as he took hold of his huge, erect manhood, caressing it with his left hand, causing it to pulsate and swell even more. In his right hand, the quirt dangled menacingly. He sneered at her. "Welcome to your new life, slut!" He grabbed a handful of her wet hair and pushed her head downwards. "You are about to become a slavegirl! Now, what do you think about that!" He loosed her hair.

Rachel knew that she must be dreaming all this. It was a lucid, nightmare, which would end when she woke herself. She screwed up her eyes, and shook her head, but nothing had changed. Then there was a blur of movement to her left and she cowered as Elizabeth Stone picked up the dog-noose and slipped the rope around Rachel's neck again. The noose tightened, just enough to prevent Rachel freeing herself.

Then Rachel's head was reeling, as Hartman cuffed her alongside the ear, scrambling her mind. "I asked you a question!"

Shaking the pain away, Rachel mumbled. "I don't know what you mean."

He sighed deeply. "Then I'll explain properly." He looked down at her, grabbed her hair, and yanked her head back, "You're being abducted you stupid slut! You're going on a little journey." He sneered at her. "To North Africa. There you'll either serve Sheik Abbas, in his household, or you'll be sold to the highest bidder. Simple as that. You're a slavegirl." He shrugged, "As to what sort of slavegirl -" He shrugged. "That depends on how much you impress the Sheik!" He sneered and shook his head. "And there'll no escape." He loosed her hair and pushed her away, contemptuously.

Rachel was horrified. All those stories she had heard; the books she had read so avidly. They were based on truth! The white-slave trade still existed. Girls like her were still abducted and sold into a life of slavery and abuse? Horror of horrors, she was about to become a part of the evil peddling in female flesh; an unwilling, victim of these monsters. There was no doubt. Hartman wasn't lying to her. And that needle. It alone would explain why she stayed still, docile and submissive. Just as she would have to be, to enable them to get her out of the country. She trembled, frightened, yet bemused that there was a certain warm tingling in her vagina. But why? This time it wasn't a sexy, game in the privacy of her rooms. It wasn't in her imagination. This time it was real. She was being kidnapped and she would become a slavegirl! The startling truth made her suck in a deep breath. She felt her jaw go slack as her mind recoiled and she shuddered. God! And that quirt! Oh dear God. She didn't want to feel that again.

She realised then, the quirt was the least of her worries. She was half-aware of Elizabeth Stone grinning at her, as slowly, she pulled on the pole, forcing Rachel's head upwards, on a level with Hartman's waist. and now she stared again at the man's penis. The drug, whatever it was, was also telling her what she was expected to do. Unable to draw away, she leaned towards the huge member in front of her face.

At the same time, Hartman pulled his foreskin right back and waved the huge bloated head of the weapon in front of her face. "Now you sexy little bitch," he said, "it's time to show me what you can do! Suck me gentle and suck me deep! And when I come into your mouth, you will swallow every drop!"

Rachel knew she had to comply. He could shred her back with that quirt. She swallowed a sudden surge of bile, as she caught the stink of the stale urine on the man's penis. Feeling unclean and sluttish, she cringed, as he nudged the vile thing towards her lips.

She knew she had to comply, or be whipped, and she had to

make it look good. Forcing herself, she slid her tongue languorously around the evil-tasting weapon, to begin teasing him with her soft tongue. She gagged a little, as the massive cock invaded her mouth, to thrust against the soft skin at the back of her throat. She dribbled saliva all around the huge weapon, partly to get rid of the bitter taste of the filth and partly to lubricate her soft, full lips. She moved her head about the awesome thing. Sliding her tongue around the tip, she tried to ignore the vile taste. Then, surprising her, she felt the welling-up of her juices as she tasted the first slight weep of his semen salty-sweet, now that the stale taste was going.

The huge weapon began to pulse as Hartman started to thrust his hips more eagerly, pushing into her mouth; his urgency and his passion beginning to rise, and he moaned, entwining his fingers in Rachel's hair. Rachel struggled now, trying to pull away from him, but it was useless. Using the noose, Elizabeth Stone forced Rachel's head closer to Hartman's loins all the time and Rachel began to grunt like an animal as the thick shaft rammed home into her mouth, all but choking her.

Seemingly oblivious of the naked girl's distress and intent only on his own sexual gratification, Hartman shoved himself savagely into the back of her throat. Pushing the tender flesh aside, he roared out as he widened her gullet for the passage of his huge member.

Hardly able to breathe, Rachel gagged and heaved, her saliva flooding into her mouth, as her throat was invaded by the man's awesome penis. The huge head swelled even more as he shoved ever deeper into her mouth. She was gasping for breath now and her limbs flailed, ineffectually, as the woman pushed Rachel's head close to him. Hartman ground Rachel's face into his groin, roaring out his passion. "Come on, bitch! Make me come in your mouth!"

Just as Rachel thought she could stand no more, the man's

pipe seemed to grow to enormous size and there was a sudden, scalding surge of semen jetting into her throat.

Grabbing Rachel's ears, Hartman rammed her face savagely against his lower belly, forcing himself right into Rachel's battered throat.

She struggled, her naked body bucking against his thighs; her hands grabbing wildly about his legs; she gurgled her protests as she tried to breathe, and she began to kick as she felt herself suffocating. It was hopeless. With her face held, hard against his loins, Rachel was forced to swallow. A shudder coursed through her. Groaning, she tried to hold back the vomiting reflex, as the thick salty, liquid slid down her throat, on its way to her stomach.

Hartman pulled away from her, and giggled. "You won't need much training, will you?"

Gasping; heaving, coughing, Rachel turned away. Feeling degraded, used and dirty, she felt the sperm rise into her throat again and she made to vomit again.

Hartman growled angrily and his huge paw enveloped her mouth and nose. "Swallow it down, and answer me, bitch!"

Once more, Rachel was forced to swallow and finally Hartman loosed her as her struggles ceased. She trembled and turned away, lowering her head in abject shame.

Hartman brandished the quirt over her shaking body. "I asked you a question. Answer me, or I'll rip you to shreds with this!"

"But I don't understand." Rachel quavered.

Hartman sighed wearily, "What part of 'answer me' don't you get, you stupid bitch!" Then slashed the quirt across Rachel's buttocks, standing impassively, as the screaming girl writhed at his feet.

Eventually Rachel recovered and looked up at him, tears in her eyes.

Hartman just spat into her face. "I will ask you just once more." He shook the quirt for emphasis. "You're a slut and you won't need much training. Is that right?"

Rachel was now fully aware of her predicament. She knew what she had to say. Licking her lips, she looked up at him. "Yes Sir!"

Without warning, the quirt cut across her buttocks again and another line of burning pain forced a squeal from her. Involuntarily, Rachel fell to her side and rolled onto her back, cowering before him.

He leaned over her and raised the whip once more. "You call ALL men MASTER! UNDERSTAND SLUT!"

Fearfully, Rachel nodded. "Y-yes Master!" The word seemed strange; she was bewildered as she tried to sort herself out and to understand. Why was she submitting to this abuse? She still wanted to laugh at this ridiculous situation, at this madman who seemed to think she was his slavegirl. She wasn't an innocent. Even before her recent interest in bondage, she had been well aware that many people had perverse fetishes. She grabbed at the straw of hope. Perhaps this was just a game to them? Maybe, when their lust was sated, they would let her go? Even as the thoughts formed, she knew it wasn't to be. Even if they were just fulfilling their own fantasies, they could hardly let her go afterwards. The sudden fear then! God! they might murder her, to keep her quiet! Oh God no! Even the horror of abduction and slavery would be preferable to that. At least she would be alive. Perhaps it would be best to play along for now! Her mind whirled in confusion! Much as she wanted to, she knew she couldn't make herself resist. Good God! It even seemed natural to call him Master!

Hartman laughed loudly. "You learn fast." He grabbed her hair and pulled. "Stand!"

Rachel screamed as her scalp burned and frantically got to

her feet.

Gently then, Hartman caressed her stomach and the swell of her genitals with the whip. Then, abruptly, he lifted the quirt to shoulder height to slash the handle, savagely, across the breasts.

Rachel's screeching battered about the studio as she clutched at the hurt, trying to crouch down, but unable to do so, held upright by Elizabeth Stone, with the dog-noose in her hands. Rachel did manage a slight movement, but it was an unwise thing to do, for she merely suffered four more stinging lashes across her presented buttocks.

Then Elizabeth Stone slackened off the noose and Rachel dropped to the floor, scrabbling for the door to the changing rooms. She had to get out. Naked or not, she had to get away from this freak. She would be injured, badly, if she didn't avoid that lash!

She was wasting her time and after three more slashes, Hartman finally cornered her against the raised surround of the Jacuzzi. He laughed as he surveyed her cowering form. "I am quite sure we can train you to be an obedient slavegirl." He turned away from her and began to get dressed again, grinning at Elizabeth Stone. "She'll do Mrs. Stone. We take her to the van and I will pay you the ten thousand in cash."

Rachel, forgot her pain. Her mind was numb. So horrified, she was barely able to comprehend what she had just heard and seen. Dear God! This pair of maniacs had procured her! No! Worse! She had been sold! Like an animal! Just as if she was nothing but a carcass. Dear Lord, she had been sold like... like a slave!

Her heart fluttered as she realised what it meant. The white-slave trade really did still exist; and, Dear God! She was to become a part of it. This really was happening to her. She was being abducted! Soon she would find herself being sent abroad.

Sent abroad to what! Oh God! Who was this Sheik Abbas? And where was she to be taken to? What was to happen to her? Was she really going to be auctioned off, like a chattel, to the highest bidder? Or would money just change hands, resulting in her finding herself in some dingy foreign brothel, to be used for the pleasure of others?

Mentally, Rachel shook herself. She was being stupid. This was some strange, but realistic nightmare. Soon she would wake. But then her heart sank, for she knew. It was hopeless. She knew this was real enough. The burning welts on her flesh, the filthy taste still in her mouth, told her she wasn't dreaming.

She could delude herself no longer.

She was a chattel and she belonged to this man.

He had abducted her and eventually he would sell her.

Into slavery!

Now she knew full well what would happen to her.

She would be used as a plaything to satisfy the lust of perverts.

As Rachel shuddered with the terror, she realised her bowels were loosening and suddenly she was unable to control her bladder. With a keening wail of anguish, she felt her own urine running down her legs, and she began to sob with the shame.

They came across to her, and Hartman passed the quirt to Elizabeth Stone. Then he took the dog-noose and tightened it once more. He pushed Rachel's head down to the pool of urine on the floor, and sneered. "This isn't a toilet, slut! I ought to make you clean it up!" He laughed out loud as Rachel began to sob, almost demented now, as she thought of the horror of what he was suggesting. But she needn't have worried, for with a contemptuous laugh, Hartman tugged her head upwards again. "On your feet, slut, and come here!"

Helped upwards by the noose, tight about her slender neck, Rachel obeyed, to stand meekly before him.

He grinned and took a hypodermic needle from his pocket. Expertly he held it up, squirted a few drops of liquid from it and then plunged it into her thigh.

Rachel winced, but merely stood still, blinking, feeling the semi-drowsiness overtaking her.

Hartman nodded, and began to caress her flanks. He started to croon gently to her. "You really are a superb creature!" He allowed his hands to explore Rachel's sex lips.

Elizabeth Stone chuckled. "Not a virgin Ernst!"

Hartman leered and pushed his finger against the resistance of Rachel's tight anal ring. "Around the back she is."

Elizabeth Stone laughed. "My beloved husband must be slipping!" She stepped closer to Rachel and grabbed her chin. Squeezing tightly, her thumb and forefinger pressing Rachel's cheeks, painfully between her teeth, Elizabeth Stone looked directly into Rachel's eyes. Then she spat straight into the helpless Rachel's face. She retained her hold on Rachel's chin, keeping her head still as the glob of saliva dribbled downwards. "You see what you get for trying to steal another woman's husband!" Without waiting for a reply, Elizabeth Stone loosed her grip on Rachel's face and pushed her captive's head backwards.

Hartman steadied Rachel and then continued exploring her intimate parts. He suddenly smiled, looking up at Elizabeth Stone. "She is getting really wet. I think we might have a natural, here."

Elizabeth Stone shrugged. "I don't suppose it will matter to the Sheik." Then she grinned, and pointed towards Rachel's downy sex-mound. "Although, with all that dew running down her legs I'd agree. She does seem to be enjoying herself." The woman's expression became bleak and as she swung her hand in a wide arc, to give Rachel an almighty, back-handed swipe across the face.

Rachel yelled out, and tottered, her head full of bright light, her ears roaring.

Ignoring the wail of pain and shock, Elizabeth Stone turned away. "Take her to the van. The sooner I see the back of this baggage," she said, "the better I shall like it."

3 - Rachel's Journey Begins

It was chilly outside in the yard and the cool air raised her naked skin into goose-bumps. It was also gloomy, no light but the weak tungsten safety lights. She realised that they must have turned off the exterior floods; not that it would have mattered. There was no one around the club perimeters at this time of night. No one who could help her anyhow.

Rachel had slowed a little, then drew in a gasp of shock as Hartman's goad sank between her buttocks again. He didn't give her a jolt, but she still yelped, as the end almost burrowed into her anus. Instinctively, she increased her pace.

"See that, Mrs. Stone," Hartman chuckled. "She's learning fast!"

"All the better for her then!" The woman shoved Rachel between the shoulder-blades. "Maybe it will save her from too many whippings."

"Huh!" Hartman grunted, "I shouldn't bank on it!" He gave a throaty chuckle, "Where she's going, whipping a white-girl's arse is a National Sport!"

"For the one with the whip, Ernst!" The woman chortled.

"Or the goad!" Hartman touched the goad to the nape Rachel's neck, and gave a short jolt, forcing her to stagger before increasing her pace yet again. "See what I mean? She's a natural!"

The bullying pair were still chuckling as they hurried Rachel around the corner of the building, into a wide space, near the rubbish bins.

There was a white panelled truck, parked in a pool of brighter light which spilled from one of the large squash court windows. The van's lights were on, the engine was running over quietly and the back doors were closed. As Hartman pushed towards the van, the driver's door opened and a young, well-built man climbed out to walk towards them.

Another gasp of shock, as Rachel recognised him. Taylor! One of the maintenance men. She had always disliked his odious manners and suggestive chatter. She had to admit though, he had a well-developed physique. His arms were massive, bunched muscle rippling below short sleeves of his tight fitting white shirt. Even through the material Rachel could see the wedges of solid flesh that made up his torso and she saw the bulge in his crotch between the firm, meaty thighs that threatened to break out of his tight stone-washed jeans.

There the attraction ended, though, for he was as ugly as Hartman, with close-set shifty eyes, a large, hooked nose and thin cruel lips. As he saw the naked Rachel, a gleam of sadistic delight shone in his eyes and his face twisted into a grin, showing her blackened, broken teeth. Even from a couple of yards Rachel caught a whiff of his stinking breath and she shuddered.

The man had a whippy cane in his right hand and he pointed the bamboo at her trembling form. "Very nice Mrs. Stone." The cane touched Rachel's right breast causing her to draw back. He ignored the movement, "Always guessed she had nice tits." The cane travelled slowly down her belly and hovered around her hips, "Good body," Taylor continued. "This slut should go well on the block!" He pulled the cane away. "Not such a stuck up bitch now, eh!" The cane sliced through the air like lightning and Rachel screamed out as the bamboo cut a stripe of burning agony across the side of her left thigh. Then another blow, equally painful burned into the other leg.

Taylor just grinned, and opened the rear doors of the van. "Time to go, sweet thighs!" he said, as he jerked a thumb towards the van. "Room for one downstairs!"

Rachel's hand went to her mouth to cover her scream of shock at the strange sight in front of her. The interior of the truck had been divided into four compartments, with a horizontal platform half-way up from the floor and a vertical wire mesh screen along the centre-line. Cages! And all but one of them occupied! By kneeling, naked white girls! Although all Rachel could see of the girls, were their rounded, stretched buttocks and the soles of their feet, separated by an iron bar which had been clipped in place between their ankles, and secured to the floor of the van.

She could hear their anguished cries, sounding strangely muffled; disgusting almost as they grunted and gurgled like pigs. And the stink! Oh God the smell! Rachel gagged as she saw the damp patches of urine on the floor of the van. God! It was disgusting! Rachel felt her heart go out to these unfortunate wretches, as she also noticed that their arms had been fastened behind their backs and their wrists were secured to the top of their cages. Then Rachel's heart gave a great leap of fright as she realised she was going to join them at any moment!

There was no time for further speculation, for Hartman jammed the goad into the crease of her buttocks, gave her a jolt and ignoring her wail, shoved her to her knees.

Taylor was behind her then, and she made a half-hearted attempt to rise. But the cane slashed into the top of her buttocks,, and instinctively, her hand went behind her, reaching for the site of her pain.

Taylor chuckled in her ear. "Too easy slut!"

Rachel's heart dropped as she felt the handcuffs click into place. Then a pair of rough, uncaring hands came around her head and before she could struggle, a leather collar was slipped around her neck and fastened to the rear.

Hartman snarled in her ear, "Head up bitch! Now!"

Shivering, trembling in fear Rachel, swallowed and did as she was told. Then her horrified yelp was smothered as a foul smelling leather muzzle was slipped over the lower half of her face. And a bitter tasting, rubber tube was forced half-way into her throat. A hard metal ring in the muzzle was lodged behind her teeth and she began to gurgle in protest. Shaking her head, trying to get rid of this awful thing.

It was a waste of time. She sobbed into the muzzle as she felt the straps secured tightly behind her head. Now she could understand why the other three wretches in the van were making such disgusting, gurgling noises.

She yelped into the muzzle then as the cane striped across her buttocks and Taylor hissed, "get in bitch. On your knees like the other sluts."

Shaking with horror, Rachel got to her feet and went submissively to the van. She was helped by a shove in the back so she stumbled, sprawling headlong, stopping only when the upper half of her body slammed into the floor of the van.

By now, Hartman had gone around to the front of the van and he was inside, leaning over the back of the drivers seat. He grabbed Rachel's hair, and dragged her into the tiny cage, ignoring her pained, muffled squeals as he pulled her right forwards. Then her picked up a short length of chain that was secured to a ring in the floor of the van, and working quickly he snapped the chain to the front of Rachel's collar, forcing her head right down to floor level.

There was very little room in the tiny cage, and Rachel could feel the rough splintery surface of the wooden panel above her scratching into her back. Then a hand on her buttocks, shoving her further forwards, before she felt the cold metal rings being placed about her ankles, keeping her legs in contact with the floor.

So now, she was crouched on her knees, in a cramped cage. She was chained, collared and muzzled. She was gurgling into the muzzle, trying in vain to stop her saliva from welling up and dripping from the muzzle. But just like the other three girls, she could do nothing about it. Now Rachel had to believe. She really was being abducted. This was no game. No one was going to allow her to go. As the awful truth struck home, she began to sob into the stinking leather muzzle. Oh God! What on Earth was to become of her?

Then she yelped into the muzzle as there was the jab of another needle in her right buttock. In moments, she felt woozy again and she barely heard the van doors being slammed shut; the moaning and gurgling of the others suddenly seemed far away. Then everything was drowned out by the revving of the engine as the van pulled away.

She groaned again, and blackness overcame her.

The van lurched on through the night, carrying its cargo of female flesh to an uncertain future.

Rachel recovered consciousness slowly, becoming aware that movement was difficult and that she was somehow cramped up, with her arms and legs secured. As full awareness returned, the first things she noticed were the pitch darkness and the awful stench; nauseous odours compounded of stale sweat, urine, and filth. She tried to move, but couldn't - her arms were fastened behind her back, and her wrists were secured to the rear of a thick metal collar which was secured tight up against her chin, forcing her head up. There was also a sore prickling all over her scalp, and she knew that her hair had been pulled upwards against its roots, and was secured somewhere above her.

She knew she was on her knees, and the discomfort across her shins told her that the floor beneath her wasn't solid, but consisted of crosswise iron bars, close together, and almost breaking her knee-joints apart. She could also feel bars pressing down on her back, and her collar was secured to some kind of grille in front of her, to judge from the feel of thick rods that dug into her shoulders and upper arms. She could also hear the moans and sobs of other girls, punctuating the throb of an engine, and from the slight roll, she gathered that she was aboard some kind of boat. Then she gagged, all but vomiting as she became aware of the dried and half-dried filth that covered her back, and realised where the slimy waste had come from. Obviously, there was someone above her, no doubt suffering the same severe bondage as herself.

Rachel understood immediately what had happened to her and her heart began to race, as she realised that the terrible ordeal in the Health Club had not been a dream. She had been abducted, and she was most definitely on her way to God knew where, to face a life of abuse and slavery. It had all been too real, and worse, she just knew that what she had suffered so far, would be nothing compared to what was to come.

She began to tremble as horrific ideas stuttered through her mind. What was going to happen to her? Oh God! Why her? What had she done to deserve this? But then she knew that. She had been foolish enough to meddle with a rich woman's husband. Lawful or not, this was to be her punishment.

Her shaking increased and she felt her bowels loosen. Oh God! This was a far cry from the silly games she had played in her room and with Charles. This was real. Only too real. She was really in trouble, and there was nothing sexy or enjoyable about the position in which she now found herself.

She tried to shout, not with any hope that anyone would listen, but more to make contact with whoever else was in here with her; to share the misery, she knew the others would also be feeling. She merely heard herself gurgle into some kind of stiff, rubber half-mask, or gag that had been secured tightly around her lower face. In fact, the thing fitted her face so closely, it seemed as though it had been moulded to her lower jaw.

She could breathe easily enough, because there was a hole in the gag, but she couldn't speak, because her mouth was filled by a thick, unyielding rubber tube, pressing down her tongue and almost touching the soft palate the back of her throat. The tube turned her moans to wet gurgles, and her taste buds were being assaulted by the bitter taste of rubber. Instinctively, she wanted to spit the tube out, but just a few brief tries told her the thing was immovable. All she did was hurt her tongue and splather even more saliva through the tube.

There was no blindfold over her eyes, but there was no light whatsoever and, try as she might to see anything, the darkness was absolute. All Rachel knew was that she wasn't alone, for she could hear the sound of metal scraping and jingling and the desperate gurgles and moans of others, no doubt, abducted just like her and surely bound in the same manner. A hapless cargo of female misery, weeping into their gags and struggling, hopelessly against their chains and the cramped, confinement.

She shifted against her confinement again, trying to ease cramped muscles. The movement merely caused further discomfort, and she sagged into her chains. At least, she reflected, it wasn't cold. On the contrary. The atmosphere was heavy and the warmth was dragging sweat from every pore. Once more, She tried to adjust her position; to close her knees, but she was prevented from doing so by a rod, fastened between her lower thighs, spreading her knees and thighs wide, forcing her buttocks upwards against the top of her tiny prison, the exaggerated posture also causing her vagina and anus to gape wide.

Then there was the sudden blinding glow of light, as the place was flooded with light. Blinking away the dazzling lights, Rachel sucked in a horrified gasp, as she saw the full extent of her predicament. Directly opposite her across the steel floor, there was another blonde white girl. Her head was jutting out from the barred front of another cage, just like Rachel's. This girl also had a mask covering the lower half of her face, and was spluttering through the wide hole in the centre, no doubt also suffering the evil tube in her mouth. Now Rachel could see why her head was forced so far upwards, for the girl's hair had been worked into a plait, which was tied tightly to the floor of the cage above, just as Rachel knew her hair would be fastened. Not only that, above the girl there was another cage; yet another young female, this one a dark-haired, white girl, in the same dreadful bondage.

Rachel could barely move her head to the side, but she was just able to make out the rest of the opposite wall, which consisted entirely of these cages; two tiers of three, each tiny prison occupied by a naked, sweating, filth streaked white-girl; Just like herself, all chained and gagged exactly as she was, all forced into the low, tiny cages. The only part of their bodies not in the cage was their heads, which stuck out into the narrow aisle between the two banks of cages; twelve captive girls, each of them muzzled, and splathering their saliva, as they gasped and moaned, struggling in vain, to find comfort in the cramped cages.

At the edge of her vision, Rachel could just make out the head of a girl on her right. That meant there would be another six cages on her side of the compartment. She swivelled her head slightly to see that she had been right. All the heads poking out from the front of the cages reminded her of ranks of battery hens; except there was no feeding trough below their heads. And even if there had been, with these muzzles around their mouths, how would they eat? Rachel was soon to find out.

A door in the end of the aisle suddenly slammed open and a huge bloated white-man stepped into the compartment. Almost as one, the girls turned their heads in frightened expectation, towards the doorway.

Almost choking, Rachel felt her stomach leap with fright. Hartman again! He was half-naked, the rolls of his pasty white, belly hanging over the waist band of his jeans, and again, his face reminded her of a gargoyle. His little, piggy-eyes were glinting deep in the crevices of his blubbery cheeks and he was licking his thick, wet, lips; lips that reminded Rachel of rubbery slices of raw liver. In one hand he held a steel jug, full of a slopping mess that reminded her of pig-swill. Poking out of the filthy slop, there was a length of rubber tube with a funnel at one end. In his right hand there was a metal pole about three feet long, furnished with a brass tip at one end and a rubber handle and trigger switch at the other.

Rachel shuddered and moaned into her gag as she

recognised the pole for what it was. Another goad! Not quite like the one this brute had used on her at the Health Club, but a goad nevertheless. And it would be no less painful if it was applied to her.

Hartman looked about the compartment, clearly not caring about the stench. His face moved into the twisted grimace, that served him as a smile, showing his broken, discoloured teeth. A wheezy chuckle started as he pulled the rubber tube out of the jug. Drops of thc swill spilt onto the deck. He cackled again and swung the tube about, so that splatters of the swill sprayed about, landing on the naked flesh of the girls nearest to him. He laughed aloud, as in vain, they tried to withdraw from him, into the tiny cages. He put the pail down on the floor.

"Feeding time for you sluts!"

Rachel knew what was coming and the knowledge sent shivers of terror through her. Clearly, she wasn't alone in her fear and disgust, for as the compartment was suddenly filled with the fearful muffled cries of the girls, as they struggled in their chains, protesting into their unyielding muzzles. She could almost read their minds. Now they all knew. There was no denying the desperate position they were in.

As the evil Hartman swaggered along the narrow passageway, he slid the goad along in his hand until he was holding the rubber handle, with his forefinger on a small trigger switch. All of the girls struggled, their chains rattling, their frightened breathing coming noisily through their muzzles. Like Rachel, they must have experienced the goad already. Probably even Hartman's goad. They didn't need to be told its purpose, nor that of the jug and rubber tube. They were going to be force-fed!

There was a half smile on his face, as he began to look at each of the girls in turn.

"Now then. Who's going to be the first to eat breakfast!" He stopped, turned and moved a pointing finger slowly about the imprisoned girls. He was still chuckling, clearly enjoying the fear he was instilling in all of them. Then Rachel's heart gave a great leap of terror as he suddenly stopped by her cage, turned to face her and looked down at her. "Blondie I think." Then he laughed. "She's our little fitness instructor." He looked down at her in contempt. "Just a skinny slut who looks as though she needs a meal." He grabbed Rachel's plaited hair and pulled her head up higher, causing her collar to dig painfully into the nape of her neck. "Say please slut!" he taunted her. "Pretty please!"

Rachel began to struggle, trying to plead with him, trying to ask him to release her. But she knew it was hopeless. All he did was put the goad between the bars of the cage, probing between her legs until he could sink the tip of the fearsome thing into her sex.

Now Rachel was suddenly screaming into her muzzle, even the thick mask failing to muffle her agonised yells as the surge of electricity turned her into a quivering wreck, her spine arching towards the floor of her cage, forcing her filth streaked buttocks even higher. The girl above Rachel, obviously fearing she might be next, also began to scream. Then she lost control of herself.

Hartman merely laughed at them as he withdrew the goad. He looked at the captive above Rachel. "Christ bitch!" he said. "What are you going to do when it's your turn for the goad?" He giggled. "This mare underneath you will be in a real mess when we get to the Island." He chuckled. "I think I'd better change you over." He pulled Rachel's head up again. "After I've fed you all."

He stood up then, and looked around at all of the caged wretches. "Right then my beauties," he went on, "that's a little demonstration as to what will happen if you struggle or disobey. And if you still don't learn -" He paused and then replaced the goad in Rachel's sex. "It's a bigger ration of Mister Goad." Giggling, he gave Rachel another jolt.

She screamed again, frantically jerking against her chains, wailing, unable to control herself.

The gloating sadist pulled the goad clear, and surveyed his terrified charges once more.

"Now, remember, you do just as Hartman tells you. You won't like it, but you'll do it!" He giggled. "Oh, I nearly forgot! You sluts don't call me Hartman. You're allowed to call me Master instead!" He giggled at his weak attempt at humour. "Got it?"

Immediately, the girls all began to nod and gurgle into their muzzles.

Hartman began to gloat once more. "You learn fast!" He nodded. "Good! Otherwise it's pain!" He looked down again at Rachel and she began to shake, expecting more of the goad. But this time Hartman reached for her hair again and raised her head. For a moment, he stared contemptuously at the shaking Rachel. "No more struggling bitch!" With a distorted sneer on his ugly face, he shoved the tube into the hole in Rachel's muzzle. "Swallow, bitch! Swallow!"

Rachel was gagging now, as the tube disappeared into the hole, inch by inch, and she began to thresh about in her chains as she choked, trying to throw up the rubber tube. But it was hopeless. Soon the tube was completely down her gullet and grabbing her chin, he shoved Rachel's head even further back against the collar. Then he began to pour the glutinous mess from the jug, into the funnel and Rachel's struggles became wild, as the cold swill began to distend her belly. Finally, she could hold it no longer, and began to retch. But Hartman merely grinned at her, and grabbed her throat, just above the steel collar. His fingers closed tight and none too gently, he massaged her throat, forcing the food back down into her stomach.

"No throwing up, slut! We want to sell a slave, not a bag of bones!" He bent and peered into her terrified eyes. "You throw up and you get Mr. Goad! Right?"

Shutting out the thoughts of the evil slime she had been forced to swallow, Rachel managed to control the vomiting reflexes. She gurgled her acquiescence into her muzzle, nodding as best she could.

Hartman grunted satisfactorily. "And just remember it!" Then callously he snatched the tube from Rachel's gullet, wiping the end of the tube on her hair, before retying her plait to the bars above. Then, one by one, he went around the cages, to repeat the procedure, feeding each girl her ration of the swill. He was just about to leave the compartment when quite suddenly, the girl opposite Rachel let go, and spewed the contents of her stomach, all over the aisle.

"If you didn't like your food bitch, then try the taste of this!" He was grinning all over his ugly face, as he unfastened his fly and released his erect manhood from his jeans. Feeding his penis into the hole in the slave's muzzle, slowly and deeply, he began to fuck the helpless girl's mouth. The pitiful wretch was soon struggling to breathe against this purposeful invasion of her mouth and she began to shake and thresh about inside her tiny cage, her muffled wails, turned to gurgling as the slow, rape of her mouth went on. Then Hartman started to approach his climax, his movements quickened and his hips began to thrust harder and harder against the girl's face. Oblivious of her struggles, he finally came, in a great burst of passion and frenzied jerking, emptying his sperm into the slavegirl's throat.

When he withdrew, he looked down at the retching, gasping slavegirl, heedless of the stray sperm that dripped from her muzzle. He grabbed her plait and pulled her head up a little to peer into her face. "If you can't stomach your gruel bitch, then I suppose I'll have to spoil you with cream every day!" Cackling, he then pressed his huge weapon against the exposed portion of her face and expressed the last few dribbles of sperm from himself, wiping the surplus across her forehead and into her hair.

"Sorry, but we got no strawberries to go with it!" Laughing at his weak joke, he wiped a another weep of his semen across the girl's face, then re-zipped his fly, before swaggering from the compartment, slamming the door behind him, leaving the cargo of misery to their suffering.

5 - Arrival At Sarinka

For Rachel and her fellow captives, time had ceased to have any meaning.

There was no way of telling night from day, and Rachel had long since lost track of the number of times they had all been fed. Even if she had known that, she could only guess at the frequency, but it seemed they were given food about twice a day that. If you could call the stinking swill they served up, food.

It was a miracle almost that Rachel had been able to keep the stuff down. But she knew she had to.

How long had they been on the boat? Rachel tried to guess. God! Two days? A week?

However long, it was enough for Rachel to have become accustomed to the slop they forced down her throat at regular intervals. There must be a conditioning process going on, for she knew she always felt hungry, just before feeding time. When the terrible ordeal of being force-fed was over she actually had to admit to feeling that her hunger had been satisfied. In fact, during her enforced idleness she was well aware that she had put on weight. The collar about her neck was feeling much tighter than it had when she had first discovered the thing was around her neck. From time to time, as her buttocks and other prominent parts of her naked body, banged into the bars of her cramped cage, she could tell that her bones were much more cushioned by flesh.

Groaning into her muzzle, Rachel shifted position again, trying, in vain, to get comfortable. She wouldn't be able to take much more of the pain of being chained in this cramped, tiny prison. She had only the vaguest notion of where they were being taken, had no idea how long the voyage would be and her mind was full of wild ideas of the terrible things that would happen to them when they got there.

Sadness flooded her mind. Much as she had no real idea where they were going, Rachel was even more certain why all of them had been abducted. Their bodies were of value to these inhuman monsters. She, along with all the other girls, were destined to end up in some filthy brothel. If that was the case, she understood why they were all being allowed to gain weight. She knew all about Middle Eastern men preferring their women on the plump side and she trembled as an awful notion occurred to her. It seemed that these monsters were actually fattening them all; fattening them to suit the perverted tastes of the evil men who would soon have access to their bodies? Then an even worse thought struck home. Perhaps they were being fattened up just like beasts, for the market. Oh! God! No! Please! This had to be some perverted game. These people would let them go when they had tired of fulfilling their warped fantasies.

However, listening to the moans and sobbing of her companions, Rachel knew that was a forlorn hope. All she could look forward to for the moment was the prospect of being released from these awful animal cages. To her horror then, Rachel found herself almost praying for their arrival, knowing that, despite the unknown horrors awaiting them all, for her, the voyage couldn't end quick enough.

Then there was a sudden consternation as the whole cargo of slavegirls started to babble and splutter into their muzzles with a mixture of fear and expectancy. The reason for all this was that, quite suddenly, the thrum of the engines had ceased, and the boat was rolling gently from side to side. Rachel knew they must all have the same thought in their heads. Had they arrived at last!

Sadly, she realised the truth. She desperately hoped so! Whatever these monsters were going to do with them, it would be a wonderful relief just to be taken out of these cages. Maybe they might even clean them all of the filth.

There wasn't long for them to wonder, for the door slammed open and the hold was full of bright light. Hartman was there, dressed in filthy jeans, and tattered vest. He had his goad in his hand and he roared out. "Silence you sluts!" He waited until all the girls had fallen into mute obedience, then her walked up to the first cage, opened it, and dragged out the wailing, frightened occupant, a small, delicately-built brunette. Callously, he allowed the chained girl to drop to the floor, oblivious of her scream of pain as she crashed to the iron decking. He unfastened the iron rod from between the girl's thighs, and then the goad did its work again as Hartman shoved the tip of the thing in between the girl's buttocks.

The helpless girl screamed and scrabbled about the deck, Hartman grinning down at his tormented victim. He pulled the goad away from the girl, and then lifted her to her knees, by her hair. One more touch of the goad between her breasts and the girl fell silent, suffering her torture, clearly knowing it would not cease until she bore it in silence.

Hartman nodded. "Sensible bitch!" He looked around the tiny, stinking compartment. "All you bitches realise right now," he warned, "you suffer in silence. The more you scream, the more you get!"

Then, he unfastened the girl's arms from behind her collar, and released her thighs from the spreader. He shoved the goad between her shoulder blades and gave her a tiny burst, ignoring her as she stiffened, almost sitting up on her knees. He grabbed her head and pushed it down again. "Head down! Palms on the deck!" he ordered.

The girl obeyed, hanging her head submissively. Satisfied, Hartman bent towards her ear. "And you stay still, bitch! Understand?"

The subjugated slavegirl nodded and remained motionless; unprotesting, as Hartman shackled her collar to the cage beside her head. He giggled at her then hawked up a great globule of saliva, he spat on her back, before turning away to go about the business of releasing all of them from their cages. He unfastened each girl in turn, releasing the thigh spreaders and unshackling their arms from the rear of their collars. When Hartman got to Rachel, he dragged her out into the narrow aisle and, yanking her hair, turned her to face the doorway, as he had done with all of them. He now had the line of girls, on hands and knees, all facing the doorway. Next, he went down the line again, warning them to stay on all fours. As he reached each girl, he lifted her head by the hair and pushed it forwards so the girl's face was pushed between the buttocks of the girl in front of her. Finally satisfied, he took a long length of rusting chain from a hook on the wall and, stepping over each girl in turn, he began to shackle them into a coffle.

This chain was secured to the leading girl's collar, then it was passed down the front of her body, through her legs, before being threaded through the collar-ring of the girl behind. He repeated the process all along the line, until he got to Rachel. With Rachel being the last in line, he pulled the chain through, viciously, laying it between her buttocks, before taking it up her back to padlock it to the rear of her collar. Rachel, struggled, whimpering, as the links cut deeply into her sex, and she gurgled into her muzzle.

She merely earned herself a slash from Hartman's quirt. Ignoring her squeal of protest he bent over her and grabbed her plaited hair. Pulling her muzzled face up towards his, he snarled at her. "And if you don't keep up with the coffle, my little slut, you will be in for an uncomfortable time." As if to emphasise his words, he gave the chain another tug pulling it even deeper between Rachel's sex-lips. Then he shoved the goad between her buttocks and nudged it past the tight links of chain, almost sinking the tip of the fearsome thing into her body.

Rachel stiffened, waiting for the surge of power, but nothing came. Hartman just chuckled and removed the goad. Then sweeping his quirt in a flat arc towards Rachel's unprotected flesh, he slashed her across the backs of her thighs. Rachel wailed into her muzzle, and pitched forwards, colliding with the girl in front of her, her face sinking in between the soft globes of the other girl's buttocks. All the girls began to splutter into their gags, and they were shaking in terrified anticipation as Hartman delivered another savage blow to Rachel's taught, offered buttocks.

Then Hartman was squeezing past the coffle of kneeling slaves, towards the doorway. Reaching the doorway again, he unshackled the leading girl from the steel bars, and lifted the heavy length of chain to smash it down into the buttocks of the brunette.

"Crawl, slut! Out the door and just keep going."

His goad touched the second girl briefly, eliciting a pained, muffled scream from her. "And you all keep in time, or we'll be here for ever," he cackled then and, as each girl passed him, he gave her a taste of the goad between the shoulders.

And so it went on, the coffle of misery, shambling along, trying to keep in step, but failing, and for their trouble, earning themselves either a kick in the ribs or a blast from the goad, as they crawled along, gangways, struggled up companionways, until finally, gasping and spluttering, they found themselves on the upper deck of the large boat, the hot sun burning down on their naked, filthy bodies.

Rachel, her heart hammering in fear, her mouth dry, risked a glance about her. To her left, she could see a limestone jetty and a small huddle of buildings. One of the buildings had a large entrance and she could see the vaguest suggestion of pillars inside the gloomy place. Obviously it was some kind of warehouse. Then, from one of the smaller buildings, there appeared a half-dozen men, dressed in the long, flowing robes of Arabian dress and all carrying a rifle. Rachel felt her heart miss a beat, It was true then. They must be in the Mediterranean.

On each side, the buildings and jetty gave way to a sandy, shore-line, but it seemed very short; enclosed at each end, by the, dazzling empty blue of the sea. Rachel guessed, they were either on a promontory or an island and albeit that she could see only a short stretch of land, enclosed at each side by the empty sea, the scenery did suggest the North African coast. She felt the nervous fluttering in her stomach. It was all to real, and she had no doubts now. If she needed any confirmation, she got it as the line of men sauntered over towards the boat, talking and giggling amongst themselves, pointing at the coffle of sobbing girls as they were herded off the boat, and onto the sand covered jetty.

Hartman slashed the quirt across the leading girl's back, ignoring her muffled wail.

"Halt!"

The line of shaking, moaning girls came to a standstill and Rachel began to catch her breath in frightened sobs. Oh! God! What now!

She was soon to find out.

"Stand up, sluts."

But that was easier said than done for all of the girls. They had been chained in their cages for so long, their legs were barely able to support their weight as they tried to stand. One by one the girls tried and failed, tottering over, pulling their neighbour down with them. All this did was earn them all savage slashes from the quirt, until, finally they all managed to stand, holding onto one another for support as their weakened legs threatened to give way.

Hartman stood for a moment, surveying the coffle, as they stood there, wobbling, and tottering. The evil sadist grinned at them. "Step over the chain and get it in front of you. Move!" The goad touched the breast of the leading girl and she jumped, expecting a shock. Nothing came but Hartman's sadistic giggle as he watched the girls disentangle their legs from the chain, arranging it so it hung in loops across the front of their filth-streaked, sweating nakedness.

Rachel was acutely aware of her vulnerability as she stood there, in full view of these awful men. Her heart was beating irregularly and she felt faint, knowing that already the hot sun was beginning to scorch her back, even through the layer of filth she had all over her back and buttocks.

Completely uncaring of the girls' discomfort, Hartman walked up and down in front of the line two or three times, occasionally stopping to inspect one or other of the captives more closely. Then he stepped back and pointed to his right, towards the wall of a building.

At about shoulder height there was a long line of huge rusting steel rings set into the stonework of the building. Turning to the Arabs, Hartman said: "Up against the wall with them! One to a ring!"

Immediately the whole line of girls began to wail into their muzzles. They had all seen the men with the rifles and they all drew the same conclusion. The men came across, laughing and using a combination of kicks, hair-pulling and slaps and pushes, they bundled the terrified girls over towards the wall of the building.

The girls' fears were unjustified, for Hartman, laughing at them, said. "Stop flapping sluts. No one's going to shoot you, you stupid bitches." He looked at them as they leaned against the wall, their panic subsiding. "You're too valuable for that." Then he stepped close up to Rachel, to grin into her muzzled face.

Instinctively, Rachel began to breathe faster, in her panic, her saliva dribbling through the hole in the muzzle. Instinctively, she drew her head backwards, away from him, but he merely reached forwards and hooked his fingers beneath the edge of the muzzle. His fingers bunched against her throat, causing her to retch, as he pulled her head forwards slightly. "You stink, bitch! Christ do you stink!" Still grinning he loosed the muzzle and took a key from his pocket. In moments he had unlocked Rachel from the chain. He turned towards the Arabs. "I'll see to this one first. Take the others into the display room. Set them up ready!"

Again the men began to mutter eagerly among themselves as the moved towards Rachel's companions. There was the loud sound of leather swishing through the air, the smack of whip against flesh, all mingled with the muffled cries of pain, as the girls were taken across to the huge entrance, of the darkened building.

Rachel, still terrified watched helplessly as the line of girls was herded and shoved through the doorway into the darkness.

Hartman returned his attention to Rachel, and, grinning, he lifted her arms, and padlocked her wrists to the short length of chain, hanging from the ring in the wall.

Rachel hung her head in submission, knowing it was useless to resist. She would have to bear whatever it was they were going to do with her.

He raised his hand to grab her chin again, chuckling as Rachel's eyes widened in a mixture of fear and pleading. She gurgled into the muzzle, but Hartman shook his head. "I know what you're trying to say! Waste of breath slut! You're here and here you stay!"

He sneered, spat into her face.

Rachel cried into the muzzle and tried to shake her head, to get rid of the slimy globule of saliva, but Hartman merely cuffed her alongside the ear. "Keep still!" he growled. Then he turned towards a couple of the Arabs, who had drifted out of the large building. "Rig a hose!" he said. "It's time to wash this little bitch down!" Again the men began to laugh and chatter, as eagerly they set about preparing a hose, connected to a water main by the large warehouse. Then they stood; giggling and chattering among themselves; making obscene gestures towards the terrified Rachel, who waited, shaking with fright, her arms shackled to the ring in the wall.

Then Hartman stepped aside, and raised his arm. "Wash the slut down!"

Rachel was suddenly being thrown from side to side, her hips, shoulders and elbows being smashed into the stonework behind her. The water hit her like a battering ram, knocking the breath from her body, and she squealed frantically into the muzzle, certain she would drown, as she tried to draw breath. It was futile, the water pressed her against the wall, then as the angle of direction changed she would be twisted in her shackles, so her back and buttocks were exposed to the stinging onslaught of the water.

It went on for what seemed like minutes and when it did finally stop, Rachel hung against her chains, sucking in as much air as she could through the mesh of the muzzle. Her body was quivering with efforts to lift herself up properly, but all the strength seemed to have gone from her limbs.

Hartman had come across to her now and, grabbing her hair, he lifted her head to gaze into her terror stricken face. "Better now, slut?" he cackled, and, unlocking her chains, allowed her to fall to the uncaring stone floor, where she lay prostrate on her belly, still struggling to breathe.

Hartman landed a vicious lash across her unprotected ribs. "On all fours, slut!"

Rachel's yelp of pain splathered into the muzzle and whimpering she obeyed, wondering what terrors were to follow now.

Giggling to himself then, Hartman did no more than straddle her body and allow his weight to settle onto the her bowed back. His quirt laced into Rachel's buttocks. "Move mare! Take me across to the Despatch bay!"

He grabbed her hair and pulled her head upwards, showing her the large hall about thirty yards away. Another slash of the quirt. "Move I said! Time for a real bath!" He giggled again as the tormented Rachel began to make her painful, laboured way across the paved area, gasping and panting, almost collapsing under the weight of the gross creature who was riding her as if she was a pony. Her head was bowed and her breasts were heaving with exertion, but she knew she had to keep moving or another whipping would be the result. That or another taste of the terrible goad.

6 - Escape!'

Head down, submissive now, Rachel started the laboured crawl towards the shadowy entrance, her back almost breaking under the weight of the grotesque monster sitting astride her. She was gasping and spluttering, trying to breathe through the wire mesh in the centre of the muzzle, her saliva was seeping from beneath the leather, to slick her neck and her upper chest with a slimy film. Each time that Hartman lashed his quirt into her buttocks, she howled into the unyielding leather muzzle, and jumped; as if trying to evade the constant, stinging blows of the quirt, whilst realising she couldn't.

Eventually she reached the entrance to the shadowy building, and now she could hear the moans and sobs of her fellow captives coming from inside the building. She was urged inside; yelling out as she suffered another crashing blow from the quirt. It was pitch dark in here after the glare of the sunlit yard and pillars, her eyes were unable to adjust quickly enough so that she wavered and bumped into one of the massive, stone pillars. Yelping as the hard stone cracked her head, she veered sharply, almost unseating the massive Hartman. Again she yelped into the muzzle as this time the quirt lashed into her buttocks and Hartman's voice cut through the air.

"You almost had me off then you little mare!" he snarled, and administered yet another slash of the quirt to her right flank. "Watch what you're doing, slut!"

That was when the stench hit her; even through the muzzle and she felt her stomach tightening as the bile started to rise. She screwed up her eyes, swallowed as best she could, suppressing the urge to vomit; knowing at the worst, it might choke her, and at the least, displease her lumbering fat rider; resulting in yet more lashes from the quirt. But the stink! God! The rank smell of unwashed human flesh and waste; it was like a wall! They had just washed for her down, and now she was to be put into another filthy place. What was the matter with these people? Didn't they realise they were dealing with human beings and not animals? Rachel suddenly stopped worrying about it for suddenly, Hartman grabbed her hair.

Savagely, the beast pulled her head backwards, her neck cracking in protest at the uncaring treatment. Hartman maintained his grip as he dismounted and stood up. Then, twisting his hand into Rachel's locks, he pulled her upright, until she was straining on tiptoe, grunting with pain, her body quivering with the effort to bear the torture. Hartman twisted his hand even more, pulling Rachel's hair against the roots, causing her to squeal into the leather again. Then, with his other hand against the swell of her buttocks, he pushed her towards the pillar she had just bumped into.

Now that her eyes were adjusting, Rachel could see much better; but what she saw horrified her. There were two lines of the pillars, which were about eighteen inches in diameter. Most of the upright columns had a naked, sweating girl chained to the stonework; arms and legs, wrenched backwards, behind the pillars and secured with handcuffs on wrists and ankles. The girls' bodies were chained close to the pillars, secured with thin, wicked looking chain, which dug into tender, shining, sweating flesh. Now Rachel was aware of the agonised gasps and sobs, as each muzzled girl suffered the constraint of her bondage. Heads down, in total defeat and submission, they sagged against the thin, cutting chains and sobbed their misery into their muzzles. Then all thoughts of the other girls were smashed from Rachel's mind as she was slammed into a pillar herself. Again she had no time to worry about the terrifying sight, as her breath whooshed out. Before she could recover, she was twisted around to face Hartman. She gurgled into her muzzle, trying to plead with him. Futile.

Hartman merely lashed her across her stomach, causing her to double over in agony, her lungs heaving as she fought for breath. He loosed her hair and she fell to her knees, just as Hartman lifted the whip, smashing it down across her shoulders. Rachel screamed as the lash curled around her body, cutting into the side of her right breast, and she huddled into a ball.

Now she cowered before the evil Hartman, gazing up at him in terror; gurgling into the muzzle, trying to beg for mercy, even trying to call out the word. "Master!" Then, she suddenly realised she was actually free of her chains. She didn't have to stay within range of Hartman's lash. She was suddenly seized with hope, with the knowledge, she didn't have to stand for this treatment.

Her eyes had adjusted to the gloom now, and just thirty feet away she could make out another doorway in the building. The door was wide open and beyond she had a glimpse of a low, stone wall, and a sloping bank of brown stubby grass, scorched by the searing heat.

The oblong of daylight beckoned her, and without considering that she really had nowhere to go, that she was naked and muzzled like a dog, she knew she had to make a dash for her freedom. She had to try. As Hartman's arm went back to deliver another blow of the whip, she sprang up, screaming in anger and frustration. Nimbly, she side-stepped and leapt at Hartman, her hands clawing for his eyes.

Amazingly, the fat sadist reeled backward, taken completely

off-guard. He raised a thick slow, arm to fend her off, but he was too late.

Rachel's nails raked down his face and the bloated pig roared out his anger and pain. Wasting no time, Rachel took advantage of his confusion, and was off, running flat-mad for the open door, hearing Hartman's yell of anger, but taking no notice whatsoever. She had to get away! She was barely aware of the shouts of the men, or of Hartman's voice strident voice, ringing out. "Catch the slut! Stop her and bring her to me! Move!"

Then she was into the hot sunlight again, and in one bound, cleared the low wall. She hit the stunted grass, her feet slipping beneath her, as she began to career down the slight slope. Soon she was at a second low wall, her sweat running from her naked body, her lungs heaving, as she struggled to breathe through the fine mesh that covered the hole in her muzzle. But she knew she had to keep running; anything, anywhere to get away from these monsters.

She managed to keep on her feet, ignoring the bristly stubble sticking into the soles of her feet, as she slid down towards a wide ditch at the bottom of the slope. The ditch was full of scummy, smelly water, but there was no time to worry about it. She had to run. Regardless, Rachel jumped over the line of stone edging, alongside the ditch, to lose her footing. She fell, rolled and unable to stop herself, she slithered towards the water below.

That was when she realised that the yells and shouts of her pursuers were fading; even becoming less frequent She frowned. They didn't seem to be getting closer to her; almost as if they didn't care; just the occasional shout, and questioning yell, as if they were just letting her know she was being pursued; that sooner or later, she would be captured.

No way, she thought to herself. She was fit. She could run,

keep ahead of them. She made a sudden resolve as she thought of the rifles. If they did manage to reach her, she wouldn't stop. They wouldn't catch her. They could shoot her before she would give up; far better maybe to be killed than face a life of abject slavery at the hands of these monsters.

Then, a questioning thought. Where was she going?

It didn't matter.

She was free.

Had to keep moving.

The fact that she was naked just didn't matter; she could find a way around that later. Once she got clear, she would surely come across someone who would help her. She took a flying leap into the water, screaming out with all her strength, trying to ensure none of the filth got inside her muzzle. She floundered for a moment, gasping and coughing into the muzzle, but finally getting her balance. Then, standing waist deep in the murky water she realised her mistake. She wasn't in an ordinary ditch. She was in a stinking, drainage channel! The channel emerged from a high, steep bank to her left, and disappeared into a tunnel to her right. Between the surface of the water and the tunnel, there was about two feet of space and she realised she would have to brave a difficult wade along the tunnel, if she was to escape. She had no option, despite the fact that she didn't know how long the culvert was, where it would come out, or if she would even be able to breathe inside the circular shaft.

Mustering her nerve, she began to wade towards the tunnel, and paused only long enough to take a quick peek into the void. Her heart leapt with joy. There was daylight, just a few yards ahead. Her hope raised, she took as deep a breath as she could and ducked into the tunnel, to begin wading towards the crescent of light ahead.

If the ditch had been rank, this was a thousand times worse.

Within a few feet, she was gasping for breath, longing for the oxygen that was virtually non existent. Her stomach rebelled at the stink and the feel of the slime squelching between her toes, increased the desire to vomit, each movement causing even more rancid smells to erupt around her. Even the muzzle was not proof against it, and she knew that she would become unconscious, if she didn't get fresher air. Yet somehow, she found the strength to go on, to ignore the filth underfoot, and the fact that the mess was also plastering her long hair to her aching shoulders. But suddenly she was there; the light causing her pupils to close up again. But at least, she could get fresh air at last!

She reached forwards trying to grasp the stone work of the other entrance to pull herself through. Her face crashed into the steel mesh that she had been unable to see and she vented a frustrated scream into her muzzle. She sucked in fresh air, but that was the only reward she would get for her tortured struggle through the culvert. She began to sweep with frustration as her fingers wrestled with the thick mesh of the steel grating blocking the exit. More in desperation than with any hope of success, she grabbed the bars of the grating and shook with all her strength, but to no avail. The thing was immovable. Her spirits dropped like lead and she groaned into the muzzle. There was nothing for it. She could stay here until she suffocated, or drowned, or she could wade back again, and face the wrath of Hartman. She didn't relish more of Hartman's treatment, but the choice was no choice at all. She didn't want to die here, like a rat in a trap. If she was going to die, horrible as it might be, death in the open air, at the hands of Hartman was preferable to that.

God! She realised suddenly, even a life of slavery was better than dying here in this filthy, scummy drain. Sobbing with anger and frustration, Rachel took as much of the foul air into her lungs as she could and turned around to make her shambling way back towards Hartman and her fate.

The stench rose and hit her again as finally she splashed back into the open air. She retched into her muzzle and at the edge of her vision, saw the bloated, grinning Hartman standing at the edge of the pit. In desperation she tried to undo the straps of the muzzle, but her fingers were not strong enough to wrestle with heavy buckle, and in any case, there was a padlock on the thing! She was really panicking now. There MUST be a way out! She glanced frantically about her. But where to go? There was no way out!

She had tried the filthy tunnel. Where the water emerged from the small hill, now ahead of her, there was just no room to get through at all. The surround to her right was too sheer to climb and, to her left, the evil Hartman, his stumpy, fat legs wide astride, cut off the only other retreat. He was grinning like an ape and the terrible noosed-goad was in his hands!

Oh God! That goad again! Please No! No more of that!

Rachel began to tremble and her stomach leapt with frustration, and fear. There was nothing for it but to surrender to him. She must just hope to Heaven the fat bastard, didn't put the goad into the water. Shaking her head she screamed defiance at him, her cries even breaching the gag inside the muzzle. She began to wade towards him. Cringing inside Rachel felt the vomit rising as her feet disturbed the slime again, allowing the vile stench to bubble upwards to fill her nostrils, even through the muzzle. The water was splattering upwards too, flecking her naked body with even more of the filthy, green slime, and she suddenly realised that the level of water was rising. Then to her horror, she realised why! Her feet were sinking deeper into the slime and she was having difficulty in getting her legs clear, to take further steps. Breathing in panic again, her saliva bubbled through the muzzle, as she struggled to make progress. Rachel vented a deep sigh into the muzzle and she stifled a sob. She knew she was just wasting her time. She would be sucked under and she would drown, after all.

Hartman seemed not to worry. He just laughed aloud and reached forwards with the noosed goad. The rope dropped about Rachel's neck and a last desperate groan escaped her lips. Heedless of the filth, she sank until the tide of scum was up to her breasts, lowering her head in defeat, to begin sobbing into her muzzle.

The fat ogre boomed out. "Why didn't you say you wanted a swim, slut! I'd have thrown you in myself." Then his expression hardened, as he pressed her head downwards with the goad, his finger caressing the switch. "Now come here bitch. You and I have something to discuss."

Rachel knew she had to obey. She had tried to escape; had failed, and now she knew she would be made to pay for her stupid indiscretion. She began to tremble as she stood again and with a supreme effort, wrenched her legs free of the grasp of the slime. Slowly, she began to wade towards her tormentor. As she got with a couple of feet of him, he tightened the noose and Rachel felt herself being pushed under the tide of filth.

The thick, sludge; the stench of raw sewage, enveloped her, the slimy mess streaking all over her body. She swallowed the rising sickness, screwing her eyes up, trying not to breathe, lest she suck in the filth.

Then the shock of the goad as Hartman switched it on for a moment,

Despite the clutch of the mud, her upper body leapt clear of the scum and she screamed into the muzzle, her eyes popping. Her neck muscles standing out like cords, as the shock coursed through her tortured body. She arched backwards, the mess dripping off her tortured body, and her cries could be heard plainly even through he muzzle. Again and again, Hartman switched the goad on and off, playing her like some big fish, giggling as his helpless captive, threshed and screamed, splashing about in the filthy water. Finally he tired of the sport, and he dragged the half-conscious Rachel towards him.

Heedless of bruising her body, he grabbed hold of her filth-streaked hair and pulled her clear of the stinking ditch. Leaving the noose about her neck, he leaned over her.

"On your knees slut!"

Coughing, spluttering her lungs heaving, her body dripping slime all about her, Rachel pushed herself agonisingly to her knees. Whatever had possessed her to try to escape like that. She should have known there was nowhere to go. She should have waited for another chance; later there would have been a chance surely. But not now. They would surely not give her another opportunity. Knowing she must obey, she drooped her head submissively before Hartman. She gritted her teeth waiting for the cut of the whip or the paralysing shock of the goad. But nothing. The evil sadist simply locked the noose and began to drag Rachel along behind him as he strode towards the huge shed once more. He looked down at his struggling burden. "You won't try that again in a hurry!" he snarled, slashing the quirt into her buttocks again. Then he placed his boot against her ribs and pushed, rolling her over on her side in the damp sand.

Rachel screamed out as once more the leather cut into her unprotected flesh and she curled into a ball, knowing it merely gave the sadistic Hartman fresh targets for his whip.

Six strokes more he smashed across her back and the top of her buttocks, before grabbing her hair and dragging her over to one of the pillars. He ignored her wails and lifted her up to her knees once more, then yanked her head backwards, to glare at her. "I'm going to make sure you don't get that far again my little beauty!" He grinned at her then, and snapped his fingers to one of the men standing near the wall. "Fetch me a ten kilo weight Ahmed!" he said.

The little Arab nodded and, grinning like a chimpanzee, he scurried off

Hartman turned back to Rachel. "You can thank your lucky stars, I have to leave you fit and whole slut!" he sneered at her, and grabbed her chin, forcing her head back. He squeezed Rachel's cheeks together then spat into her face. "Slut!" .

The little Arab had returned and he was still grinning, and carrying square concrete block with a ring set into the centre of one face. There was a length of steel chain attached to the ring and dropping the stone beside the sobbing Rachel, the man handed Hartman the end of the chain.

Hartman growled at Rachel as he pulled her head right back. "We'll see how far you can get with this little necklace, shall we?" Chuckling to himself, he secured the chain to Rachel's collar and then clipped the free end of the links to the concrete block. Then he lashed Rachel again. "Pick the rock up slut!"

Rachel glanced up fearfully, shaking, half-expecting another slash of the whip. She swallowed ineffectually and picked up the rock. The stone wasn't heavy; not in itself, but Rachel knew that would depend on how far it would have to be carried. She clutched the stone to her stomach, knowing that if she dropped it she could expect another beating.

Hartman pulled Rachel's head back again and sneered at her. "You know what a bunny-hop is?"

Frowning, gasping into the muzzle, Rachel drew in a strangled breath. She knew all right and she knew what torture was about to be inflicted o her. Bunny hopping with this stone shackled to her neck was going to be sheer hell; but she knew the alternative. That whip! Jabbering into the muzzle, now, she nodded.

"So start hopping, slut, and don't stop until I tell you." The whip slashed into her buttocks again. "And don't drop the rock!"

Rachel wailed, jumped forwards and began a tortuous bunny-hop along the aisle between the rows of pillars. It was hopeless. She managed maybe six hops before her trembling thighs gave out and the rock slipped from her grasp. She stumbled, sprawled headlong and smashed down on top of the rough block, yelling out as the sharp edges raked into her tender breasts, tearing skin from her unprotected nipples.

Hartman ignored her predicament, merely sauntering over to her and slamming the whip into her thighs. He bent over her and grabbed the chain at her collar, lifting her face close to his. "I told you to hop!" He shook her head from side to side. "So hop! Get some air between those feet and the ground!" He giggled. "Or I'll have you bunny-hopping from your knees! Got it!"

Once more Rachel picked up the rock, and wincing into the muzzle, began to hop again, screaming into the muzzle as each time she landed, the whip sliced into her buttocks. But she stuck it for about fifteen yards, and finally, Hartman shoved her with his foot, sending her sprawling towards one of the pillars. "That'll do for now slut." He left Rachel where she lay, gasping into the filthy sand, and turn towards Ahmed again. "Get me a bamboo pole Ahmed and some baling string."

Once more Ahmed scurried off to return with the items, which he handed to Hartman.

The evil overseer nudged Rachel, with his foot. "On your knees slut!"

Rachel obeyed struggling to her knees reaching for the stone without even being told to.

"Leave the stone for now!" Hartman snapped. "Put out your hands, palms up."

Trembling still, Rachel obeyed and mutely allowed Hartman

to tie her wrists, with about two feet of the baling string hanging in a bight between them.

"Pull you elbows back!"

Again Rachel obeyed silently; then sucked in a strangled breath, as she realised what he was going to do.

Savagely, Hartman shoved the pole through Rachel's bent elbows, so it was tight into the small of her back. Then, with more of the string he secured each elbow to the pole. He then tied more string to the pole in the small of Rachel's back, pulling the end through between her legs, tugging the bight deep between her labia. Grinning into her terrified pain-wracked face, he fastened the loose end to the bight between her wrists.

Satisfied that the binding was now tight enough, Hartman picked up the rock and grinning into Rachel's face he placed the stone into Rachel's upturned hands. He looked down at her sneering. "Now we can start crawling." He giggled. "Or rather you can start!" He pointed along the aisle between the stone pillars, each still supporting a bound, struggling and helpless female. "Let all these bitches see what happens to slaves who try to escape." He bent to Rachel's ear and hissed. "We got something special lined up for you slut! They won't see it, but they'll hear you scream!" He kicked her in the rump. "Now crawl slut! Crawl!"

The terrified Rachel hunched herself over the rock, clasping it for dear life, squeezing it against the tender skin of her belly. She began to crawl, slowly towards the archway at the other end of the building.

Within seconds, the coarse sand beneath her knees was sloughing off her skin and slowly the weight of the stone began to tell. Three or four times she almost dropped it, as the weight started to pull on her arms. Determined not to give Hartman an excuse to hit her, Rachel clasped the stone to her belly, holding on fiercely, as she stumbled on her knees towards the archway.

Hartman and the Arab, merely sauntered after her, with Hartman tapping the whip against his thigh, just loud enough so Rachel could hear it. He began to grin as he saw that Rachel was weakening, beginning to tremble. Soon, Rachel was sobbing into the muzzle as she tried to hold onto the rock. Once more she was gasping with fear and the effort of holding her burden. Her saliva splathering through the muzzle dripped over her breasts and she could feel the burning pain as the weight of the rock began to cramp her fingers, and pull on the tendons of her arms. Shaking, crying into the muzzle, Rachel had no alternative but to obey, and pray her ordeal would soon be over.

7 - Rachel Meets the Whip-Master

They had passed through the arched opening and she had been shepherded towards a square, stone building, in which there were no windows. Just a panelled door, made of what looked like cedar-wood. Hartman walked ahead and pushed the door open and as he did so, even in the heat of the sun, Rachel felt a blast of warmer air belch out to meet her as she struggled on with the rock slipping from her grasp. Hartman turned to her. "Stop there slut!"

Rachel, obeyed him, gratefully sucking in air, trying to ignore the sweat running into and stinging her eyes. She still clutched the rock to her body and she was beginning to tremble, knowing it was going to slip from her grasp.

But Hartman snapped. "Drop the rock slut!"

Again Rachel obeyed, then began to work her aching fingers trying to ease the cramps, to restore the circulation to her bound arms.

Hartman ignored her discomfort, and merely came over to unclip the stone from her collar.

Then the Arab grabbed her hair and with one heave, pulled her to her feet. Hartman then placed his foot against the small of Rachel's back, to shove her into the small building, so she went headlong. The pole jammed through her crooked elbows denied her the use of her arms to break her fall, and she sprawled, across the wooden floor inside, crying out as the fall jarred her body and knocked the breath from her.

As she recovered her wind, Rachel saw that she was in a sauna, although there was no fire at the moment. Yet the room was still hot from recent use, the air thick and unmoving and Rachel immediately began to perspire. But it was more of a cold sweat; a cold sweat of fear, as she began to wonder why they needed a steam room out here in this tiny shoreline settlement.

Hartman must have noticed her perplexed frown, for he said. "The Steam-Room. Makes a great punishment for unruly slavegirls." He chuckled. "Imagine being shut up in here for a few hours, eh bitch!"

Rachel groaned into the muzzle and began to whimper. They couldn't mean that. The heat outside was bad enough. In here it would dehydrate her in minutes.

Then Hartman came over to her, grabbed the pole that was in the small of her back and pressed her belly to the floor.

The little Arab stepped over then and to Rachel's surprise, released the stinking muzzle.

She turned her head briefly, and managed to blurt out: "Please. Let me go! I won't tell anybody. I promise." Desperately, Rachel tried to keep the tears from her eyes, the tremor of fear from her voice.

Her answer was a million jabs of fiery pain in her scalp, as Hartman grabbed a good fistful of her hair, and pulled her head right back. She wailed as her spine arched against the pressure of Hartman's foot. The obese bully raised his hand and sliced it across, to chop into Rachel's face, with sudden, stinging force, filling her head with a starburst of light and an insistent ringing. Rachel yelled out, but the man seemed not to notice, merely grinning into her tear streaked face. "How right you are slut!" he hissed. "In fact, from now on, you won't even speak unless you're told to, much less tell anyone anything." He loosed his grip, and allowed Rachel's head to thud to the floor again, causing another show of stars in her head. "That is," he went on. "If you could find anyone who would bother to listen to the bleating of a slave." His hand raised again, this time to slam into Rachel's defenceless bottom, eliciting another squeal of pain and resentment. "Now slut," he said. "I'm going to release your arms." He showed her the noosed goad, "You try anything and you know what to expect?"

Rachel swallowed and nodded miserably. "Yes M-Master!"

"Just be sure you do!" In moments Hartman had released the pole and the bindings around her arms, so Rachel stood naked, and unfettered, but for the leather collar about her neck. The obese bully gave her a few moments respite whilst she got the circulation moving through her arms again.

Then Hartman had slipped his noosed goad over Rachel's head, and tightening the thing, he forced her up on to her toes, ignoring her choking cries. Once more there was a blow of searing pain running through her as he gave a short jolt from the goad. Then, lancing needles of agony in her scalp as the brute grabbed her hair yet again, to twist his fist into her locks.

Rachel tried to stop herself from panicking, but she began to hyper-ventilate. A crashing blow in the stomach doubled her over, before Hartman savagely pulled the noosed goad up again, straightening her once more. Then he let go her hair, allowing her to totter around, keeping her upright with the goad, as she fought for more air.

Finally, Rachel, her eyes streaming, her stomach aching, began to recover her breath. She tried to swallow, but her mouth was bone dry as her terror began to mount. Then her heart gave a great flip, and a nervous yelp of fright escaped her lips as the door of the steam-room opened and a tall, bearded Arab walked into the room.

He was stripped to the waist, and above his pantaloons, his magnificently sculpted body rippled with sheets of fine-toned muscle. He still wore his head-dress, so his face was all but obscured. However, Rachel could see his dark eyes glittering above the black beard. His white teeth flashed as he sneered and held up a long, flexible, riding crop. He paused as he closed the door and stared, long and hard at the naked, trembling Rachel.

His lips twisted into a sneer as his gaze raked over the filth-streaked, trembling girl. "Another filthy Christian slut, Ernst!" He boomed, shaking his head. "How do they manage to get themselves so filthy I wonder?" He shrugged. "But then I suppose it is natural for pigs to wallow in filth." He sneered again and pointed the crop at Rachel. "However, she will feel the strength of my arm despite her filth."

Hartman took a handful of Rachel's hair again and held her head still, so she found her gaze locked on the new arrival. "This is Jamil Ben Kadar," Hartman said. "He is Whip-Master to Sheik Abbas." He lifted her up higher on her toes, her hair tearing at the roots, bringing tears to her eyes. "You are about to find out why he is a Whip-Master," Hartman chuckled again. "Just be thankful that Jamil won't be coming with us to the Sheik's Palace!"

Jamil chuckled, a deep throaty sound, welling up from deep within his mighty chest. Then his face twisted into a cruel grin and he stepped over to her, bending the whippy crop right before her face. "Now you will learn why you should not try to escape." He pointed to the slatted seating on the one side of the steam-room. "Stretch the slut over the woodwork!" He flicked the crop to and fro, his eyes gleaming as he relished the swish of its passage through the air. "I intend to give her something to think about." Again he flexed the crop, allowing it to spring straight, swishing the air. "And I want to hear how she screams!"

Rachel moved back, lifting her arms in an instinctive gesture of defence. Futile! She yelled out as a blast from the goad knocked her silly. Then Hartman dropped the handle of the goad and grabbed her upper left arm. The fat Arab went to her other side and between them they frog-marched her over to the seating.

Screaming and struggling, her legs wind-milling about, Rachel tried to resist.

Her reply was just the chuckling of the two men as they shoved her towards the seating.

Rachel was fit, quite strong in fact, but she was no match for the men. Struggle as she might, she couldn't break free of their grasp. Their huge hands were squeezing her arms like twin vices, and they merely chuckled, easily dodging her flailing legs, as she tried to kick out at them. Not that it would have made any difference, but she never made contact once, as they rushed her across the small room.

They slammed her, face-down, on the second level, her breath whooshing out of her lungs. She felt her breasts being squashed flat against the wooden slats, and her nipples burned as they were forced between the wooden strips. Then her arms were pulled outwards and she felt her wrists being secured to the woodwork. She sucked in a frightened gasp and turned her head to one side, to see that they were using leather belts to tie her wrists. Again she struggled, kicking out with her feet, trying to hurt them, but just wasted her time. All she was doing was providing a rather erotic spectacle for these perverts.

She sagged, knowing what was to come. The evil Jamil was going to beat her, and there was nothing she could do about it. Even as the thoughts entered her head, it was made ever more clear, as the men each grabbed one of her ankles to stretched her thighs wide. Before she could resist further her ankles were strapped to the uprights beneath the lower seat, so that she was, completely powerless to defend herself, or even resist what was being done to her.

Jamil smashed the crop into the woodwork beside her head and she jumped, letting go a squeal of fear. The huge Arab Whip-Master boomed out again. "Open the door wide, Ernst! I want the other sluts to hear this bitch screaming."

Involuntarily then, Rachel began to scream, until suddenly her hair was grabbed and her head was pulled back. A filthy piece of rag was stuffed into her mouth. Then Hartman was growling in her ear. "I know what Jamil said, bitch. He wants to hear you scream!" He chuckled. "But not just yet." He tugged on the goad, to emphasise his words. "So, when I take the rag from your mouth, you'll oblige, won't you?" He released the noose, dropped the goad to the floor and grabbed her neck in one huge hand and squeezed hard, just below the swell of her skull. The pressure of his grip made her feel dizzy, but she still struggled against him, trying to spit out the filthy rag.

Hartman merely pulled her head even further back. "WON'T YOU!" he shouted.

Rachel subsided, knowing she was finished and nodded slowly.

Hartman removed the rag from her mouth and chuckled. "Now you WILL scream. As much as you want." He giggled.

"It might help you keep your mind off the pain."

Rachel stared to sob then. "Please. Let me go. I haven't done anything to you."

Jamil's voice cut in. "That is true, my little slut. You have done nothing to my friends. But," he added, "you tried to escape. For that you must be punished. You and your fellow slaves must learn. Such behaviour will not be tolerated." He placed the crop on Rachel's trembling shoulders and softly traced it down her spine. "In fact, any transgression will result in severe punishment." Then he lifted his arm high, and brought it down in a scything arc, flattening out at the bottom of the swing, so the crop seared horizontally into Rachel's taut, offered buttocks, the blow instantly raising a line of reddened fire on the soft flesh.

Rachel had never experienced pain like it. Her agonised scream bounced around the room as the sudden blaze of intense agony caused her buttocks to contract. She wriggled, still yelling, trying to bleed away the withering pain, but before she noticed any difference, the second blow fell, and her body jerked upwards, against the leather straps. A hoarse scream burst from her lips as the restraints on her wrists and ankles stretched her joints. Then her screams were almost continuous, each one merging into the next as the crop rose and fell, burning, blazing pain across her buttocks. Rachel, of course, couldn't see, but she knew, the flesh of her behind was being raised into fearful ridges of blue and red welts, as blow after blow ripped into the sensitive flesh. Then the nerve endings in Rachel's skin began to give up the effort, so that the sharp agony became a dull-ache.

Her tormentor seemed to sense this natural anaesthesia and suddenly the crop found a new target, this time tracking a searing welt across the tender flesh, just below the swell of Rachel's upthrust buttocks. Rachel was beginning to understand why

Jamil was called a Whip-Master, as the beating went on. The savagery of the beating was causing her to jump upwards and forwards, in an instinctive effort to get away from the punishing crop. But this merely caused her more pain - as her movements forced her weight against the tight leather bindings, so they scored into her flesh.

Then another line of heat, this time lower still, as the sadistic Jamil altered his aim, to begin the scourging of the backs of her spread thighs. This was followed immediately by another cut, just above her bent knees. He clearly knew exactly what he was doing as he started all over again, and began to work systematically, gradually moving the blows upwards again, until once more, he was slashing the whippy crop into the red-raw flesh of Rachel's battered arse-cheeks.

Beside herself with pain now, Rachel was hoarse, her screams blending one into the other as the crop rose and fell, again, and again, crashing into the tight-stretched skin of her defenceless, bared behind. Another awesome blow slashed into her and with her eyes streaming tears, she began to beg for mercy, trying to twist around in wild panic. She knew it was useless but she was also aware that she would have to make the man stop before she was whipped to death.

Then, as if he could read Rachel's mind, Jamil ceased the onslaught. Even above her sobbing, Rachel could make out the rasp of the sadistic man's breathing, as for a moment there was respite. Rachel twisted her head around and through tear-streaked vision saw the bastard standing to one side, the crop hanging from his hand.

"Perhaps now you will think twice before you try to escape again, bitch," he spat. "Not that you will get another chance." Then he raised his arm and the crop hissed through the air to thunder into Rachel's flesh again.

Rachel was done with screaming. Her throat was sore, dry,

cracking almost. Her backside was inflamed, to the point that the nerves were completely deadened. She certainly felt the blow, but now she merely whimpered, and then clenched her muscles as the crop sliced through the air yet again, to add another wicked stripe to the mess of welts that Rachel knew would be on her flesh. Then it ceased again and Rachel heard the man step back, breathing heavily.

Now Hartman was speaking into her ear, a half-chuckle in his voice. "How do you like your new life, slut?" He didn't wait for a reply. "Not much I shouldn't wonder." He giggled. "Now you see what disobedience gets you." Another sadistic chuckle. "And all because you couldn't resist messing about with another woman's husband." A pause then. "Well, where you're going you won't be doing any messing about." He grabbed her hair and shook her head for emphasis. "It will be you who will be messed about with." He slammed his open palm into Rachel's inflamed behind, extracting a harsh groan. "And you will be getting used to the feel of a crop across this little arse of yours. And a few other things besides!" The man straightened. "There's plenty more to come, my little slut, of that I can assure you!"

Rachel whimpered trying to keep her buttocks from tensing, her hips from wriggling against the fearful pain that was engulfing her rear end. Somehow she knew. Wriggling was precisely what they wanted to see, but her backside was hurting dreadfully and it was almost impossible to keep still.

She heard Jamil chuckle again. "That's right, Christian bitch! Jiggle those soft buttocks about! Such a sight will ready us for the next part of the proceedings." Then there was one more terrific, searing blow from the crop, and Rachel started to black out. She hovered on the brink of unconsciousness, just slightly aware that Jamil had dropped the crop and had stalked out of the room. There was a fearful nagging in her brain, as she wondered what the bastard had meant by 'the next part of the proceedings'.

But in her heart she knew.

She was soon to find out she was absolutely right.

8 - The First Test

Mercifully, they were unfastening the leather bindings from her limbs, and Rachel whimpered as they hauled her to her feet, the movement aggravating the pain in her buttocks and thighs. The mist of agony was making her feel dizzy, and her mouth was slack, open and she was dribbling slightly, her saliva running down her naked front. The slightest movement sent fresh waves of agony through her throbbing red-raw buttocks and thighs. She was so preoccupied with the centre of her pain and the stupidity of her rash escape attempt, that she barely noticed that Jamil had returned. Then she shuddered as through the mist of pain she heard the terrifying Whip-Master's voice.

"Bend the slut over Ernst. I want to see if she is ready for us."

Rachel made no effort to resist as Hartman applied pressure on the noose, and as she was bent forwards, she merely sucked in a tired gasp of air as a rough hand was suddenly shoved between her thighs, the blunt, uncaring fingers impatiently spreading her labia, seeking the depths of her sex hole. She was in so much pain; the agony gradually consuming her whole mind, and, seemingly, she had lost all will to object. She just stood there, submissive, obedient even, as Jamil worked his hand right into her sex-passage. Then she groaned, and her heart fluttered as without warning, she felt the first stirrings of her juices.

The obscene massage went on and she tried to suppress her mounting desire, knowing she didn't really want this, but knowing also, there was very little she could do to prevent her natural, physical responses taking over.

Then the problem vanished as the hand was withdrawn, and she was jerked upright again, the noose tightening around her neck. Jamil shoved his hand beneath her nose. "There slut! Smell yourself!" He pushed his fingers between her lips and into her mouth. "Taste your own juice!" he sneered. "It seems you found the beating somewhat satisfying. Maybe you are beginning to like this treatment?"

Rachel almost vomited as the man forced his fingers down onto the back of her tongue, then she swallowed, instinctively, as her own juice moistened her sore, dry throat.

Jamil chuckled, as he took his hand from her mouth. "Ernst! I believe she likes the taste of her own filthy slime!" He dried his hand in Rachel's hair, and then grabbed her chin, holding her head upright. He stared into her eyes. "It might be that she also likes the flavour of another woman." He shrugged. "In time, I have no doubt she will find out." He squeezed her cheeks, so her teeth scraped into the soft flesh inside her mouth. "That's right isn't it?" he loosed her and stepped back.

Rachel drooped her head in shame. This man had no right to treat her like this, and he also had no right to assume she was a slut just because... Her mind was a mess of conflicting thoughts. How could she explain? True, the juices from her own body had tasted quite sweet, had been welcome in a way, moistening her ravaged throat, but she had been more or less forced to swallow. It wasn't because she liked it for God's sake. Then, sadly, she realised. It didn't matter what she felt, wanted or needed. To these men she was quite clearly, nothing; less even than an animal. Mutely, she shook her head, then looked at her tormentor. She managed to croak through her burning throat. "No! Please... Please! Let me go. I really won't..."

A sharp slap across her face cut her off. "That is very true slut! From now on, you do nothing unless you are told." Jamil snarled. "And most of that you will not wish to do." He sniggered. "Not at first, anyway." He added mysteriously.

Hartman broke in. "Jamil, my friend. If you want to fuck her, let's hurry it up. I have to get the slut to His Excellency." He pulled the noose tight again and guided Rachel towards the benching. He pushed her against the woodwork, so her shins barked on the front rail. "Up there slut!" he growled. "And be quick about it. On your hands and knees."

Jamil grabbed Rachel's hair and, leering at her, he twisted her around, then forced her back so she plumped down on the slatted seat, causing her to cry out as the movement aggravated the sore flesh of her bottom. Jamil grinned in her face. "If your pretty little arse is too sore to sit on, then why don't you do as you were told and get on all fours?" He patted the wooden seat. "Now move slave! Get up there! Turn side on to us." He giggled. "I need room to service you. In front and behind!" Another wicked chuckle as he took control of the noosed goad, guiding Rachel onto the seats.

She flinched, stiffened, waiting for a shock. Nothing came and she swallowed, stealing a glance at her tormentor.

Jamil cuffed her alongside the ear. "Hurry!" he said. "You were given an order. Do it! NOW!"

Groaning inwardly, Rachel obeyed, clambering up onto the lower seat, adopted a hands and knees position, before turning so that the slats ran along the length of her body.

Jamil pulled her head lower with the noose. "This time your arms and legs are free. There are no belts to hold you." He ran a hand over her haunches. "You will surely find that I shall make you long for sexual release. But," he warned, "you stay as still as possible. That way, I get all the enjoyment."

Rachel, knowing full well what he meant, lowered her head in embarrassment. She knew she was going to be raped by this sadistic bully and there was absolutely nothing she could do to stop him. If she screamed out, it would be pointless. There was no one who would hear anyhow. At least, no one who would care. She also knew she would have to stay still, or be punished. Also, in order to do as Jamil had said, she knew she would have to grip the wooden slats, or she would be battered about between the sadists and the wall in front of her. Swallowing her fear, she grabbed the slats, her small fists, wrapping around the wood.

Jamil's laugh boomed out then. "See Ernst! The Christian bitch is readying herself for me." He snorted. "She is all but begging for me to start!"

Hartman dismissed Jamil's remarks with a wave. "Jamil, it doesn't matter whether she likes it or not. It's for you to enjoy, not her." He grabbed the goad. "Now, for Christ's sake Jamil, hurry it up! I'm behind schedule as it is."

"You should learn patience Ernst!" the big Arab smiled, then shrugged. "But, as you say, His Excellency shouldn't be kept waiting too long." He dropped his pantaloons. "Who takes her first, you or me!" He caressed his hardening prick, so it jerked, towards full erection, swinging about like the boom of a crane.

Hartman shrugged. "I already had my fun with the bitch." He jerked on the noose again. "I got plenty of time for more, later on."

Jamil grinned delightedly. "Ah! Yes Ernst." He pointed to the goad. "Then please make sure you pull that noose tight. Pull her right back onto me!"

Rachel could hardly believe what she was hearing. They were talking about her as if she wasn't here, or as if she didn't understand them. The enormity of her situation struck home. Oh God help her! Between them, they would half kill her.

Then Rachel yelled out as Hartman loosed the goad, and grabbed her hair. He twisted and her head was forced up. She was obliged to loose the wooden slats and as her shoulders lifted, her firm, well rounded breasts pushed forwards, showing them that, despite the embarrassment in her expression, her nipples were suddenly hard and swollen, throbbing even.

"Oh Yes!" Jamil breathed. "Such breasts. Such nipples." He caressed the trembling Rachel's upper body. "Sheik Abbas will really like this one." He leered at her and Rachel shivered with fear as she saw the crazed expression on his face, the fierce lust in his eyes. Then Jamil stretched out a hand, to lift her left breast. He squeezed, hard, and Rachel winced, biting her lower lip, trying not to cry out. The pressure intensified, until she could stand it no longer and she yelped out, her hands reaching for his wrist, to tear his hand away. She was wasting her time. All she got for her trouble was a hard smack on her sore buttocks from Jamil. "Keep still slut!" Then with a chuckle he loosed her, so her breast fell forwards again.

Her breast was throbbing with the pain, the bruise clearly beginning to form and she sagged again, smothering her sobs, just wishing they would get on with it and maybe then leave her alone.

Hartman licked his lips. "Yes. Okay Jamil! So they're nice tits." He tightened the noose a little. "Now hurry it up friend. I just told you, I have to get this bitch on her way."

That was when Rachel experienced the first fluttering in her stomach. Suddenly, she was breathing more heavily and her pulse was beginning to race. A warm glow was spreading through her belly. With difficulty, she tried to regain her composure; knowing she must deny herself sexual arousal. That would only increase their enjoyment. But it wasn't easy. Her confused mind was playing games with her. After all, wasn't this what she had longed for, in her lonely bed, on those long, sexy afternoons of pleasurable masturbation?

Of course it was!

But it was different now.

There was no escape for her.

She was being obliged to perform and, much as she knew she wanted to be taken by this evil man, to submit to him, the absence of choice was taking the edge off the experience. She swallowed again knowing she ought to scream out at them; force them to leave her alone. But that was futile, she knew. They would just see it as a way of having even more enjoyment from taking her body. Again she tried to deny the throbbing desire, that was pulsing away inside. The she gasped aloud as she felt her genitals begin to throb, her labia started to swell outwards, like a flower, to expose her wet, burning sex-hole and her prominent, tingling pleasure bud. She was suddenly longing for stimulation. It was all she could do to prevent herself from clawing at it herself, to squeeze it and to sink her own fingers deep into her body.

She felt shame, yes, but that was again pushed aside by the lust, as she began to pant, wanting Jamil to begin his assault of her body. Oh God!. She groaned inwardly, What was wrong with her? She shouldn't be feeling like this, with the looming prospect of being taken by a monsters like this. Yet, denying it was useless. The plain fact was, she was hot for sex. Right here and now.

Nothing had happened with the Steam-Room equipment, but even so the space was suddenly smaller, hotter and it was forming the nucleus of her whole being. The air was hanging heavy with naked lust and Rachel trembled with pent-up desire, as she waited. Then, again she shuddered, knowing Jamil was playing with her mind, teasing her just biding his time.

Her throat was still dry and her breathing was beginning to rasp as she tried to calm herself, ready for the impending onslaught. She could also hear the two men breathing, and once again, fear shouldered aside her desire.

Oh God! She prayed, Please let them hurry up and be done with her. She screwed up her eyes, trying to gather the strength to give Jamil what he wanted. As for what was to come, she could, in the old fashioned sense, relax and think of England! Of England? God! Think of anything, just so long as she satisfied this pervert and survived. A glimmer of hope then. Maybe, she could escape after all. Despite the beating, the warning, she knew she had to try one day.

And she would. She would get another chance...

Rachel jumped then as the quiet was disturbed by Hartman's voice. "Push that arse up slut, and hold your head high." He encouraged her with a jerk of the noose. "And get your mouth open wide."

Clenching and unclenching her buttocks, clamping her teeth against the pain juddering through her tortured buttocks and hips, she obeyed, gripping even tighter on the wooden slats beneath her.

She knew they were looking at her, she could feel the intentness of their gaze and she suddenly wanted to recover her modesty, to shield herself from their lustful gaze, with her hands. But she sucked in a gasp of surprise as she felt her nipples suddenly harden, felt her stomach flip with a twitch of nervous anticipation, felt her labia begin to throb, to swell and to pout, exposing her vagina.

Still she couldn't look at the two men, but she had no illusions about the sight that she must be presenting to them. If she had harboured any illusions they would have been dispelled by the ragged sounds of their breathing, as they too began to reach full arousal.

"Higher with those buttocks my little slut!" Jamil's crop tapped her reddened buttocks, slipped between the red-raw globes and began to tickle her sex lips Rachel gasped, expecting more punishment. Nothing came and, obediently she shoved her hips up even further, peaking her buttocks, painfully stretching the ravaged skin of her shapely bottom.

"Lift up your head slut and put your hands on your head."

Rachel obeyed, arching her back, so her breasts jutted out even more. Her mouth was open, ready, and her gaze was directed at the cedar wood panelling in front of her.

Then, surprising her, Jamil was in front of her, kneeling on the wooden benching, grinning, his huge penis fully erect, the foreskin pulled right back exposing the shiny, purple glans. "First, I want to see how you suck a real man my little slut!" Grabbing her hair he pulled her head back against Hartman's noose and without any further hesitation, he lunged straight into her ready mouth.

Then, unexpectedly, Hartman dropped the noose, and yelled out. "Oh Fuck it! I got to have the bitch!" Instantly then Rachel felt her vagina invaded by Hartman's gigantic weapon, and she emitted a smothered squeal as the force of his entry, widened her passage, exciting the sensitive tender membranes inside, pressing her clitoris hard against her pubic bone. She spluttered her saliva around the shaft of Jamil's huge tool, the gristly organ completely filling her mouth, stretching her lips wide, as the man began to pump in and out of her face.

Then from behind again, there was Hartman, his hands scrabbling into the sore mounds of her buttocks, his fingers pulling her body against him, so she was being bounced back and forth between the two of them. Almost in perfect time, each man sank himself into her body, the cock in her mouth swelling, flattening her tongue and Hartman's huge monster, spearing into the depths of her belly.

Rachel abandoned herself to the assault, and her spine arched like a bow, as she groaned with each mighty thrust from Hartman. She was just able to breathe, each time Jamil withdrew from her mouth; surprising herself at the ease with which she took this huge thing in her mouth. Groaning, Rachel allowed her throat to relax, so the bloated penis slid right into her gullet, the heat of the thing spreading through her chest.

Despite Jamil's boasting manner, he didn't last long and within a few more thrusts, he was leaning back, hanging onto her hair, yelling out his lust as he pumped his copious load of scalding sperm into Rachel's mouth. The hot creamy liquid slid straight down her throat, and even before she realised it she had swallowed the whole load.

Hartman, in his own passion, snatched her arse-cheeks wider apart so he could lunge even deeper into her gaping, wet sex. In moments he had thrust right into her, plumbing her depths, making her feel as though her whole belly was taking him. His heavy fat thighs slammed against her thrashed buttocks as he rammed himself right home; again and again, thrusting into her, feeling massive, filling her, stretching her slippery sex-hole wide. Much as she wanted to deny it, Rachel knew she was boiling to a climax herself; ashamed of what she was doing yet somehow relishing the fact that she was being used as a mere sex-object, knowing that she could do nothing but kneel there and take every thing they wanted to give her.

Jamil had slid from her mouth now, and his sperm trailed across her face. Eagerly almost, she grabbed for the penis, slipping it back into her mouth, sucking it dry, draining it of every last drop of semen. Jamil was gasping with desire again, lunging into her, mouth, clearly desperate to regain his erection. But he seemed to be finished and with a dismissive gesture he withdrew from her and grabbed the handle of the noosed goad again. She moaned in true passion as Hartman lunged once more, her back bent into an even greater bow of pleasure, as his weapon lunged. She shoved her buttocks towards his thrusting, her breathing becoming ragged as she allowed her mouth to go slack, to gape, her saliva and the remnants of Jamil's semen dripping from her mouth, unheeded as the warmth of lust overtook her. She bucked against Hartman again her sore buttocks, burning anew as he ground up against her with each thrust.

She slid along the slatted benching, fingers losing grip on the timber and beneath her breasts swung to and fro, in abandon. Her orgasm was rising quickly now and she fought for every breath, as she tried to hold onto the delicious sensation as Hartman began to quicken his movements. Jamil, sensing Hartman's approaching climax, tightened the noose and dragged Rachel back towards Hartman's lunging, hips. The Whip-Master cried out. "Come Ernst! Give to the slut. Flood her out my friend. Let it go!"

Hartman responded to the Arab's urging and his movements quickened, his loud breathing turning to groans of passion. Finally he arched back, thrusting right into Rachel's body, Yelling aloud as his climax overtook him.

Rachel squealed in pain and pleasure as she felt the boiling love cream jetting into her and she clenched her thighs, as the sperm continued to spurt, his prick thudding deep into her, stiffening, swelling, pulsing his load, draining into her abused body. She was so filled with this huge member that the sperm squelched out of her, to run freely down her thighs. Gasping, straining, squealing, she squeezed her thighs together again, still trying to retain him, to contract her muscles so she could milk every last drop from him, as she had her own orgasm. Now she paid no heed to the red-raw striping on her flesh, intent only on keeping that gorgeous fat cock inside her; almost praying for the release of her boiling, threatening climax.

There was to be no release for Rachel though, for suddenly Hartman withdrew and there was the immediate blast of a shock from the goad. Then another, and yet one more.

No orgasm for Rachel!

She yelled out in anguish as consciousness drained away.

9 - Rachel is Left To The Villagers.

When Rachel recovered consciousness, she realised that she was in the open air again and that the sun was burning her back. Groaning wearily, she tried to lift her head, but a chain clinked, then pulled at her collar. She was shackled to a huge block of stone, far too big and heavy for her to move, let alone carry. Apart from that she was unfettered, and she breathed a small sigh of relief for that small mercy; although it was clear that the block was just a means of preventing her from escaping, should she have recovered, and found herself alone. Not that she would try that again! In any case she was still naked. Had she really expected to be any other way? Not really. Slavegirls, it seemed, didn't wear clothes. She suppressed the sadness as best she could. It was pointless. It made nothing any better.

She managed to get to her hands and knees, wincing as the movements reminded her of the beating she had received from Jamil. Then she risked a glance about her. It seemed she was in a new place altogether, for she didn't recognise any of the stone buildings that surrounded the large square of hard-packed, sandy earth. In the centre of the square there was a large pole, on a raised platform.

Then she jumped, as behind her, Hartman's voice brought her to full awareness. "Are you with us then slut!"

She looked up. The sun was behind him and she blinked in the glare, just able to make out that it was indeed Hartman. She tried to speak. "Please! Tell me. What -"

Hartman raised his arm and a quirt thundered into Rachel's back. "Shut it, slut!"

Crying out, she cowered from him, but he caught hold of her hair and dragged her to a seated position, oblivious of her cries as the hard earth aggravated the bruising on her buttocks. He bent and without a further word, he unshackled her from the stone. Then he placed his foot against her ribs, and dug into her side. "On all fours!"

Miserably, Rachel obeyed, smothering a sob as the pain in her backside began to throb.

Hartman chuckled. "Hurts does it?" He grabbed her buttocks and squeezed, chuckling as another squeal of anguish escaped her. Then, he stooped over her and in moments, had fitted another muzzle around her face. Then he got astride her back, as he had before, and the quirt sliced into her buttocks. "To the pole slut."

Head down, Rachel obeyed, struggling to bear the weight of the fat sadist as she crawled across the sandy square towards the pole.

The quirt continued to land on Rachel's naked, sweating buttocks, aggravating the bruised skin, as she struggled with her burden across the open square. The sand was taking more skin from her knees, as she struggled to hold the evil Hartman upright, knowing full well, the consequences should she let him slip to the floor.

Each time the quirt landed she all but collapsed, but through sheer determination, managed to retain her position as she shuffled along on her knees. Soon though, she was at the platform, and she was allowed to pause. Now she had a chance to see through a gap in the surrounding buildings. She caught a glimpse of open countryside, and the glint of sunlight on a patch of sea. Clearly they were on an island, so what had been the point of her escape attempt? Her effort had been hopeless; there was nowhere for her to go, and now, as the quirt landed again across her shoulders, Rachel cursed her stupidity, for even trying such a foolish stunt.

Then Hartman grabbed her hair and yanked her head back. He delivered a sharp kick into her ribs and her breath exploded from her body. The bullying overseer pulled her head right back and glared down at her. "Jamil's punishment was bad enough, but now, you'll really find out why you shouldn't have tried to escape!" He grinned at her then dragged her over to the pole in the centre of the open space.

More skin was sloughed off her knees and elbows as he pulled her towards the pole.

Hartman paid no heed whatsoever to Rachel's injuries, and finally he fetched her up against the thick post and stopped. Then he grinned at Rachel again. "Time for a posting slut!" he said. "Except you ain't going anywhere!" He laughed out loud as he pulled Rachel into a seated position, by dragging her upright by her hair.

She gasped into the muzzle again as he shoved her head forwards, roughly, uncaring that she almost choked against the pressure from her collar. He took her arms and pulled them behind her, yanking at her limbs, crossing her wrists. In moments he had tightly bound her wrists together, and, chuckling at her, he spun her around on her bottom, so she was facing the tall pole.

Rachel began to pant into the muzzle as she noticed the

crosspiece that was set into the pole about four feet up from the base. Crying into the muzzle, she tried to shut out of her mind, the agony that was soon to come; for surely, Hartman was going to suspend her from the crosspiece?

But he didn't. Instead, he suddenly pitched her backwards, and she yelped into the muzzle as her head hit the stone floor, with a sickening thud. Blinding lights flashed in her head and she felt herself losing her grip as unconsciousness threatened. She was unable to stop him doing just as he wished with her, and she screamed into the muzzle again as, before she realised what was happening, Hartman had dragged her close up to the pole, so her legs were spread to each side of it, the base of her spine cracking painfully against the rough wood.

Her tormentor bent down and quickly tied Rachel's wrist-bindings to the base of the pole, with more baling string, before lifting her legs and lower torso clear of the floor. With a savage heave, he bent her knees over the crosspiece, ignoring her squeals, as her shoulders slid along the rough, sandy floor.

In moments he had secured both of Rachel's knees to the crosspiece, so that most of her weight was exerted on the backs of her bent knees, and her head was being forced into her chest, forcing her steel collar into the underside of her neck. Hartman wasted little time. Pleased by her agonised struggles, he bent each leg downwards, to tie one ankle to each wrist.

Rachel was soon gasping into the muzzle, her head bent forwards, so she was forced to look upwards along her tortured body, her knees spread wide across the horizontal spar, her genitals gaping wide, the hot sun beating down on her unprotected skin.

Hartman stood up and looked down at her, then he waved to one of the men, busy inside the shed, finishing the job of securing the rest of the slavegirls to the pillars inside.

The man came over to him. "Effendi?"

"Water for the slut!" He pointed to the inverted Rachel. "Just a mouthful." He grinned at Rachel, again. "Then we'll leave her to roast for a while."

The man hurried off to reappear moments later with a goatskin bag. He squirted water into the hole in Rachel's muzzle, just enough of the precious liquid to slake her thirst, but no more.

Hartman looked down at the naked, tortured Rachel. "You stay here for three hours. Later I'll come and move you. The sun should put a nice glow on these titties eh? And when you're done to a turn, I have another surprise for you." He bent down and peered into her agonised face. "That is, if you've been a good little slavegirl. Afterwards, you can go back under cover with the rest of the sluts." He shrugged. "If you upset me, I'll demonstrate another way of tying you to this pole." He patted the woodwork almost lovingly. "You'll be surprised at the permutations we can work out with this." He leered at her. "And not one of them is any less painful than another!" Then he lifted the quirt and brought it down in a vicious slash, right into the spread vee of Rachel's thighs, smiling with glee as the trussed victim jerked against her bonds, her screaming wail audible as such, even through the muzzle.

The whip descended once more and again Rachel's body lurched involuntarily upwards, causing the tight bindings to cut into her lacerated wrists and ankles. Immediately her hips began to move and her moans welled up as she tried to ease the burning agony in her genitals.

Hartman merely laughed aloud. "That's one variation! Just to keep you awake slut!" A nudge with his toe. "You get one stroke every hour." He tucked the quirt into his belt. "That's if you're good!" He leaned over her. "If not, then you get more." Again he nudged her with his toe. "So it's up to you my little slut!" With another laugh, he spat on Rachel's defenceless body, before turning away to walk off, leaving her to suffer in the burning Sun.

Hartman moved lazily as he blinked away his comfortable sleep and his vanishing, erotic dream. For an instant he frowned, wondering where he was. Then he remembered, and a broad smile stretched his fat, rubbery lips. Strange how coming to the Middle East always threw him. He stretched again. He had a good life all round though. To him fell the responsibility of obtaining attractive, preferably white, females for Sheik Abbas; either for his Excellency's own delight, or for the Sheik to sell on, at a fat profit. Hartman was a modern-day version of a Middle Eastern Elite Guard and he felt he was important. At the back of his mind though lurked the unsavoury notion, that he was no more than a pimp; a procurer of female flesh. So what, though. He was paid well enough and the more attractive and voluptuous the flesh he gathered, the better the Sheik liked it; and the happier he made Hartman, with bigger and better rewards.

Being Sheik Abbas's Chief Procurer also had its more physical perks. That was what Hartman really liked. The complete freedom to treat the sluts as he felt fit. To torture them, use their bodies, whenever and however he fancied. His eyes glittered and he licked his lips, as he thought about the scores of beautiful girls who had fallen beneath his whip. Lying here now, he could almost hear their screams, as his whip had slashed into their unprotected flesh. Yes! Life was good.

So what if he went too far sometimes? Whilst he had never actually killed one of the sluts, the fact remained that, if one of them did keel over, it wouldn't really matter. The Sheik wouldn't want weak stock anyhow. As for marking the merchandise, well... No problem! The Sheik took no interest in the slavegirls, until they were brought to him for assessment. After that, unless he kept a particular slavegirl for himself, his only concern for the rest was how much had been made from the sale of their hides. In fact, most of the time, the Sheik didn't see the sluts at all, relying on Hartman's judgement on what to sell or retain. So, if Hartman injured one of the bitches, he merely pushed another into the line, while the less fortunate wretch was left to lick her wounds, as it were.

He stretched again, and got up from the bed. This time, Hartman had brought his latest captures to Dashika, a small oasis in the province of Mashtuk; ruled by Sheik Abbas. In this small settlement, the villagers, knowing Hartman's relationship with their venerated Sheik Abbas, were only too eager to offer Hartman and his brutal cohorts the simple hospitality of their village.

The room that Hartman had been given was in the basement of a substantial stone building, the main building in the village in fact. The place was probably one of the coolest structures in the village. Even at this lower level though the place was still humid, sticky and warm. Without sophisticated air-conditioning, the humidity couldn't be avoided in this part of the world and Hartman had more or less got used to the sultry heat of this virtually barren country.

It was still quite early in the morning and Hartman was pleased with the peaceful night he had passed in blissful sleep. He smiled to himself as he thought briefly of the unfortunate slavegirl, the stuck-up slut he had lashed to the pole in the sunlight, yesterday.

How had that little bitch spent the night?

He smiled again, more cruelly, as he thought of the mare. In acute discomfort, no doubt. Then a frown gathered. He had made a mistake with that one. She had managed to get clear of the Colonnade. She had already suffered under Jamil's whip, and had been given an enforced dose of 'sun-bathing'. Yet,

Hartman guessed, she would still need the lesson reinforcing. It usually took some time to convince slaves like her that escape attempts were futile. She would have to learn; and be left in no doubt as to what would happen to her, if she tried again.

Hartman's feature twisted into a sadistic grimace as he remembered the slut's aborted escape attempt. He fingered the still sore slashes she had raked down his cheek. Hartman and his group of 'catchers' had been ready for any escape attempt by any of the herd of sluts they had bought to the Island yesterday. It had been no problem to recapture her and return her to the 'fold', for her first taste of slavegirl discipline. But even so, if he met the Sheik by chance, and he still bore traces of the slut's attack, he would look foolish; his pride would be damaged. That was something he wanted to avoid. So, just the day before, he and the seven other men of his hunting party had entered this dusty village, to 'rest', as Hartman had put it.

Again he fingered the scratches. Feisty little bitch. He had to give her that. She was fit too! Might even find herself turned to good use in one or other of the troupes of fighting slavegirls, which many of the rich merchants in this area kept for their amusement. Hartman chuckled then. That was until a slave lost too often. Then the fighting slave would often be pitted against Dobermans or some other breed of huge dog. They would soon prove how fit a slave was; or wasn't! And who would finish up with scratches!

Hartman rubbed the last of the sleep from his eyes and went across to the unglazed, arched window, to gaze out across the courtyard. The square served the village as a marketplace; an open, sandy space where goods were exchanged and frenetic bartering took place at least three times every week. In fact, anything of any importance was conducted in this bleak, dry, dusty square. He looked towards the centre of the square, and the platform.

Last night, he had altered the slut's bondage slightly, shackling her slender arms to rings in the stone platform, so she was spread-eagled, on her back, with her knees bent and chained cruelly over the cross piece. The slut was still there of course. Where could she go? Chained like that. She would have suffered, for sure. As a way of payment to the villagers, last night Hartman had told them they could abuse the girl as and how they wished. Just so long as they remembered her arse and her slash were 'out of bounds', as it were. Finally, he had removed the muzzle, to give easy access to her mouth.

He let out an amused grunt. During the night, someone had seen fit to place a large block of stone beneath the slut's back, lifting her upper body further against the restraints of her wrist chains. This had the effect of making her mouth even more accessible, with her head draped over the edge of the stone. She made an erotic sight, although her pain must have been indescribable, as her arms were being pulled downwards from her shoulders and her shapely legs were spread wide over the crosspiece.

Her feet were pulled right back beneath her thighs, so that her sex-hole was fully displayed and even from here he could even make out the blonde, sweat coated hairs of her quim, glistening as the droplets of moisture caught the rays of the early sun.

Hartman grunted to himself with satisfaction. The hairs would soon be removed; the slut was of less value with a hairy crotch; Arabs liked their slave-girls to be shaved, so they looked like young girls, at least around the genitalia. So, her pubic hair would be shaved. Although, Hartman decided, as this bitch had given him so much trouble, he was going to enjoy actually pulling most of the frizz by hand. That was if she was going to be sold on the block as a pleasure slave. If she were designated as a galley slave, or a pony-girl, she would retain the hair, so she would sweat more as she worked, causing greater discomfort between her thighs as she lathered up.

Hartman shrugged. That was up to Sheik Abbas. For the moment the slut was stretched out; on offer; so any local man could amuse himself with the tethered beauty's mouth.

Hartman shrugged mentally. That was her fault. She shouldn't have tried to escape.

Even as Hartman looked at the prostrate, defenceless girl, a shambling figure emerged from the dawn shadows of the building surrounding the squarc. The man was obviously a beggar; a filthy specimen, unclean, unshaven, remnants of food coagulated in his facial hair, his tattered clothing stiff with the grease of countless spillages and innumerable days without washing.

The man shambled over to the offered prize of the girl's body and shaking with lust he began to play with the unprotected breasts, allowing his hands to wander over the taught abdomen. Then he lifted himself upward so he could straddle her, facing her head. His weight squashed her rounded, breasts into her ribcage. At the same time he manoeuvred his engorged prick towards her open mouth.

In moments, the peasant was forcing the naked white beauty to suck his swollen cock and it was clear he wouldn't be happy until she had swallowed his entire offering of glutinous sperm.

To Hartman, this was no more than the slut deserved. She was a bitch; a stuck-up, English slut, who needed to be taught a lesson.

For her part, Rachel was trying to shut out of her mind the filthy stinking creature, who was raping her mouth. She had to suck off the loathsome swine; there was no alternative but at least she could try to blot everything out. Then she realised, the sooner she finished this odious task, the quicker she would get a few moments respite. And so she began reluctantly, to use her tongue to excite this filthy beggar.

With rasping groans, the man finally began to twitch his hips faster and his movements became more and more frenetic as his moment approached. Then with a wheezing roar he finally allowed his sperm to erupt, at the same time withdrawing from Rachel's mouth, so his hot, sticky semen sprayed over her exposed face, neck and shoulders.

The man's shuddering slowed and, gasping out his lust, he climbed off Rachel's prostrate form and readjusted his filthy garments. Stepping back from the helpless Rachel, he spat on her face, cursing her in Arabic. Then he bent to her again, to wipe his hands in her hair, before turning away to shamble off back into the maze of streets leading off the square.

Rachel was fighting back the tears of shame and disgust. The night had been long and brutal. She had lost count of how many of the villagers had used her mouth for their sexual gratification. Men and women, for God's sake! The women maybe had been the worst. She had been forced to lap out their filthy crotches, and suffer their evil kisses. Then most of them, their lust sated, had straddled her body and urinated over her, the final insult to a captured, white Christian slavegirl. And some of the men! After they had used her mouth, they had stood off from her to lash her with whips and straps, raising angry, red wheals on her defenceless flesh.

But maybe this was the end of her present suffering. There were few people about now, at this early hour. Maybe, once rid of this vagrant, she would have a brief respite from the torment. Then she realised the reality of her new, still strange predicament, Just because it was another day, would anything change? Surely a new day would mean nothing new for her. If nothing else, she would face another long crawl, carrying her burden of the heavy rock back to the display hall.

Rachel shuddered as she wondered what more tortures

awaited her. She had yet to meet the Sheik; but to judge from the behaviour of these cruel people, she could expect him to be the most vile man a white girl could ever meet. She shocked herself then as an insistent voice told her that the Sheik was no ordinary man; she was no longer an ordinary girl. The Sheik was a cruel, Arabian Master and she was a mere slave; worse even, as she realised she was a Christian slave; an object of the vilest contempt for these Arabian men.

Still chuckling to himself, Hartman was content for a moment or two, simply watching the spectacle unfolding before him. The morning sun glancing off the bright sandy square told him that the day promised to be another hot one. Typical of the days here in the interior. He smiled to himself as he watched the gross villager forcing his fat cock deep into Rachel's gulping mouth. He wondered how long the man could hold out against the energetic sucking of his prick by the gorgeous offering left for him, and any other casual passer by.

The slut's melon sized breasts crushed under the man's weight as he pumped his bulk up and down above the defenceless girl. The ugly brute was forcing himself deeper into Rachel's mouth, and her own drool was running from her mouth as she struggled to bring this brutal assault to an end.

Soon though, Hartman had tired of the spectacle. Besides, it was inflaming his own desire and he decided he would send for a slavegirl for himself. But he wouldn't fuck the bitch! He wouldn't shaft her mouth either. He grinned to himself as he looked at the dog-whip hanging on the wall of his room; he would lash the unfortunate slut. Then, he might fuck her. Unless he decided it would please him more to merely masturbate, until his sperm jetted over the helpless form of the mare! Still grinning, he reached for the bell-rope beside his bed.

Hartman had left the slavegirl where she lay in her chains, sobbing into the rush matting on the floor, her collar attached securely to a ring in the wall at the head of the bed. She hadn't had much idea how to pleasure a man, but then she would learn. So instead of sex, Hartman had amused himself with the whip and the goad, and a set of body chains. He had gained his final satisfaction by masturbating himself, the sight of her helplessness being all the stimulation he needed, using her as if she was no more than a living version of a magazine picture. When he had finally climaxed, he had jetted his seed into her open mouth, forcing her to swallow.

Then, indifferent to the wretched slavegirl's misery, Hartman had dressed and now he was making his way down the staircase at the side of the house and head down toward the square. Just as he rounded the corer of the house, yet another villager had just finished pumping a copious stream of hot semen deep into Rachel's mouth. The stinking, ugly creature held Rachel's nose so she was forced to swallow the entire load. Exhausted, then, the vagrant flopped down over Rachel's face and lay there until he could compose himself. He then got up off her abused body and began to wipe the remaining slime from his softening penis across her face and into her hair. The vagrant had finally hoisted himself upright, to lean over Rachel's filthy, abused body. The man grinned and gave her labia a savage pinch; laughing at the screech of pain issuing from Rachel's lips.

Hartman couldn't read the filthy villager's mind, of course, but it was a sure bet the ogre would be hoping the slavegirl would still be here later that night; would be telling himself what he would do with the defenceless, offered white beauty. Hartman grinned then. The little shit would be unlucky. Inside three hours, they would be on the way to Sheik Abbas again.

As he watched the man dismount the slut, Hartman admitted to himself that he rarely found such valuable flesh as he had in this one. She was treasure. There was something about her that seemed to make men want to degrade and abuse her. The Sheik, Hartman reflected, might well keep this one.

Hartman came over to where Rachel lay and looking down at her body he felt another surge of lust in his loins. Her long, beautiful legs were spread wide and gobs of dried and half-dried semen were splattered all around her genitals. Not being able to actually fuck the girl, the men had mostly amused themselves by masturbating and aiming their spunk at her belly probably to see if they could hit the target!

A grin moved on Hartman's face as he saw some of them had succeeded, and her pubic hairs were matted with the stuff, some of it still slithering down the inside of her thighs. Her mouth was covered with a coating of spunk and her body bore slash marks where many of the villagers had used whips or sticks on her.

Hartman decided that he would leave later that afternoon to begin the rest of the journey to the Sheik's compound. He had an idea of what would happen to this sensuous white slut when they got there. He knew that a cruel cage awaited her and he also knew of the Sheik's fierce temper at the audacity of any white slavegirl who had attempted to escape. Well, Hartman decided, one of the men could clean her up, give her water, and she could stay where she was until it was time to leave. A few more hours in the sun; an occasional turning, would give her a nice tan. The Arabs liked a white slut, but they also appreciated a slave that had a nice golden, colour too.

He looked down at her in contempt. "I'll leave you here until we move on slut!" He spat into her face. "And no screaming. Or it's the whip!" He grinned then and hefted his goad. "Or maybe some more of this." With that, he turned away and walked back to his room, and the waiting slavegirl. There was an hour or so to while away. Plenty of time to use that little slut again, before they got the consignment on the move again. As with the stuck-up bitch, out there in the square, another hour or so of degradation and abuse would give her a foretaste of what life as a Christian slavegirl was all about.

10 - Displayed For Sheik Abbas!

The whole world seemed to be spinning around and there was a dreadful whirring in her ears, as, slowly, Rachel recovered. She looked upwards towards the roof, able to make out the rough stone in the gloom, the meagre light coming from a low wattage, wire covered light fitting in the domed ceiling.

Where the hell was she? The last she remembered was being released from that awful pole, in that poky little village, and shackled, by the neck, to five other girls in a coffle. Then they had been whipped and goaded into the back of a canvas covered lorry, where they had been told to curl up together in the filthy straw that covered the bed of the truck. There had been a quick drink of water for each of them, before they had been allowed to sleep. Sleep? A drugged sleep no doubt, Rachel decided. The bastards had given them drugged water, of course.

And now?

It was hot and she was sweating profusely and there was the stink of unwashed human flesh, and stale wastes. Even through the muzzle she still wore, the stench was almost unbearable.

Her eyes flickered, and with a groan she tried to move. It was impossible. She was lying on her back, and there was something pressing down across her throat, something rough, with jagged splinters around it. Her wrists were clamped beside her head and she realised she was in some kind of pillory. She tried to move her legs, but again, she couldn't. They were aching like hell and she realised her calves had been forced back beneath her thighs, and that there was something thick, hard and unyielding jammed across her legs, behind her knees.

Another dungeon! God, how much more did they think she could take?

A further groan escaped her lips, and she splathered into the muzzle as she tried to turn her head. All she managed to do was sink more splinters into her flesh, as the pillory gouged her neck. She tried to roll her gaze to the side, managing to see enough to realise she was not alone in the room.

Then, as if on cue, the room was filled with the groans and sobbing of other girls, as they too recovered. She was between two other girls, both of them white, one a redhead the other, a brunette. Both of the girls, like Rachel, were muzzled, and they were moving their heads about in terror as they tried to understand what was happening to them. Their futile struggles merely added to the agony and, like Rachel, they soon realised their struggling made thing worse; only increased the discomfort.

Eventually, all three of them settled down, just grunting and moaning into their muzzles, as the pain went on. It was clear to Rachel that the three were not alone and that there were other women in the room, across the other side, beyond her feet, where she couldn't see.

Then the whirring of a motor began again.

For one moment, Rachel thought they were going to bend her back even further, but this time, she had things wrong. Now she realised that, with her two companions, she was being tilted upwards and forwards, so that eventually, she felt her weight being transferred to stretch her ankles and lower legs, as the pillory she was chained into slowly became upright. Now she could see the other three girls across the space, about ten feet away. Two white girls and a gorgeous black girl, each of them chained as she was, their necks and wrists pinioned, their lower legs bent beneath their bodies, and strapped to the heavy spine of the pillory.

Rachel could now see how she was displayed, her thighs forced back beneath her, with her hips spread wide so that her genitals were on full view, as were her, soft, rounded, thrusting breasts.

The room was full of the moans of tortured girls as the agony continued. Then the door at the end of the room crashed open and in walked Hartman, his obscenely fat body wobbling, a grin on his ugly face and his grotesque belly straining against his vest, hanging over the thick leather belt. In his right hand he was holding his beloved goad.

His grin widened as he made straight for Rachel.

He stopped in front of her and leered into her face. The goad found its target as Hartman forced the metal tip into Rachel's vagina. He giggled as he gave her a sharp jolt of power, causing Rachel to arch away from the upright forcing her head and wrists down against the pillory. He treated her to another short shock, then said. "Time for inspection." He looked about the room, his gaze encompassing all of the wretched girls, hanging in their pillories. "The Sheik is to decide what's to become of you all." He sniffed. "This is the initial inspection. After this you'll be assessed by Sheik Abbas, so he can decide what to do with you."

Then the door scraped back on its rusting hinges again, and the imposing figure of an Arab walked into the room. Sheik Abbas? It had to be! And my God! Rachel shuddered.

The Sheik was holding a chain leash, at the end of which there was a naked white girl on all fours, by his left leg. The chain was attached to a heavy, deep leather collar and the girl's head was being forced up high, as the Sheik pulled on the chain. Sheik Abbas stopped, jerking savagely backwards on the chain, causing the girl to choke against the thick, studded collar as she pulled up sharp. The Sheik looked down at her with contempt, then kicked her in the side. "Sit!" he hissed.

Immediately, the naked slave adopted a dog-like sitting position beside him, crouching with her hands held between her thighs, resting on the floor. She was trembling, cowering almost, her panic-stricken gaze on the whip that the Sheik had tucked into the waist band of his caftan.

Rachel sucked in a frightened gasp as she took in the red and blue welts on the girl's white skin, the bruises on her buttocks and the filth on her sweating body.

The Sheik looked around at the room, gazing contemptuously at the trussed group of girls, his shipment of human misery. Then an evil grin showed. "No doubt you sluts think you are suffering." A hoarse chuckle escaped him, as he went on. "You have barely started. This is luxury, compared to what is to come." He looked down at the pitiable slavegirl by his side. "Down!" he snapped.

The girl immediately lay on her side, curling her legs up, resting her head on her outstretched arms. It was amazing how dog-like she looked. The Sheik snapped out another. "Sit!"

The wretched girl scrambled back to the crouching position again, but it wasn't fast enough for the Sheik and the whip slashed into her defenceless buttocks.

The girl wailed out, but her cries were not those of a woman. Instead the sounds issuing from her were the yelping cry of a dog in pain. The whip slashed into her again, and once more her dog-like cries sounded through the room. The Sheik sneered at the wretched creature, then snapped out. "Speak!"

The girl began to bark and yap, like a dog, her hoarse voice cracking, tears in her eyes, an expression of utter degradation on her pretty face, as she was forced to debase herself in front of the other slavegirls.

That didn't seem to bother the Sheik, for he lifted the whip to smash it into her flesh again. "Cease!"

The girl fell silent, and sat, still crouching, shivering in fright, beside her Master.

Rachel felt her heart go out to the girl, in her humiliating position. Then realised, with horror. This could easily be her, in a very short time.

The Sheik looked about the room again. "You see how very suited this bitch is to her new role." He chuckled. "It took her some time to stop screaming as a woman would scream, when whipped." He shrugged. "But she eventually got the idea." He caressed the naked slavegirl's bruised and battered flesh. "I whip her only when I want her to do something." Another sadistic smile. "Or stop doing something! Or when it pleases me!" He shrugged. "She now voices her pain only as a dog." He looked down, at the slavegirl. "Isn't that so bitch?"

The slavegirl yapped once, and then licked her chops, as would a dog.

The Sheik took something from his pocket and held it up, It was a dog biscuit, shaped like a large bone. He looked at the cowering girl. "What do you say bitch?"

The girl adopted a begging position, and began to pant and whimper, asking for the tit-bit.

The Sheik grinned contemptuously again and dropped the biscuit.

The slavegirl caught it in her mouth, then crouched down on her belly and began to eat the bone-shaped biscuit, holding it between her extended arms, crunching the biscuit with her head to one side, using her back teeth. When she had eaten it, the Sheik yanked the chain again. "Fours!"

The girl got to all fours, again, and looked up, waiting for the next command. Rachel was horrified at the adoring look on the girl's face as she stared up at her master.

The Sheik merely took her over to the wall and fastened the chain to a ring set in the stonework. He slashed her with the whip and snapped. "Down!"

The girl dropped to her belly again and lay half on her side, like the dog, they had virtually turned her into.

God, Rachel thought, if they could condition a girl to behave instinctively, like that and love it, what couldn't they makc any of them do?

As if her had read Rachel's mind, the Sheik boomed out. "So my little sluts! You see what we expect of you! There was one example of how you can be trained." He paused. "To behave exactly as we wish!"

Then he licked his lips and cast a slow gaze over all of the pilloried girls. His eyes lighted on Rachel and with a cruel smile on his face, he lumbered over to her. He paused in front of her for a moment, then reached out to remove the muzzle.

Finally free of the vile tasting muzzle, Rachel made to speak, but the Sheik grabbed her hair, pulled her head up, and then growled at her. "Silence! I'll tell you when to speak." His fingers were then suddenly prising Rachel's jaws apart, pulling her lips back, baring her gums as he inspected her teeth. "Open wider!"

Rachel obeyed, and the thick, strong fingers were in her mouth, probing, exploring her gums and the soft tissues inside her mouth.. He took her front teeth between forefinger and thumb, tested her incisors, to see if they were tight. Then her did the same with all of her teeth, ignoring the retching of his helpless slave. Then he grabbed her tongue, twisted his fingers around it and pulled it right out, dragging it down over her chin, as far as it would go, again unconcerned about Rachel's struggles and retching. He loosed her tongue, shut her mouth then allowed his hands to wander all over her body, pinching and kneading her flesh, squeezing her buttocks, her breasts, and teasing her nipples, which, to Rachel's surprise had suddenly hardened, beginning to push out into small peaks of desire.

A satisfied smile appeared on the Sheik's face as he noticed this, then his insistent fingers were forcing their way between Rachel's well shaped labia, wriggling their way into her moistening sex-hole.

Rachel knew she could no longer resist this massage, degrading as it was. She felt her spirits drop as, of their own volition, her juices began to flow. She felt her cheeks begin to redden as the shame overtook her and she moaned, closing her eyes in a childish gesture, as if it would mean no one else could see her wanton behaviour.

The lubrication helped the Sheik to get his fingers right inside her sex-passage, and she sucked in a gasp of air, half pain, half pleasure, as the man's blunt fingers slid I right inside her warm, moist passage. Then the Sheik began to masturbate her, slowly, gently, his fingertips teasing her vaginal lips and seeking her clitoris. Rachel began to squirm involuntarily, as his fingers played with her distended pleasure-bud, touching, rubbing, causing her to try to close her legs on his hand. Next, he nipped her clitoris between finger and thumb, and started to roll her pleasure bud around, pressing it right into the crevice of her sex. He was grinning, as Rachel's heavy gasps became louder and her moans turned from moans of distaste to sound of genuine pleasure.

Rachel was soon whimpering, trying to fight the rising desire, but failing even to dull the rising ache of her passion as her pleasure began to mount. Again she tried to clamp on his hand, but with her legs wrenched back behind her it was almost impossible. All it did was heighten her frustration, as she wriggled her hips, pushing them towards him, like a common slut, all but pleading with this awful man to push his hand, his whole arm even, into her body.

All thoughts of her suffering, the fear of her possible fate were vanishing in the mist of her desire. For now she was intent only on gaining as much pleasure as possible from this abuse of her body, as the Sheik slowly and expertly brought on her natural responses, responses which she knew would end in a delicious, shuddering climax.

Now, Rachel's cries and whimpers filled the room, as the Sheik went on an on, teasing caressing and squeezing, his fingers opening and closing inside her, stretching and relaxing the muscles of her vaginal passage. Finally, Rachel could stand no more. She opened her mouth and gave vent to a wild, shrill scream of passion. A delicious warmth spread through her belly and deep inside, her juices began to flow; Her involuntary climax was as swift as it was shattering and she squirmed and wriggled, whining, whimpering, begging for more of the Sheik's hands and fingers. She was suddenly oblivious of the pain in her wrists, ankles and neck, she ground her hips against his hand, and she shoved herself towards the Sheik, like the slut she knew she would eventually become, trying to force his hand deeper into her own body.

But the Sheik grinned at her and merely withdrew his hand. He stepped back gazed at the groaning, frustrated Rachel as she hung limply in the pillory, her whole body shining with perspiration, her blonde hair hanging damp and lank, her chest heaving as she whimpered and mewled, trying to close her thighs together, trying to deny the feelings of lust as her juices welled from her vagina.

Then the Sheik lifted the whip and smashed it across her belly.

Still lost in her deep sexual desire, Rachel barely felt the blow, and she merely grunted, squirming again, thrusting towards her tormentor, grunting to him, willing him to continue with the delicious massage of her sexual parts.

The Sheik raised his eyebrows in a surprised expression, then took his arm back, and swung the lash forwards, viciously this time, right across Rachel's thrusting, defenceless breasts.

This time Rachel did scream out, and she tried ineffectually to get her imprisoned arms to the hurt. Sobbing now, suffering the sear of that last blow, she returned to the reality of her misery. As well as the pain of the lash, she could also feel her cheeks burning with shame, as she recalled what had gone on and the way she had debased herself, willingly almost, in front of her fellow captives.

The Sheik turned to Hartman. "I think we have a natural here Ernst?"

Hartman nodded enthusiastically. "Oh yes Excellency. She will need some training, but I think she will come around nicely!"

Sheik Abbas nodded in agreement, then said. "Take her to the Discipline Room! I will carry on with a full assessment!"

He turned away with out waiting for a reply and went across to his dog-slavegirl. He unhitched the chain, gave the subjugated girl one wicked slash with the whip then growled at her. "Fours!"

The girl scrambled to her hands and knees then, submissively, she allowed herself to be led, at her Master's heel, from the room.

Hartman stepped over to Rachel, then sneered at her. "Slut!" He bent, picked up the discarded muzzle and fitted it back around Rachel's mouth. After buckling the thing behind her head, he unshackled her from the pillory, setting her on her knees. He allowed her a few moments to get feeling back into her lower legs, then pushing the goad between her buttocks, he shoved the tip slightly into her anus. A swift jolt from the goad was enough to get Rachel to her feet.

Hartman slapped her rump with his huge hand. "Run, bitch! Run! Move that arse."

Rachel obeyed, sobbing as the goad landed across her buttocks. Then, with a deep blush of shame and embarrassment, she ran towards the door, her buttocks jiggling, her breasts bouncing about.

He was close behind her. "Turn left!" At the same time he landed another slap across her jiggling buttocks as she obeyed, running out into the cool of the long, stone-walled corridor.

Hartman did not run her very far.

After about fifteen yards, her slashed the whip into her thighs. "Halt and turn left!"

Gasping and wincing, she obeyed, rubbing at her sore thighs. Then another searing blow from the whip landed across her buttocks and she screamed out, her hands going for the hurt again.

Hartman's voice sounded loud in her ear. "Leave yourself alone, bitch!" he snarled at her, "Go through that door and kneel in the centre of the room!"

She obeyed, walking into a huge, round room, about thirty feet in diameter. The place was dome-shaped with white emulsioned, stone walls. Around the perimeter there was an artificially surfaced running track. Inside the brown circle, the rest of the floor, was fitted with a heavy, shag-pile carpet. Obediently, Rachel went to the centre of the room and knelt on the shag pile.

Hartman came up behind her and she felt the sudden prick of a needle in her right buttock.

Moments later the darkness closed in on her.

Rachel came around again she was still kneeling, totally naked, in the centre of the large room. She wasn't alone. Hartman was beside her, holding her upright. Also, Rachel was aware that she was in the presence of the Sheik again and she bowed her head, instinctively, as she saw him sitting in a huge armchair that was placed atop a large dais. Knowing her place now, Rachel waited, obediently, for either the Sheik or Hartman to give her another command.

Hartman prodded Rachel's buttocks with the whip. "Offer yourself to the Sheik, slut!" he hissed.

Shaking with fear of the whip, Rachel nodded her head. She was so confused and bewildered. It seemed impossible that, so recently, she had been a free woman in a normal western world. Now, she found herself naked, in chains, trying to come to terms with the awful truth that she was being considered as a mere slave; the sole property of a grotesque, greasy sadist; an Arabian Sheik, who expected her to obey any command instantly, and to do whatever was required of her.

Rachel groaned to herself, as she tried to remember. It was hopeless. Over the last days, in common with all new arrivals, she had been kept permanently under the influence of some drug or another. So much to remember. So much whipping and torture. It was difficult to know what they expected of her. Again she groaned, in fear, trembling as she tried to recall her recent lessons. Her memories were fleeting, yet she knew this wouldn't worry Hartman. To that sadistic monster, she was a mere piece of saleable flesh. Just another slave who must obey. Any failure to comply, regardless of the reason, would result in punishment. Then, as Hartman's whip cracked again, Rachel suddenly remembered. Obediently, almost in a conditioned response, she sank to all fours and crawled towards the Sheik.

Hartman flicked Rachel's soft, white buttocks again with his wire whip, and pushed her towards the Sheik. "This bitch is learning Excellency. Almost eager." Hartman leaned forwards to watch carefully, as his charge lowered her head to the floor.

Submissively, Rachel touched her lips to the rough woven carpet tiles, as close to the Sheik's feet as she dared, without actually touching them. Then she turned around completely, and forced her buttocks upwards, spreading her knees to expose her genitals and anus to the Sheik. "I offer m-m-myself to you, M-M-Master!" Rachel quavered, her lips trembling uncontrollably, finding difficulty in uttering the words.

The Sheik grinned. "Indeed, she does seem eager." His grin became a leer. "Or is it just fear of the goad Ernst!"

"Of MY goad, Excellency," Hartman sneered, and almost lovingly allowed his goad to slip through his fingers until he had hold of the handle. He gently touched it to Rachel's forehead.

Instinctively, Rachel screamed out and reared up, falling backwards against the dais. She slid down, and yelped as the back of her head hit the edge of the platform.

Hartman just laughed. "You see Excellency. I never even switched the thing on!" He stepped forwards then and this time, shoved the goad into the soft flesh of Rachel's belly. He gave her a short dose, gloating as Rachel screamed out her agony.

"On your belly! NOW!"

Sobbing, trembling in fear and clutching at the soreness around her navel, Rachel obeyed, rolling over onto her belly.

The Sheik nodded, a cruel smile still on his face. "She is indeed becoming conditioned." He looked down at Rachel, her whole body shaking with fearful anticipation, and he placed his foot on the back of Rachel's neck, pushing her face into the rough carpet. Then, ignoring her terrified shaking, he stooped down, and once again she had to suffer the indignity of his examination of her private parts.

His podgy hands began to wander all over Rachel's body and yet again, he explored her exposed flesh, fondling and squeezing her belly and her pert, upthrust breasts. "I think I was right, earlier today. I may have made an error in buying this creature." He looked at Hartman. "She's not very big! She may not have the strength to pull a cart."

Hartman shrugged. "Well, she is a Christian, which is what many of you friends prefer. She is also a natural blonde and she has the build of a pleasure slave." He allowed the goad to trace across Rachel's back, chuckling as she shivered, cringing from him, waiting for the shock to hit her. He lifted the goad away. "But, she was pretty fit when we took her, Excellency. I think she'll muscle up enough to pull a cart or a cutter's oar."

The Sheik fingered his chin. "Hmm! Or maybe she would look better harnessed to a gig."

Hartman grinned. "At the worst Excellency, she will be worth money as a pleasure slave."

The Sheik nodded. "You are right Ernst." He resumed his examination of Rachel's genitals, oblivious of her frightened shaking, and the stiffening of her body. "Not this time slut!" he remarked as he clearly realised Rachel was fighting the urge to surrender to the caress. He grinned wolfishly as his fingers then explored the pucker of her tight little anus. "Ah! She's a virgin back there Ernst!"

The fat man chuckled. "That's a bonus Your Excellency. If she doesn't make it as a galley slave, then I'm sure we can find a purchaser who is prepared to pay extra for the privilege of opening her up."

Hearing all this, Rachel sobbed and raised her head, about to plead with the Sheik to let her go. Prepared to do almost anything, she opened her mouth to speak. She was silenced immediately as the Sheik growled at her. "Stay still slave!" Then he wiped his fingers on Rachel's bent back, and straightened up, turning to Ernst.

"You can only do your best Ernst. See what you can make of her." He glanced at the cowering Rachel, then prodded her with his toe. "Supplicate yourself!"

This confused the Rachel again, and she looked up at him in panic and silent puzzlement.

The Sheik spat in her face. Growling his displeasure, he cuffed her. Then angrily, he grabbed her hair, and viciously twisted his wrist around, throwing Rachel to the floor, face upwards. He loosed her and knelt astride her body, trapping her upper arms with his knees.

Shaking her head, Rachel tried to plead with him, to let her up. It was a waste of time.

The Sheik slid his knees forwards and trapped her head between them, taking a tube-gag from a bag near his chair. He rammed the evil instrument into her mouth, and, twisting her head to the side, he secured the gag at the rear of her neck. He stood up and pushed her away with his foot. "If you won't speak bitch, wear the gag!" Then, casually, he took his dog-whip from his belt and began to whip her.

Sobbing, writhing, scrabbling about the floor, Rachel tried desperately to avoid the lash, but all she did was provide more targets for the singing leather as it sang through the air. Time after time the leather cut into her tanned flesh, curling wickedly about her abused body, the Sheik ceasing only when Rachel had stopped struggling and curled herself into a sobbing, protective ball. She moaned and began to roll off her knees, almost unconscious with the pain.

Hartman sighed wearily, and stepped across to a large brass tap near the doorway. He filled a bucket with cold water and. going back to Rachel, he splashed the stuff over her battered body, to bring her spluttering back to full consciousness. As she regained her senses, Rachel cowered away from them, sobbing into the gag.

Hartman ignored her cries. "You were told to supplicate yourself. For the last time, I'll tell you what to do!" He grabbed a great handful of her hair, lifted her head and hissed into her face. "You get on your belly and go over to the Sheik." He shook Rachel's head. "You wriggle towards him, like a snake. All the way. When you reach your Lord and Master, spread your arms to the side, and kiss the floor. Then you kneel, lean backwards grab your ankles and offer your sluttish body to His Excellency." He tightened his grip on Rachel's hair and shook her head from side to side. "Now do you understand?"

Rachel, stifled her sobs, and nodded, mumbling into the tube-gag.

"Good!" He shoved Rachel towards the Sheik. "Now! Supplicate yourself!"

Like the obedient slavegirl she was becoming, Rachel lay down, on her belly, her shoulders and buttocks quivering with fright. Awkwardly, writhing, as she had been told, she slid across the floor, wincing as the rough carpet fibres aggravated the fresh welts on her skin. When she had reached the dais she did exactly as Hartman had told her. She got to her knees and bent backwards, grabbing her ankles and arching her taught body towards the Sheik. She stayed still, straining her gorgeous breasts towards her Master.

The Sheik made her stay in the position for about ten or fifteen seconds than, he got up and looked down at her, a sneer of contempt on his face. "Now you know what is meant by supplicating yourself." He leaned forwards and caressed Rachel's offered breasts. "You won't forget, will you slut!"

Frantically, Rachel shook her head, gurgling an unintelligible reply into her gag. Then she wailed as the Sheik slashed her offered breasts with the whip. But she knew she had to maintain her position, or suffer more slashes. Quivering she held still, her shapely breasts heaving in fear, as she panted into her gag.

"Now!" the Sheik went on, "hands on the floor again!"

Needing no further telling; fearing more of the lash, Rachel placed her palms on the carpet, lowering her head in submission, still sobbing into the gag and trembling, her heart hammering. Oh God! She thought, was she going to end up like that wretched creature, in the Display-Room. Was she destined to spend her life acting like a dog, just to amuse these perverts? She sagged then, realising that whatever they wanted to do with her, she had to obey. Her head hung lower as she waited, submissively, for the next command.

The Sheik turned to Hartman. "I wonder how well she runs Ernst? Fetch me the coach-whip please."

Hartman chuckled. "Oh yes!" Eagerly, he stepped over to a rack on the wall and took down a well-oiled, long handled whip with a thin, whippy end. He cracked the whip in the air, the noise causing Rachel to flinch and suck in a panic-stricken gasp of air.

He passed the whip to the Sheik and once again the room reverberated to the crack of the whip as the Sheik tested it, allowing the end to flick Rachel's buttocks. She straightened up with a muffled squeal, her hands going to her buttocks, seeking the fresh weal she knew had been added to the tender stripes already on her flesh.

The Sheik laughed. "On your feet, Mare. Up! Quick!"

Again the whip cracked, this time just in front of Rachel's face.

She needed no further bidding, but scrambled to her feet, splathering into the gag, an expression of bewilderment in her eyes.

The whip flicked her across the buttocks again, the stinging end curling about her hips to sear the base of her belly and she jumped, squealing out in pain as the leather aggravated her already reddened skin.

The Sheik cracked the whip again, "Now slut! On the track and start running! All around the room." The whip cracked again. "Move!"

Rachel sobbed turned to him to plead with him, but she never had chance to even open her mouth as another flick from the whip bit into her legs. She turned and ran towards the perimeter track.

Another flick from the whip started her running. "Knees up slut!" the Sheik barked. "Knees up and keep moving!"

Miserably, Rachel started to jog around the track, lifting her knees high, her face reddening with shame as she realised how she must look to these men with her boobs bouncing about, and her buttocks wriggling enticingly.

"Faster!" the Sheik screamed at her, and the whip landed again, this time curling wickedly around her upper body, the tip cutting into her tender nipples.

With a muffled yelp of pain, Rachel all but tripped, as this time the whip seared into her flesh, just below her buttocks, the leather wrapping itself around her legs, to leave its mark on the taut muscles at the front of her thighs. She started to run now, her knees jerking up higher into an exaggerated trot. Her breathing was becoming heavier and more laboured. She knew she was fit, knew she could run well and for long distances. But this was something different. This time she was running in fear, with a whip cracking at her flesh, a man screaming at her to go faster, and with a vile gag wrapped around her face, stifling her, restricting the supply of much-needed air.

Even so, she began to move into her stride, not far short of a sprint. But still the whip slashed into her body, the Sheik giggling and shouting with each slash of the thin leather whip.

Soon Rachel's breathing became ragged, and she began to stumble as she tried to evade the lash, and keep her footing on the slippery carpet.

But there was no respite, and the madman kept her moving with well-aimed strokes of the supple leather, so that hardly a part of her upper body and legs was untouched. As she started to lather up into a sweat, the friction between her thighs and buttocks, was working the moist film of perspiration into a thick, slippery foam, as though she were a horse. Her torso was dripping with her sweat, the pain of the whip made worse by the moisture on her skin. Each time the whip landed, the leather threw up a misty spray of perspiration around her and, unashamedly, now she was crying into the gag, crying out, asking, begging for the torture to stop.

She was wasting her time. Even had the evil sadist been able to understand her gurgling protests, she knew he would stop only when he was satisfied. And so the crazed man kept shouting at her, the whip kept slashing into her tender skin, until breathing became almost impossible. She just could not take any more and finally, she stumbled to sprawl onto the red surface. She cried into the gag again as the tough surface of the track added its fiery scraping to her already burning, tortured flesh.

Casually almost, the Sheik stepped over to her, cast aside the coach whip, and drew a riding crop from his belt. He laid the crop across Rachel's glowing buttocks, eliciting a screech of agony from her. "ON YOUR KNEES!" he roared, leaning over the terrified Rachel. "I'LL TELL YOU WHEN YOU CAN LIE DOWN, MARE!"

Fearfully, Rachel scrambled to her knees once more, trembling violently in fright, her pain-wracked breathing splathering through the gag, seeming to fill the room. Head down, she waited for her Master, a cloud of steam rising from her sweat-soaked body.

The Sheik looked at Hartman. "She runs well." He ran his hands softly over Rachel's dripping flesh, allowing his fingers to stray into the crease of her buttocks. He straightened up. "Stay on all fours, bitch!" he warned as he leaned over her. "I'm leaving you with Hartman for a while. As you will have gathered, as well as knowing how to use the goad, he's an expert with the whip. I can assure you he can cut you to the bone."

He grabbed Rachel's hair and pulled her head right back, to stare into her terrified eyes. "Or he can subject you to unknown agonies, without leaving a mark on your hide." He grinned. "Such a pretty hide, and one for which we can charge out patrons dearly. So don't make it necessary for him to leave any more marks on your skin. UNDERSTAND?"

Rachel nodded frantically. She didn't want any more of that whip. Trembling now, she remained on all fours before the Sheik and sobbed quietly into her gag. She knew they were winning. She would have to obey them or be whipped and tortured. Oh God! What had she done to deserve this?

Her thoughts were interrupted by a slash of the Sheik's whip into her shoulders and she cowered away from him. He looked down at her. "This one will make a fine pony-slave, Ernst." He smiled cruelly and bent, once more running his hands over Rachel's tortured body. "We will sell her on, I think. She will soon be well-furnished, and she'll train on. She will carry a rider well!"

He stood with his hands on his hips, the crop still in his grasp. "When she is on the auction block, we must remember to emphasise her qualities in that area." He turned to Hartman. "She will fetch a good price." He grinned at Hartman. "Now, take the mare away and get her fit for the slave-market."

"Oh yes Excellency. I shall enjoy doing that!"

The Sheik nudged Rachel with his toe. "Soon you will be in the Middle East. Then you will find out what REAL fitness is, and you will learn how a slavegirl behaves towards her Masters." He caressed Rachel's long, blonde hair, then turned to Hartman. "Make sure you keep that mane of hair in good condition, Ernst." He chuckled again, gave Rachel another savage slash with the crop and stalked from the room.

Hartman was still grinning as he came over to Rachel. In moments, he had shackled a chain to the slave-collar. He pulled savagely on the chain. "Come on, slut! On your feet! I've work to do so move that arse!"

Still panting from her exertions, her saliva still dripping from the gag, slicking over her naked body, Rachel struggled upright. Submissively, she bowed her head and allowed Hartman to lead her from the room, and along the corridor.

They didn't go far. Within a few yards, Hartman snarled. "Halt and face left!"

Rachel obeyed, mutely, to find herself in front of a heavy pair of green, plastic, flap-doors. There was the strong smell of human waste and urine in her nostrils, and she could see pieces of straw sticking out beneath the doors.

Hartman prodded her with the whip, herding her through the swing doors. The room was small, rock-walled with three wooden stalls built into the wall in front of her. The stalls were lined with straw bedding and each was provided with a large slave-ring and a trough. Over against one wall there was a huge pile of rotting, fermenting, soiled sweepings from the stalls; a midden of human excrement and straw!

The stench was vile, but Hartman didn't seem to notice. He yanked angrily on the chain. "Come on!" He snarled at Rachel, dragging her towards the stinking heap. Unceremoniously, he threw Rachel into one of the stalls and clipped the chain to the large ring in the wall. "Now stay there! I'll be back." He paused. "Eventually" Without another word, he turned and left the stinking room, abandoning Rachel to her misery.

12 - Prepared For The Slave-Market

Despite the trouble the slut, Rachel, had caused him, Hartman was beginning to realise she was becoming one of his pet acquisitions. Since she had been put into the pit, with the 'roaches, she had begun to mellow a little. Yet, in any case, there was something different about the little slut. Stuck up she might be, but she was really stacked.

His piggy little eyes gleamed as he peered through the grille of the girl's cell. The slut had been sleeping for about four hours, and her breathing was deep and rhythmic, but Hartman knew, any moment now, she would wake from her drugged sleep.

His gaze roamed over the luscious captive animal lying on the bed. He leered then and rubbed absently at his hardening prick, as he continued to survey the unconscious girl. Just an hour before, Hartman had prepared the unconscious slave for the auction storage room and now he felt his cock pulse again, towards a full erection. She definitely looked real sexy. Handling her had been a real buzz! Placing that neat waist into the iron belt. He rubbed at his crotch again, as he let his thoughts roll. He remembered how soft and smooth her flesh had felt beneath his hands, as he had explored the superb body at will; the way in which he had caressed the silky smooth flesh; assessing the firmness and shape of her magnificent breasts. He had allowed his fingers to invade her most intimate places, forcing aside the hood of her clitoris so he could pinch and stroke the sensitive spot. Even in her unconscious state, she had started to juice up and had groaned, stirring as, unknowingly, she had responded to his touch.

As he had to do with all new slavegirls that were to be sold, Hartman had also fitted the girl with a leather, half-hood, so it covered the upper half of her face. The tight fitting hood was pulled taut, so it clung to the upper half of her head, pulled down at the rear to be secured to the ring in her steel collar; hidden beneath the fronds of her soft, blonde hair, which fanned out from beneath the hood. The half-hood served to emphasise the soft, fullness of her lovely lips and the shapely line of her smooth jaw-line, and of course it made her completely unaware of her surroundings. That was the main purpose of the hood. When she awoke, she would experience pure terror. And while she was in the storage room, another little refinement that the hood possessed, would make her agonising wait seem like purgatory; dulling her senses, so she would be all the easier to handle on the auction platform.

Then Hartman's cruel, lined features moved into a cold smile, as, almost on cue, the girl stirred. Beneath the thick rolled edge of the hood, her mouth formed into a lazy smile; her hands began to explore her own body, as if reassuring herself she was really awake. The girl murmured, 'So I was dreaming after all.' She moved and started up, causing her chains to jingle. The girl drew in a sudden gasp of fear and now, her mouth moved into a horrified 'o' as her hands went to the thick metal band clipped around her slender waist. The girl sobbed, 'Oh God! It's true! They kidnapped me.' Her head drooped and her shoulders rounded into a ball of misery as her body began to shake.

Then, as she realised she had the hood over her eyes, she stiffened in horror and her hands went to her neck, feeling for the heavy steel collar welded firmly around her neck and the chain that led from the steel band to a ring-bolt cemented into the stone wall.

She couldn't quite reach the collar. Her hands were manacled together and the chain between her wrists was short, doubled through a ring in her waist-band.

Hartman watched, fascinated, as the girl tried, in vain, to reach the stiff, unyielding, half-hood, her hands opening and closing in frustration. Terrified, she began to shake her head, as though trying to throw off the hood.

The sadistic Hartman chuckled again. There was no chance she would even budge the thing.

Still struggling, the slavegirl began to scream out, 'Please! Help me! Someone, help me!' Her head was swinging wildly and blindly about and she was clearly, beside herself with terror.

Hartman indulged in a quiet chuckle. He grunted and his features became impassive.

"Slut!"

The girl stopped struggling, clearly realising it was futile. Resigned almost, she began to explore her body again. Her hands wandered over her soft skin, over her belly, feeling all around the tight waist-band. She traced the contour of her small waist and the swell of her belly; as though trying to ascertain the body she couldn't see was truly hers and that she really was in bondage.

Hartman rubbed at his crotch once more. Now he could get her ready for the storage room; leave her hanging by the elbows, to wait, and suffer, before her turn on the Auction block. He really was going to enjoy that. He picked up the leather hold-all beside his feet and reached into the bag. He took out a small, remote controller, pointed it towards the girl and switched it on.

He grinned as the girl suddenly started up, screaming. Her head moved frantically from side to side as she tried to reach her ears; tried to remove the hood. Useless. Inside the hood the little refinement had began its work. The built-in 'walkman' that Hartman had just operated was now filling the girl's ears with piercing, deafening, white-noise; it would be driving her crazy.

Hartman grinned, satisfactorily. The 'walkman' idea had been his own and it worked to perfection. The continual screaming noise invading the mind of this slut would turn her brain to temporary mush, so she would be a virtual zombie as, later, she was put through her paces on the block.

Still grinning to himself, Hartman opened the cell-door and stepped across to the vulnerable slavegirl where he stood looking for just a moment.

Obviously, the wretch couldn't hear him, yet somehow she seemed to sense he was there. Her head turned, blindly towards him, her lips slightly parted, her breasts heaving, as she began to shake in fearful anticipation.

Hartman delved into the hold-all and took out a hypodermic syringe. With practised ease, he administered the Pentathol; not enough to knock her out; just enough to make her compliant and unable to resist. Not that a slavegirl's resistance bothered Hartman. It gave him an excuse, if he ever needed one, to cut the whip across their tits, or the into rounded cheeks of their tight little butts. He stifled a groan, and rubbed at his growing erection.

He switched off the Walkman then, and stooped to delve into the hold-all again. This time he took out a leather muzzle, with a hole, in the centre, the hole designed to take an erect penis. From the inside edge of the hole, a short length of thick rubber tubing protruded. Smiling cruelly, Hartman placed the tube against the girl's lips.

She stiffened in shock, and raised her hands as if to push him away. But he merely shoved the tube harder against her mouth, holding her head still with his free hand.

At first she resisted, refusing to open her lips. Turning her head aside, she clamped her mouth tight. Hartman shrugged and reached for her left nipple. Viciously he pinched the sensitive bud, between finger and thumb, causing the helpless slavegirl to yell out. He stifled the girl's cry by forcing the stiff tube down her throat. Expertly, he took the muzzle straps behind her head, to secure them tightly over the leather of the hood, the girl grunting with pain as the straps cut into her flesh.

Then Hartman grabbed her neck chain and released it from the wall. He draped the chain between her thrusting breasts, allowing the free end to slide off the bed. Falling to the stone floor, the links made an almost musical tinkling and Hartman whistled a snatch of 'Take These Chains From My Heart'. Then he grinned into her face, 'And put them round your tits, eh slut?' He released her hands and dropped the manacles into the hold-all. Spreading her feet apart, he growled at her, as she protested, mumbling into the muzzle.

With a rasping sigh, he turned her around and pulled her delicious rump into his loins, rubbing himself against the velvety skin. He allowed his erect cock to rest between her buttocks, and began moving his hips back and forth. The tip of his massive weapon slid over the bridge of sensitive flesh dividing her vagina and her back passage. He pulled her hips back against him and let out another groan of pleasure. A slight weeping of semen lubricated his prick, as it slid over her soft flesh. Then he drew right back and shoved his prick upwards, so it rested against the base of her spine, nudging into the hollow of her back. A few more enjoyable thrusts, almost sliding, in turn, into her anus, and vagina before he ceased and stepped back.

He bent to reach between those glorious buttocks, to grab a huge handful of her soft, rounded sex-lips. A few moments of gentle fondling and soon the girl mewled; whining into the stiff leather of the muzzle as, despite herself, her juices began to flow. She even bent forwards, pushing her buttocks against him, but he knew this was an instinctive reaction to the frustration she would be feeling; frustration induced by the Pentathol. Not that it mattered to Hartman. He didn't really want to shag the girl. With free access to any of the sluts that came under his supervision, he always felt spoiled for choice.

Then, suddenly she tried to clamp on his hand.

He let out a chuckle and loosed her love-mound, to put his left arm tight about her belly. Expertly, he bent her over, to thrust his swelling prick against the puckered flesh of her anus.

She began to struggle now, as he nudged his tool a fraction of an inch beyond the dry entrance to her anus, before withdrawing again, laughing at her. It would be great to ram his cock into that tight little arse, to force himself upwards, deep into her. He resisted the temptation. The girl's arse was virginal. If he tried to open her now, her passage would split. This didn't matter to Hartman; he would enjoy hearing the bitch scream as her flesh gave way. The trouble was, she would be so tight, opening her would hurt him too. For now, the slut could hold onto her tight little arse-ring.

Shrugging, he stepped back a little more and pushed his hand between her legs again. This time he grabbed the chain, pulling it savagely backwards between her legs. The links cut deep into her hot, swelling genitals, parting the small globes of flesh, scragging deep into her wet sex-lips, wresting a cry from her. Pulling her upright again, he nestled her buttocks against his thighs once more. Then he took the chain right up her back and secured the links to the rear of her collar, fastening it in place with a padlock.

Now, her leather encased head fell forwards, in defeat. She whimpered into the muzzle, as he allowed his hands to wander over the soft, golden flesh, Gently he fondled the swelling roundness of her belly, assessing the tightness and firmness of her pert breasts. The slavegirl shuddered for a moment, then gasped into the muzzle as suddenly, Hartman pulled her arms behind her and fastened her wrists together with handcuffs. Then he bound her elbows together, with a length of rough twine. He stood back for a moment, then, grinning.

She turned towards him, as if pleading.

She was wasting her time.

Hartman just growled into her ear, "On your knees slut."

Awkwardly, the girl obeyed and sank to her knees. She was still shivering with fright; her mind would be shattered with bewilderment; wondering what was happening.

Next Hartman took the end of the twine up towards the top of her head. Pulling her hooded head upright in the collar, he secured the end of the rope, to the ring in the top of the hood; this restraint forcing the girl to hold up her head, stretching her throat, above the steel collar, showing off the white softness of her neck.

Satisfied, Hartman moved round to the front of her, taking hold of his rampant dick as he did so, grinning into the girl's masked features. He grabbed her chin and forced her head further backwards, so she gasped and splathered through the muzzle. Then he began to wave his monstrous tool beneath her nostrils, so should would be able to smell his arousal, "Any resistance, and I'll take that muzzle off so you can lick this feller clean!" He leaned towards her, "After it's been up inside you." He chuckled, "Both ways!"

The terrified girl nodded her head as best she could, her fearful gasps breaching the confines of the muzzle.

Hartman growled at her, pulled her to her feet and turned her to face the door. "Now we walk." He patted her delicious rump, "And don't bump into anything will you!"

Obediently the terror-stricken girl moved towards the door.

"Turn left and run!" Hartman snapped.

Again the girl obeyed, breaking into a trot, her buttocks jiggling, her breasts swinging freely about as she ran blindly along the corridor. She was screaming now, as she tried to evade the savage slashes from the thin, leather whip that cut, repeatedly, into her defenceless buttocks. Then, purposely, Hartman reached his foot forwards, tripping the girl, so she went sprawling in front of him.

The hapless girl wailed into the muzzle, as unable to cushion her fall, the breath was knocked from her body as she crashed into the bare earth. Immediately Hartman began to beat her. Finally, growling his displeasure, he grabbed the few exposed fronds of her hair and dragged her to her feet again. "Mind you don't trip again, slut!" Another slash of the whip and he pushed her onwards again, continuing his regular persuading with the whip.

About a minute later, Hartman pulled her to a halt, and pushed her through a metal-framed doorway. They were now in a cold, forbidding room, empty and gloomy, lit only by a weak bulb in the centre of the ceiling. Beside this bulb there was a thick length of chain hanging down for about three feet, terminating in a thick iron hook.

Grabbing her shoulders, Hartman manoeuvred her into position beside the chain.

Unaware of where she was, of what was happening to her now, the girl was shaking in every bone of her body. Suddenly, urine began to run down her legs, as fear overcame her control. This merely earned her another slash of the whip. He came closer to her and pushed her back against the chain. Grinning into her face, he placed the hook into her elbow bindings. He still had the manacles that had been on her wrists, and he laughed, as he slashed the connecting chain across her thighs. The slavegirl screamed into the muzzle. Almost involuntarily, her legs had bent and, stooping down, Hartman clicked the manacles about her ankles. Then he grabbed her lower legs to stretch them wide apart, clicking each anklet of the leg irons to ring-bolts set about five feet apart, in the stone flags beneath the chain.

The girl's breathing was becoming frantically laboured and her eyes widened in terror, and she struggled uselessly against her bonds.

Hartman leered at her and ran his hands over her belly, allowing his fingers the slide between her sex-lips. His thick fingers began to caress her clitoris and she groaned into the muzzle as she tried to resist the insistent massage. But Hartman didn't stop. He knew exactly what he was doing, and how best to do it. He just kept on, rubbing, pinching squeezing and caressing her clitoris, cupping her swollen labia in his hands, squeezing her love-mound as if he was squeezing a lemon,

Soon, despite her obvious discomfort, the captive girl was forced to give in to her natural desires and she began to writhe, gasping into the leather muzzle, even pushing her self towards his hand as the delicious massage went on. Hartman leaned towards her ear, and said, "Sluts like you, used to torment men like this. Like they did my father! In a Prisoner-of-War camp." His breath began to rasp, "Then when he was hard, they cut off his rampant dick and left him to bleed." Hartman's breathing became more ragged, "I just love to get revenge for him. You haven't got much to cut off," he sneered, 'but the Sheik will have you snipped anyway, and it's me who does the snipping." Another pinch of her sex-lips. "Bye-bye clitty!" he laughed.

Then suddenly, as if realising this was all part of her torment, the wretched girl sagged into her chains and began to sob into the muzzle, shaking her head, trying to make him stop. He walked back to the chained girl and slowly took off the half-hood, chuckling as the girl screwed up her eyes, as she adjusted to the light from the bulb.

Then, Hartman stepped back. Still grinning he then walked behind her, laughing aloud as she tried to turn her head to follow his movements as he went to a large chest set against the rear wall of the room. He opened the chest and took out a huge plastic dildo. Sauntering back to his helpless captive, he held up the obscene looking thing before her face. He leered as her eyes widened further and he ran his fingers across the roughness of it, making a clicking sound as if he was running his nails over a comb. The girl began to shake violently and even through the muzzle, he could make out her gasping as No! No! No!

He leered at her, "Yes Yes. Yes!" He shrugged and slowly stripped naked himself, before, bending towards the stretched vee of her thighs, slowly moving the dildo up the inside of her right thigh.

Now the girl's struggles merely made things worse as the huge dildo inched its way toward her vagina, then she screamed out into the muzzle, as the wicked instrument nudged into her still wet vagina. Then with one savage lunge, the thing was deep inside her body and her agonised scream breached the muzzle, her body arching back in agony as the dildo was rammed right inside her wet sex-hole.

Hartman was giggling with insane lust now and he was sporting a huge erection, as he began to work the dildo slowly in and out of the helpless girl. He started to croon at her. "Relax lovely. Just relax. The heat from your juices will soften the spikes then it won't be so bad. Just relax."

The girl's movements were now becoming less frantic, as

the thick, spiked shaft continued to penetrate her body, and very soon she was again reacting as if she was actually enjoying the experience. She was now hanging limply against her chains, but pushing her hips down onto the fearsome dildo, her head hanging; her screams turning to gasps of pleasure, her saliva running freely through the muzzle as she worked her hips against the dildo.

Gradually Hartman increased the pace of his perverted masturbation until the girl was beside herself with her passion. Then in one fluid movement, he withdrew the dildo and positioned himself between her legs. One thrust was enough and his massive organ was deep inside the hot wetness of her sex-hole. With huge lunges, forcing himself on to tip-toe, he began to pump himself deep into the defenceless girl, his massive organ, widening her vagina still further.

The girl seemed to notice hardly any difference. Still she gasped and mewled in to her muzzle as she began to ride him even grabbing hold of the wrist chains above her, so she could thrust down all the harder, each time her lunged into her. Finally his movements became spasmodic as he approached a climax and with a roar of animal pleasure he jetted his seed deep into her body, just as she let go with a protracted scream of pleasure and let her own juices flow to mingle with his love-cream.

Hartman withdrew and stood breathing heavily, looking at the wretched girl, hanging there. She hadn't passed the test. She had been too easy. He shook his head slowly. She was supposed to be an unwilling slave. It didn't look as if she was going to provide much fun in her training. He shrugged. Not his worry. That was up to the Sheik's Slave-Trainers. Maybe their ways would be a bit harder. She probably wouldn't like them at all. Another giggle to himself before, Oh No! She wouldn't like them one bit. There was going to be a lot more pain for this one. A hell of a lot more. He even felt half-sorry for her. Dismissing the thoughts, he unclipped her ankles from the ring-bolts, noting her lack of resistance. Gently, then, he bent her lower legs backwards, slipping the short connecting chain of the leg-irons over the hook.

Now the girl was suspended, by her elbows, with her legs bent back beneath her, some two feet clear of the floor. She writhed against her fetters. She tried to plead with him, begging to be let down. Her words, of course, were turned to gurgles; her saliva leaking around the edges of the muzzle, as she spluttered into the leather. A futile gesture. Finally, she realised all she was doing was increasing the enjoyment of this leering, sadist and she lapsed into soft whimpering, as she tried her best to bear the agony.

Hartman patted her left thigh, "You'll be meeting Sameer shortly. He's an expert. You'll like him." He paused, then patting her rump, he added, "But not much!"

He carefully he re-fitted the half-hood to her head. A sadistic leer still on his face, he switched the walkman back on and a satisfied chuckle escaped his lips, as he watched the girl begin a tortured, demented dance; shaking her head wildly in a vain attempt to shake the hood off her head; to release her from what he knew would sound like bedlam.

Shrugging, he turned away to leave her to her torment.

13 - The Slave Market

Rachel had no idea how much time had passed since being suspended by her elbows. All she knew was the agony seemed interminable. God! It was worse than she had been forced to suffer during her nightmare journey in that terrible boat. She groaned yet again, and a half formed prayer moved through her mind; a prayer that she would die, releasing her from the suffering. Then her heart jumped and she sucked in a nervous gasp as she heard someone opening the door, throwing light into her gloomy prison.

A huge Arabic man, dressed in a voluminous black track suit, came into the room, leaving the door open, and Rachel shivered as a freezing draught hit her. She blinked away the slight dazzle as weak sunshine streamed into the tiny room for a moment. Eclipsing the light, the man came up to her. For a moment, he stood looking at her, then sneered into her muzzled face.

"I am Sameer." His grin seemed to go even colder. "Time for slave to be sold." He took a coiled whip from his belt. "Sameer looks for good price!" He grabbed her left breast and gave the soft globe of flesh a squeeze, pinching the nipple in the web of his thumb. He grinned into Rachel's face as she wriggled, squealing into her muzzle.

"Slavegirl will show Masters what she's got!" he sneered. "Or feel whip!" He loosed her breast then grabbed her chin in his right hand and forced her head backwards. "And not forget, slut, Sameer know how to make slavegirl scream."

Almost throttling her then, he lifted her as if she were a doll and released her bound elbows from the hook. Callously, he just let her drop and she crashed to the floor. He booted her over onto her side, slamming the breath from her body as his foot connected with her ribs. He stooped, and unclipped her feet from her wrist shackles but left the leg irons around her ankles. Using her hair, he pulled her to her feet, ignoring her muffled scream of pain. Then he removed the muzzle, but placed his hand over her mouth as she made to speak.

"You keep mouth shut unless Sameer speak to you. Understand slave?"

Rachel's mind was spinning like a whirlwind as confused thoughts tumbled about. Her heart was racing and her stomach fluttered with nerves. She wanted to go to the toilet, but she knew what would happen if she disgraced herself. Fighting with the fear she gasped, struggling to catch her breath, and managed a mute nod.

The whip slashed into her unprotected buttocks, and she wailed, crouching; turning her hips away from him. Sameer just shrugged, flicked his wrist and the whip curled around Rachel's hips, like a striking snake, the end cutting across her buttocks and stinging the rear of her thighs. Again she screamed and once more she cowered from him, gasping in her terror.

He looked down at her, contemptuously, "You still have your tongue." He paused, a sneer on his face, clearly relishing the obvious dread his words had induced in her. Then he went on, "So you answer properly. Slavegirl say, Yes Master, or No Master!" He held up the whip threateningly. "Slavegirl understand Sameer?"

Eyes screwed up, clenching and unclenching her buttocks, against the fire of pain, Rachel tried to answer, sobbing, "Y-yes Master!"

"Better!" He cuffed her twice, grinning as she tried to avoid the blows. "Now, straighten." He waited until she regained her balance, pulling herself more or less upright. Snatching at her hair, he dragged her out through the doorway into an arched corridor, pushing her towards the patch of daylight at the end of the corridor, about ten yards ahead.

Shaking and stumbling along, Rachel somehow managed to keep her balance, as Sameer dragged her behind him. "Slave come!" he snarled at her. "Move!" He slashed the butt end of the whip across her belly.

Rachel gasped out her agony, doubling over, sucking in gulps of air. But knowing she had to accept the hopelessness of her position, she obeyed; she bowed her head and tried to keep up with him, staggering behind. They reached the arched exit with her face looking more bewildered than ever. She was glancing fearfully about her as Hartman pulled her into the wide space of a semi-circular arena.

The air was clear, sparkling, and out here it really was freezing. Immediately Rachel began to shiver, the cold raising goosebumps on her soft skin. A high stone wall enclosed the back of the area and, at intervals of a few feet, there was an entrance like the one they had just passed through. Opposite this wall, and about forty feet across, stood a raised platform, in front of which was a chattering crowd of people, all dressed against the cold.

The platform was about five feet high, with a flight of steps at each end, rather like a stage. There the similarity ended, for along the front of the platform there were heavy oaken poles, set into the floor, and about five feet apart. Each pole had heavy-linked, rusting chains, hanging from the top and a small cross-piece about three feet from the bottom. At three of the poles there was a naked, shivering girl, each shackled to the pole, and suffering the restraints of severe bondage.

The nearest girl was a voluptuous redhead, and like her hapless companions, she was shackled with her back to the upright and with her knees bent backwards, around the cross-piece. Her lower legs were forced upwards and her arms were pulled back behind the pole, and tightly bound by the rusting chain. A shorter chain shackled her ankles to her wrists and a tight chain-gag, pulled right back into the angle of her jaw, forced her lips into an agonised grimace, the links digging into her cheeks. Secured behind the post, the chain was also a convenient means of keeping her head upright.

Rachel could plainly see the girl's pink little tongue, poking from beneath the chain-gag. She sucked in a horrified breath. Worse! Unlike the other two slavegirls, this unfortunate wretch's tongue was pierced. A trickle of fresh blood ran from the wound,

welling up around the chain-gag; bright red mixing with her splathering of saliva.
The floor beneath the poles was littered with filthy straw and Rachel felt the nausea rise as the stench hit her. Then her eyes widened further, as she saw the heavy iron rings, set in the stonework, at the rear of the platform. Some of these rings restrained more naked girls, all shivering, huddling against the stonework, and kneeling in the filthy straw. They too bore the marks of the whip, their bodies streaked with filth and their mouths pulled into sardonic grimaces by the chain-gags they all wore, secured tightly behind their heads with padlocks.

Rachel couldn't ponder for long. From the opposite side of the arena there was a sudden commotion, the angry growl of a man's voice, the loud crack of a leather whip and the squeals of tormented girls. From the archway, Rachel saw two more, naked blonde girls being herded towards the platform. Their arms were stretched out sideways, and were tightly bound with wrappings of thin chain to a long steel bar. The bar was in turn, fastened to the rear of their high, steel collars, which forced their heads up. They were typical Scandinavian beauties, statuesque and quite lovely. Their shapely bodies had been tightly criss-crossed with more of the chain which had been used to secure their arms to the bar.

Against their tanned skin, the tight, chromed chain bindings emphasised their beauty, showing off their curvy bodies, and their pert thrusting breasts; nipping in their tight waists even more, contrasting nicely with their wide, flat hips and soft, white thighs. Together they made an extremely erotic sight, and there were murmurs of appreciation from the crowd as the pair awkwardly mounted the platform steps. They wore no gags, and now Rachel could actual hear their teeth chattering as they shivered, uncontrollably from the cold and sheer terror.

Rachel's heart went out to them then as she saw the expression of utter despair and desperation on their faces. The same look that Rachel knew must be showing on her own face, the look that said they realised they were all slaves, prisoners for whom there could be no escape. Then more horror, as Rachel got a closer look at the chromed chain about their bodies. The tight chain had wicked teeth cast into the links and Rachel could see the flecks of blood where the evil bindings touched soft skin.

Rachel groaned to herself as she was forced to watch the pair of trussed beauties hustled up onto the block, where they were chained to one of the poles. No one bothered to free their arms or remove the pole which held them together and it was clear they were to be sold as a pair. Rachel soon saw why, as she noticed their facial resemblance. The two girls had to be sisters; maybe even twins. Even the bewildered Rachel, fresh to her slavery, appreciated that they would be worth more as a matched pair.

The realisation that somehow she found the sight of the two chained beauties vaguely erotic frightened her. Was she coming to accept all the treatment of those two unfortunates, and of herself, as inevitable? Was it really true that she was a natural slavegirl who might soon relish submitting to these awful people and her own baser desires?

Sameer disturbed Rachel's thoughts and snatched on her neck-chain as he went up onto the platform, dragging her behind him.

It was all too much for her and she broke down again, crying out, "Please! Let me go. Please!"

The whip shattered the still air as Sameer slashed the leather into Rachel's hips. Ignoring her scream, he said: "Slavegirl get up onto block!" He tugged her up the small flight of steps onto the platform.

"No! Please! No!" Rachel resisted the pull and made to go

back down the steps.

Sameer growled and pulled her to the floor where again he struck into her with the whip, this time across her back. "Slavegirl obey, or get more whip!" He dragged her to her feet by her hair, ignoring her agonised cries. "Now go stand by pole." The handle of the whip thudded into Rachel's buttocks, causing her to yell out in pain. Sameer placed the sole of his foot against the swell of her buttocks and pushed her forwards again.

"Slavegirl move arse, quick!"

Rachel's hips jerked forwards and she stumbled. The whip slashed into her again and wailing she scrambled upright. She suddenly gave in. Head down, in defeat, she shuffled over to the nearest vacant pole. She stopped by the pole and looked about in bewilderment, her heart racing as she took in the awful scene. Her breath began to whoop in panic, her eyes widened in terror and she sagged against the post as she looked at the expectant crowd of people below her.

All along the front of the platform, more naked, whipped, shivering girls were on display, chained to the stonework, sobbing and cowering as nearby spectators probed and prodded their defenceless bodies.

Rachel's stomach flipped in terror, but she knew she had to admit defeat. Without being told, she sank to her knees at the foot of the pole, her stomach heaving with disgust, as filth squelched beneath her legs.

Another pair of girls was suddenly dragged into the arena by an evil looking Arab. He had hold of their hair in one hand, forcing their heads backwards, and with the other hand he was pushing them along, holding the thick rope which bound them together at the waist. He hustled them to the platform and, once they had climbed the steps, he kicked them both in the backs of their knees, causing them to drop heavily to their knees.

Then he shoved their heads down low, and in moments chained their necks to rings set in the floor, so they were bent almost double, their faces half-buried in the stinking straw.

Like all of the girls in the arena, they shivered and shook with uncontrolled fear as the cold and the terror took hold of them. They turned their heads to look at the small crowd and sobbed. Most of the spectators, some women included, were avidly appraising so much displayed female flesh.

Sameer picked up Rachel's neck chain and made to secure it to the pole, but Rachel began to cry out, "Please! Don't do this, please don't!"

Sameer released the chain and once more, and the crack of the whip sounded in the still air as he slashed the leather into her breasts and belly, giving her six full-blooded strokes.

There was an appreciative gasp from the watching crowd as Rachel screamed and fell to the floor, squirming from him, tried to evade the cutting lash. Without the use of her arms, all she did was to expose more flesh for Sameer to aim for, and to cover herself in streaks of stinking filth.

Sameer ceased his onslaught, and looked down on her as he coiled the whip. His face was full of contempt for the kneeling Rachel as she hung her head and sobbed, in utter degradation.

A smatter of applause sounded and a few remarks scattered about.

"Sameer knows how to use the whip, eh!"

"Let me have a go Sameer. I'll show her!"

Others began to whisper eagerly together, pointing towards Rachel, and already money jingled loudly in the frosty air.

Rachel recovered herself and looked up at the cruel Sameer. "Please! Please! What's happening!"

"Slave, stand up!" he barked.

Rachel slowly rose against her chain, but not quick enough.

The whip slashed into her exposed thighs and belly and she yelped out, cowering from him, "Please! No More!"

"Then, slavegirl, obey!" Sameer pushed her back against the splintery pole and dangled a short length of chain in front of her face, "Or Sameer fit chain-gag." He grinned in her face. "Shut you up. Hey!"

Rachel made to protest again, but Sameer merely cuffed her across the face. "Sameer warn slavegirl no more!" he shouted, his patience obviously gone. "Now slave-bitch get lesson!" He grabbed hold of Rachel's hair, and pushed her back towards the steps, where another Arab was standing. Sameer growled something in Arabic and grinning widely, the other man climbed the steps and reached for Rachel's shackled wrists, to drag her backwards towards the steps.

Rachel began to scream at the top of her lungs as she realised she was going to get a flogging and doubtless be fitted with one of those cruel chain-gags. "Oh no! Please no! Don't. I'll be good. Please no."

A cuff across the mouth shut her up but still she struggled. It was a waste if time. The evil sadist just pulled her along as if she was a feather, towards a doorway. Still holding her wrists and now also a handful of her hair he, yanked her through after him.

In the gloom, Rachel suddenly ceased her vain struggles. She stood, placid now, but with her heart hammering; her breath coming in heavy gasps of terror, as she tried to see properly. A movement in the gloom and there was an obese white man coming out of the shadows. He came towards her.

"God no!" Rachel gasped as she realised it was Hartman. Her mind went into panic-drive and her heart all but stopped with terror, as she watched him approach.

He looked even more of an ogre than normal, stripped to the waist, and sweating in the warm atmosphere. His face emanated pure evil; his shaven head adding to the fearsome sight. There was a Satanic gleam in his piggy little eyes and he licked his lips in anticipation, as he hefted a thick broom-stave from hand to hand. He moved slightly to her left, turning to face her shoulder. Then in a fluid movement, he lifted the pole, to waist height, and swung, in a flat arc, towards her buttocks.

Fully expecting the wooden stave to thud into her bottom, Rachel moved her hips forwards to try and absorb some of the force. She had been mistaken. The heavy stave whistled through the air, landing not across her arse, but slamming against the backs of her knees, hitting her with the force of a truck. She shrieked out, collapsing to her knees, all feeling going from her lower legs.

Ignoring her agonised cries, the Arab took a big handful of her hair and pulled her head right back. He slipped his legs astride her shoulders, sagged his weight downwards and rested his own buttocks against Rachel's shoulder blades, pulling her head back, holding it up, so her collared neck was stretched taught.

With her head held firmly in the vice-like grip of the Arab's thighs, Rachel knew she was absolutely helpless. She began to scream dementedly, as the evil Hartman dropped the broom-stave and walked towards her. Then she knew she must faint as she saw the glittering dagger he had ready. The man holding her forced her head even further back, so her throat was offered to the approaching Hartman. Oh My God! They were going to cut her throat!

Hartman came close to the terrified Rachel and knelt before her, "Slavegirls must learn to keep silence when they are told!" He grinned into Rachel's face. "Now stop screaming and put out that chattering tongue."

Rachel confused now, just kept her mouth firmly closed and made small panicky, sideways movements of her head, trying to pull away from the grip of the other man's thighs, praying they weren't going to kill her.

Hopeless. The man holding her merely forced more of his weight down on her shoulder blades and twisted his hand tighter into her hair.

The sadistic Hartman placed the knife against her nose. "Or shall I cut off that pretty little nose?"

Rachel screamed out then, "Oh God! No! Don't hurt me please! I'm sorry! I'll be good! Oh! God help me!"

Hartman just grinned. "Ahmed!" he shouted.

Rachel suddenly smelt the reeking paw of the Arab engulfing her upper face, and she yelped as her nostrils were suddenly pinched together. She was obliged to open her mouth to breathe, of course, and she knew was beaten. With her heart racing, her breath stuttering in panic-stricken gasps, gingerly, she poked out her tongue. Her mouth was dry with her fear and her tongue felt huge. Hartman had no difficulty in grasping it between forefinger and thumb.

Both men were chuckling now, the Arab retaining his hold on Rachel's nose. Hartman, giggled then as he pulled Rachel's tongue right out so her bottom teeth dug into the tender membrane underneath. With a deft movement, the sadistic tormentor pressed the sharp point against the top of her tongue. So sharp was the blade that Rachel hardly felt any pain as the knife passed through her tongue.

Then Rachel's pain started, but despite her sudden, deafening screams, both men still, held onto her. Grinning cruelly into her face again, Hartman removed the knife and quickly replaced it with a round steel bar, pushing the metal rod completely through the fresh wound, before letting go of Rachel's tongue.

Immediately Rachel tried to pull her tongue back into her mouth but all she did was pull the thin bar against her teeth, increasing her pain, as the Arab let go her nose.

Hartman began to laugh. “She isn’t so free with her words now is she Ahmed?” Leaning forwards he fastened a piece of chain through a small hole in the end of the steel bit, took the chain around the back of Rachel’s head and secured the links to the other end of the rod.

Rachel was sobbing and splathering now. All she did was earn herself a couple of swipes from a switch as the Arab who had held her head, let her go and dragged her to her feet. Without pausing, he took a big handful of Rachel’s hair again, and dragged his wailing, splathering burden back out into the arena.

The crowd howled with delight as Rachel was herded back onto the platform into the custody of Sameer. Literally tongue-tied, she could swallow, but only just, and only then by forcing her tongue against her top teeth, something which increased her discomfort, adding to her revulsion at the salty taste of her own blood.

Sameer grabbed her at the neck, slamming her against the pole again. “Now slavegirl, learn. Keep tongue still or Sameer will fasten it to collar.” He inclined his head to the girl suffering on the pole. “Like that slave-bitch!” He grinned at her. “If that not work, then slavegirl’s tongue come out altogether! Understand.”

Wide eyed with sheer terror, Rachel nodded, spraying droplets of blood and saliva down her bare front. She had no doubt that Sameer meant exactly what he said.

Sameer grinned again and then turned away to face the crowd. He pointed to Rachel. “Quiet slavegirl now, hey!” He grinned at them. “And with nice pierced tongue. Give Master much pleasure with pierced tongue.” He leered and nodded with pleasure as men roared in perverted agreement.

An elegantly dressed man with a hooked nose and a grey goatee beard held up a hand, and he pointed to Rachel. “I’ll give you five hundred for her."

Sameer smiled wolfishly, then shook his head. "Slavegirl must suffer for longer." He pointed to the Scandinavian beauties, still shackled to their pole, "Twin slavegirls lot number one. They go as pair."

The tall man beamed. "All the better." He began to sort notes from his wallet.

The bidding for the two glorious slavegirls suddenly began and it was fast and furious, offers coming in from all parts of the arena. Eventually though, the bearded man beat them all down. Sameer stepped up to the chained twins. Savagely, he slashed his whip across their offered breasts, ignoring their shrieks of pain. "Sold for eighteen hundred the pair!" Sameer grinned at the purchaser. "Sameer think it must be Master's birthday!" He grinned and towards the girls, now docile and completely subjugated. He unclipped chains from the pole, detached their arms from the bar and quickly shackled them together by the neck. Then he took their arms behind their backs and handcuffed them. He pushed the pair of hapless girls towards the man and took the offered cash.

"Collect guarantee from office Sir. Money back if not happy with slaves." There was a chatter of laughter at that, and smirking Sameer said, "I hope they serve you well."

The man scowled, "They will!" He took the slavegirls' connecting neck-chain, pushed them towards the crowd, which parted to allow him passage, "Now, move sluts!"

The girls took a hesitant step forwards, clearly nervous of walking through the lecherous crowd. But their new Master was having none of it. He raised his thick cane and scythed it in a flat arc to smash the thick malacca across both pairs of exposed buttocks, raising immediate angry red whelts. The evil man just watched impassively as the screaming slavegirls collapsed at his feet, their cries piercing the frosty air. Then he grabbed both of them by their hair, kicking the nearest one in the buttocks, "On your feet and move, you little sluts!" he snapped, yanking them to their feet again. He brandished the cane in front of their faces. "First lesson! Next time it's a flogging!" Then he tugged on their chain once more, turned and stalked off towards one of the small tunnels, dragging his sobbing purchases behind him.

Rachel was slowly coming to terms with the agony in her tongue as the initial pain wore off and she was blubbering, but staring in bewildered fascination at the spectacle, scarcely able to believe what she had just witnessed. But her thoughts were broken up as there was a sudden swell of noise from the audience. She could pick out individual cries.

"Let's see the mouthy one Sameer."

"Yes! Let's have her sold off!"

"Take off the waistband Sameer!"

Sameer turned to Rachel, reaching out to remove her neck chain. Then he grabbed the waistband and deftly unfastened it, allowing it to drop to the floor. Then he beamed at the crowd, "Sameer think the little dog-bitch want food!"

Again a roar of appreciation and the crowd began throwing bits of food onto the platform, a mixture of half-eaten sandwiches, fruit and lumps of meat. Most of the food vanished beneath the layer of filthy straw and Rachel began to pant with terror and revulsion as she guessed what was to come.

Sameer, grinned at her and removed the bit from the laceration in her tongue. He shook the whip in front of the trembling Rachel.

"Slave on her knees."

Rachel swallowed her fear, wincing as the movement caused fresh pain in her slashed tongue. But she obeyed now, accepting that whatever the humiliation that was to come, it would be better than more mutilation at the hands of these monsters.

Shaking violently, she got awkwardly to her knees, her high bound arms almost causing her to lose her balance. She was already feeling nauseous with the thought of the degrading things she was being forced to do.

Being forced to shuffle about naked, on her knees in all this filth, was bad enough, but the thought of having to pick up food from the mess, then eat, made her stomach heave before she even started. Rachel knew she had to obey though, and she knelt in submission as she waited for Sameer.

Then Sameer suddenly released her arms, so she could rest her hands on the floor,

The relief was wonderful, but again the filth squelching between her fingers made he gag and heave.

It didn't have any effect on Sameer. He just snarled. "Eat! Crawl round! Eat like dog!" The whip descended and Rachel screamed out as she began to crawl about the platform, ferreting among the filth and the muck, trying to find the pieces of food,

She managed to find one slice of cold meat which she picked up, wrinkling her face in disgust trying to ignore the stink and the sight of the filth that clung to the meat as she raised it to her lips.

Then the whip slashed into her buttocks again and she dropped the meat, with a yell.

Sameer roared at her. "Dogs no got hands. Pick up food in mouth!"

Sobbing, Rachel lowered her head to the straw, gagging at the stink. She knew, though, that to be sick would earn her more whippings. Pushing her distaste and disgust aside, she began to root through the straw like a dog, moving unmentionable things aside to find the food which had been thrown onto the platform. It took her about three minutes to find enough food to satisfy Sameer's perverted mind, and she was gagging with the knowledge that not everything she had been forced to swallow was edible.

Yet, strangely there was a sudden tingling in her vagina. Not caused by what she had done but more by the fact that she had been forced to do it. There was definitely some perverse thrill to being dominated in this way and she even had to admit that the crowd somehow heightened the feeling. Again she wondered. Was she, after all, a natural slave?

Her thoughts were interrupted as Sameer administered three more slashes of his whip, to her thighs. Evidently he thought he had humiliated her enough, for he grabbed her hair and dragged her to her feet. He pointed to the filth all over her hands and lower legs.

"She need cleaning, but see how she obey Sameer. And not even trained yet!" His hand went to her crotch and expertly he felt around her sex-hole. Grinning in triumph, he held up his fingers before shoving them into Rachel's mouth, ignoring her yelps as the action caused more aggravation to her freshly injured tongue. He pushed his fingers almost down Rachel's throat, forcing her to taste her own juices. Beaming at the crowd, Sameer gloated, "Bitch gets wet, like real slave!" He pushed her towards the edge of the platform. "Kneel! Shove arse up and show sex-slash! Now!"

The crowd shouted with glee as Rachel spun away from Sameer, her breasts swinging free as she dropped to her knees in front of them. She turned to face Sameer, pushing her buttocks high and spreading her legs, blushing furiously as she displayed her intimacies to the leering crowd.. Then she sagged and her head dropped in submission, as though finally realising she was just a slave.

There would be no escape and she really was about to be sold like a beast. She knelt there, in the filth, her face inches from the disgusting mess, her whole body shuddering with shame and degradation.

Sameer poked her buttocks with the handle of his whip. "Wiggle arse! Turn around and around, Keep arse moving. Slave show what she got."

Rachel blushed deeply, but obeyed, trying to shut from her mind the image of how she must appear to the leering crowd.

The whip flicked her buttocks, and Sameer said, "Move slave. Waggle sex-hole for peoples. Let them smell you, bitch!"

As she did so, Sameer beamed at the crowd. "This fine meat." He waved an arm around the assemblage, then gave Rachel's left buttock a sharp slap. "Soft flesh. Nice for getting teeth in. Come. This really fine slavegirl." He pushed Rachel forwards. "Not virgin, but new slave. Not branded yet! Who give me five hundred!"

The bids began to come. A thin, bearded man raised his arm, "Four hundred!"

Then an ugly, heavy faced woman, said, "And fifty!"

"And fifty again!" came from another woman.

Rachel began to sob quietly to herself, hanging her head, shivering with fright, with shame and with the cold.

Sameer looked disappointed and raised the girl's head with the handle of his whip. "Come! She fine beauty. More bids, hey!"

A fat, red-faced man raised his arm. "Another hundred!"

"Thank you, sir!"

"And another!" It was the hatchet-faced woman again.

"Any more?"

There was a buzz of conversation, but no more bids. Sensing the crowd were losing interest, Sameer held the whip in front of Rachel's face, and whispered fiercely. "Straighten body slut!" He bent to her and quickly released the bit from her mouth, causing fresh blood to flow.

Relieved at the easing of the pain of the bit, Rachel shivered, then obeyed, facing him.

Sameer shook the whip in front of her face. "Come on then!" he growled.

Rachel frowned. "Please I don't understand." then she screamed out as the whip laced across her taut breasts.

Sameer growled at her. "Hurry up bitch! Sameer not wait for ever!" Again he shook the whip, giving Rachel a scent of the leather.

Then Rachel grasped what she had to do. Trembling, she leaned forwards and softly, kissed the whip.

The crowd gave a great shout of approval and Sameer stroked the long tail of the whip along Rachel's body. "Untrained, but already slave know whip! She natural slave-bitch!"

Sameer snatched the whip away and bent over Rachel to lift her head slightly. His other hand fiddled with his flies and he shook his huge weapon free of his trousers to allow it to stand up in front of her face, pushing the fearsome thing towards Rachel's lips.

"Suck, slave-bitch! Show you mean it!"

Rachel shuddered, but took the huge shaft in her mouth and began to suck lovingly at the penis, whilst trying to ignore the pain in her wounded tongue.

Soon Sameer was ramming himself into her gaping mouth and she squirmed and whimpered in agony as her tormentor grabbed a double handful of her long matted hair and began to shake her head from side to side, whilst lunging into her. Then he was at her breasts, squeezing, rubbing, pinching her nipples and half throttling her with his hand around her slender neck. His thick penis was deep in her throat. The whip handle was also playing at her genitals, forcing her to juice. Then Sameer drew away and secured her arms back to the rear of her collar again. He rubbed his hand around the wet slit of her sex, and nodding to the ugly faced woman, said, "Madam come feel!

Slut have much juice. Real slave!"

Then, quite suddenly, a waddling, fat Arab, dressed in a heavy black caftan, pushed his way through the crowd, and lumbered his huge body up onto the block. He paused for a moment, his breath wheezing and crackling in the cold air.

Rachel, slowly recovering from Sameer's onslaught, felt her heart leap with fear and revulsion. The grotesque man's face was only partly visible through the matted beard, but she could see fat, sweaty cheeks puffing and blowing, his eyes all but vanishing into the greasy folds of flesh as he twisted his face into a sneer.

Revolting though he was to look at, there was something about this man; an air of absolute authority. Rachel shuddered as she stared at his fat paws, toying with the wicked looking dog-whip tucked into his belt. Sadness and desperation flooded her mind; overtook her and she groaned in misery. The man was awful; even here in this foul place she could smell him; and she knew; she just knew! this brutish ogre was going to be her Master. She began to shake with fear and loathing as the idea of belonging to him began to soak in.

Her body started to shake with a mixture of fear and curiosity. The strange thrill; it must be just the knowledge that she was being sold! Over the last days, she had wondered if she could accept her slavery; could she learn the ways of these people; maybe, if she was to be sold to a kind or handsome Master she could even learn to be halfway happy with her inescapable fate. But this! Oh God no! There was no way she could feel anything for this bloated monstrosity.

The man's beard divided in a cruel sneer and suddenly, he stepped over to Rachel and stooped down. Casually, he slid his fat fingers into her sex.

Rachel gasped in shock and pain and tried to pull away from him, but, clearly well practised, he held her still, by the hair. Ignoring her struggles, he massaged her private parts for a few moments before nodding. "Show me your teeth!" He withdrew the whip from his belt.

Not wishing to feel that terrible whip, Rachel obeyed her mouth meekly, hiding her distaste at the stink of his breath . She opened her mouth, suffering the Arab to shove his wet fingers in, the action aggravating the fresh wound in her tongue.

Farid chuckled and turned to Sameer. "Tongue-pierced. Ready for the bit I see." He beamed at Sameer. "Maybe you knew I was coming, my friend?"

Sameer smiled ingratiatingly. "Sheik Farid! Excellency! You always welcome here." Sameer nudged Rachel's buttocks with his toe. "This one real slave! Just for Excellency."

The man began to knead Rachel's arms and thighs, assessing the tightness of her belly and the firmness of her breasts. Then he examined her matted hair. "She is filthy." His grin widened. "Yes, that is the proper way to keep these white Christian bitches!"

Farid turned to his right, where almost magically a naked Arabian girl, clean, beautiful and heavily scented, had appeared. This delightful girl was holding a steaming bowl of soapy water. An obvious slavegirl, she stood, head down at Farid's side. Without a glance at the naked girl, the Sheik, rinsed his hands, dried them in the girl's dark, luxuriant hair, then with a single wave, dismissed her.

"That is how my personal hand-maidens behave, Sameer."

He looked at Rachel again, before stepping back. For a moment he looked thoughtful. "This one I will keep in her filth, to remind her she is just a white Christian slut! A mere animal!" Once more he looked Rachel up and down. "She will pull a plough nicely." He took out a bag of coins from his robes. "A thousand Sameer. No more!"

Sameer smiled widely and then stroked Rachel's quivering

body and face with the whip. "You already kiss whip. Now slave kiss whip properly! Like she want to. Like it is man's sexy cock. Show Master what you're worth." Sameer grinned at her and lifted the whip, "Or you feel it."

Rachel, even now, hardly able to appreciate that she really was being sold to this evil monster, shivered in fright, then, leaned towards the whip and lowered her head over it, allowing it to slide into her mouth. It aggravated the wound in her tongue again, but she knew she had to perform well.

Lasciviously she began to kiss the whip; sucking and licking; sliding her tongue over the leather, as she had been told; as though it was a huge male organ. She moaned, "Oh yes Master! I obey you Master!" Twice more, Rachel kissed and sucked at the whip, moaning in abandon. But Farid made no higher offer.

Then, Sameer dragged the whip savagely away from Rachel's lips, to raise it above her cowering form. She screamed out in pain as Sameer gave her one, sudden, vicious swipe across her freezing buttocks. Ignoring Rachel's wail, Sameer barked out, "SOLD!"

Farid nodded impassively and handed over the money. He looked at Rachel. "Right my little white slut," he said slowly, "we take you away now. Soon we see how well you entertain." He leaned forwards, bent to his new slavegirl and grabbed both of her breasts, grinning as Rachel let out an anguished squeal. Then, despite his unwholesome looking bulk, Farid demonstrated a surprising strength. With an effortless heave, he lifted Rachel clear of the straw. Her shrieks rent the air, her hands tried to claw at Farid's; her legs kicked and flayed about.

Yet, struggle as she might, Rachel could not make the man release his grip. He just held her up in front of him staring into her face, his fat paws, squeezing into the tender globes of her breasts. He seemed to be waiting for something.

Then Rachel finally understood. She must bear the pain in silence. Gradually she subsided; gritting her teeth against the terrible pain. She was finally rewarded by Sheik Farid lowering her to her knees again. He didn't release her breasts completely, bending towards her face. Surprisingly, he gave her tearstained cheeks a gentle kiss.

"You see, little white-slut, it becomes easier all the time!"

He smiled cruelly then and lifted her clear of the floor once more, holding her for an instant, before dropping her, so she crashed to the littered stonework. Farid snapped his fingers and a pair of tall bronzed women emerged from one of the arched tunnels. Both women were naked, obviously slavegirls themselves. Yet they walked proudly, as they swayed their way through the crowd. They were gorgeous creatures and they were swinging their hips in an hypnotic sway, as they walked towards the platform. The crowd parted for them and there were appreciative groans from the men in the crowd as the two beauties mounted the platform and went to stand one each side of Rachel.

Both girls had high, firm breasts, with a semi-circle of inter-linked rings let into their flesh beneath each breast. The rings supported a delicate weaving of sliver chain and above their shaven love-mounds, a similar decoration had been let into the flesh, the sliver netting barely long enough to cover their exposed labia. Also, as they had passed through the little throng, it could be seen that beneath each jiggling buttock, yet more silver chain-work had been let into their flesh, so as they walked the decorative network swung enticingly against their bronzed flesh.

Each girl held a thin leather bound cane and both were smiling slightly as they tapped the wicked looking implements against their thighs. The Sheik nodded and the girls bent towards Rachel, spreading her on her back.

Rachel was shaking but she knew she dare not move away from them as they lifted her knees and together, spread them wide, exposing Rachel's genitals and inner thighs. Then they each grabbed a knee, and placed the other hand on each of Rachel's shoulders, to press her down against the floor, holding her still.

Smiling cruelly, Sheik Farid took the cane from one of the girls and with a full-blooded blow, slashed the supple leather into the exposed, unprotected vee of Rachel's thighs.

Rachel's agonised scream rent the air and she tried to get up. Hopeless. The two smiling Amazons just held her all the tighter as the cane sliced into the tender flesh of Rachel's inner thighs.

Sheik Farid administered just two blows more, to her sex-lips, all the time grinning, as Rachel screeched out her agonies, squirming against the unyielding grip of the two women.

The brutal Farid stood up, shaking his head a little. "She must learn to stand her punishment a little better I think." He shrugged again, "How long that takes is up to her Sameer, yes?"

Sameer grinned then. "Oh yes Excellency, indeed." He put the money away, and watched impassively as the two slavegirls each took one of Rachel's bound elbows, lifted their sobbing burden and dragged the pathetic bundle down from the platform, and away through the crowd. As they reached the tunnel, Rachel felt a pin prick in her left buttock and with a sigh collapsed immediately into unconsciousness.

14 - In The Palace of Sheik Farid

Throbbing, burning pain in her breasts; a raging thirst and the pangs of hunger. All of these things combined to wake Rachel, but mostly it was the pain. Automatically, her hands went to her breasts, where the evil Farid had gripped her on the block. She cried out as even her own touch caused explosions agony; shattering her mind, pervading her whole chest and abdomen.

Her face twisted in anguish as she tried to will the pain away and only when it had subsided a little did she dare shake away the last drowsiness of her drugged sleep; to move and slowly take stock of where she was.

She was lying in sweet smelling, clean straw, and she was curled up, around the tight circumference of a heavily barred, cylindrical cage of about three feet in diameter. She was still naked, but her arms had been released from the tight bindings and she could see that she would be able to move about the small cage.

She wouldn't be able to stand, for the bars above were a mere two feet or so from the floor. In any case, she was still collared, the steel band that had been riveted about her neck, seeming weightier, because of the heavy length of steel chain, that fastened her to one of the bars in the floor of the cage.

There was just a weak glow of light coming from a bulb fixed in the wall, near a steel-sheathed door, and the room was quite warm, the heat coming from a glowing brazier about fifteen feet away. The cage she was in was one of six others, spaced at intervals of about a foot around the sides of a gloomy, square room, that smelled damp and very faintly of disinfectant and human waste.

Then the pain in her tongue began to make itself felt again, and very gingerly, she swallowed. It was sore, of course, but wasn't too bad. The cut seemed already to be healing and no permanent damage seemed to have been done. Maybe she had been lucky, or Hartman had really known exactly what he was doing.

Her mind clouded then as she recalled the bloated Hartman. She had thought, after her arrival here, she would have been free of him. Whatever had happened to her, however uncertain her future in the hands of these Arabs, at least she would be free of Hartman. But that wasn't to be and she trembled as she recalled the way the bloated sadist had pierced her tongue. Then she shuddered again, as she recalled the greasy, fat Arab who had bought her body. Was she maybe in an even worse situation? Both the Sheik and Hartman to fear; to torment her; to beat her. She sighed deeply. It was pointless worrying about it. For the moment she had to accept her ordeal, as she would have accepted legal imprisonment. There was absolutely nothing she could do about it. Provided she kept her wits about her, she might one day find a chance to escape. She just had to make sure she kept herself as fit as possible, and that she was ready to take the chance when it came.

Rachel got painfully to her haunches, to look around, half hoping there were other girls in here with her, anything to hear and see another face, for what little comfort it might provide. But to her disappointment the other cages were empty. Then she drew in a shocked breath as the door crashed open and the familiar figure of Hartman eclipsed the sudden glow from outside.

Hartman! Oh God No! What now! More torture? She sobbed aloud. What had she done to be brought here? Then she hung her head in sadness; where was 'here'. She really didn't have any idea. Did she?

For a moment, the evil Hartman stood at the door, before striding over to the cage. Selecting a key from the large ring at his belt, he unlocked the door of Rachel's tiny prison, reached in, grabbed her hair and pulled her out of the cage, pushing her aside, sending her sprawling.

Rachel screamed as more agony laced her chest, and the collar dug into her neck, when the limit of the chain had been reached.

Hartman ignored her protests and just bent down to reach into the cage, unshackling the end of the chain. Then, growling at her, he grabbed Rachel's hair again, and, holding her chin tightly in his huge paw, he glowered at her. "I haven't forgotten the trouble you caused me by trying to escape, bitch!" He shook her head. "Did you think you'd get away?" he cackled. "You won't get free of me that easily!" He yanked her hair, again. "Now, on your knees! Time to see Sheik Farid again!"

Rachel barely had time to struggle to her knees before Hartman strode off towards the open door, dragging her behind him.

Shaking still, Rachel tried to keep up with him, her hands slipping and sliding about on the smooth stone floor out side the room. They were in a long, gloomy corridor lit only by weak bulbs, and seemingly endless and her knees and elbows were continually being banged against the solid surfaces and, despite her cries, Hartman just kept dragging her. At about every fifteen feet or so there was a door in the left hand wall.

As Rachel was dragged along, she began to hear muffled screams coming from somewhere ahead, the screams of a woman in terror and pain. Then there was one last long keening wail, before an eerie silence closed in; a silence broken only by the rattling of her own chain and Hartman's scuffing gait.

Suddenly, one of the doors about twenty feet ahead crashed open, spilling an orange glow into the corridor. Two half-naked sweating Arabs came out, dragging the drooping form of girl between them. The girl was sobbing, her head hanging down, her saliva drooling from her lips to fall unheeded, her blonde hair, filthy and matted, hanging downwards, and her white flesh streaked with sweat and dried blood. Rachel could also make out a livid mark on her right shoulder, as though the skin had been flayed from her back almost. God! What had they been doing to the wretched girl? What terrors had she faced. And worse! What terrors lay in store for Rachel, herself? She swallowed her fear as best she could as she watched the two men drag their half-conscious burden away down the corridor, and out of sight.

Now Rachel and Hartman had reached the door, which was still open. Hartman pulled Rachel up sharp, dragging her to her knees, before pushing her into the entrance. He pointed into the room, alive with a red-orange, fiery glow, the light sending flickering dancing-mad shadows about the forbidding stone walls.

Rachel had little time to wonder, for she yelped as Hartman's whip flicked her buttocks. "Inside bitch! Move that arse!"

Then her eyes widened, terror-bright, as she saw the large brazier in the centre of the circular room. The bright coals were almost white-hot in the centre and its heat was oppressive; already straining sweat from her pores. There was no other illumination in the place and there was a heavy, musty smell, almost pressing on her. There was another smell too. Not so strong, but recognisable. The smell of cooked meat.

Cooked meat?

Rachel sucked in a terrified gasp as she saw the irons sticking out of the brazier. Suddenly she knew. It wasn't meat she could smell. It was the stench of burned, human flesh. Burned Flesh! Oh God! They had just branded that poor wretch who had been dragged out of this place; it was that girl's scorched flesh Rachel could smell; that had been the mark on her shoulder; not flayed from her, but branded and burned from her. They really had been serious about the branding. And now, they were going to brand her!

There was no more time to think about the horrors that awaited her, for Hartman shoved her towards the far wall, where she could see two large rings set into the stonework about eight feet above the floor.

"Over to the cross! Move!"

Rachel began to sob, in fright and she turned to him; to plead with him. "Oh Please No! Please don't!" Her cries were stifled by a slash from the whip and she cried out, pulling her hips forwards instinctively.

The bullying Hartman hissed in her ear. "If you don't crawl over there, I'll lift you by your tits and carry you over there! Now move, bitch!"

Another slash from the whip and Rachel knew she was beaten, She crawled obediently over to the wall and stayed crouched on all fours, beneath the rings, her lungs heaving, her whole body trembling uncontrollably, her wracking sobs echoing about the room.

The rings were fitted with chains, each terminating in a wide steel wrist-band and Rachel knew she would soon be chained to those rings, awaiting the kiss of a white-hot iron. The only uncertainty was whereabouts on her body they would brand her. Her mind started to rebel and she felt herself losing consciousness at the though of what was going to be done to her. Yet she knew she had to hold on; somehow she knew if she fainted, they would merely arouse her again and treat her with all the more cruelty.

Then her jumbled emotions broke and it was suddenly as if she was listening to someone else. Unable to control her feelings any longer, she began to shake her head from side to side, screaming, pleading for mercy, mercy she knew would not be given. Nothing would prevent these monsters from carrying out their threat. She wailed again and her heart leapt as once again she told herself the awful truth. They were going to chain her to those rings and they were going to sink a brand mark into her skin.

Farid came into the room, his huge bulk shambling through

the doorway. He came across to Hartman. "The bitch is making enough noise Ernst! Shut her up will you?"

Hartman stepped over to Rachel and the whip slashed into her shoulders. "Close your mouth slut! Not another peep out of you!"

But Rachel was still sobbing and pleading. "No! Please don't do this to me. Please!"

In moments Hartman had leaned over her, grabbing her hair and pulling her head back savagely. The whip handle was now rammed, cross-wise, into her mouth, the thick shaft ground against her teeth. Hartman wrapped the length of the whip around her head, tying it off at the back of her neck, as an improvised gag. "Now shut it bitch!" he grinned. "In any case, you're going to need something to bite on, because I am going to make sure this really hurts!"

Still grinning at her, he lifted her easily and Farid came across to secure her wrists to the manacles hanging from the wall. They let her drop, so her feet were just touching the floor. Her arms stretched out above her and then stood back, appraising her.

Farid stroked his matted beard. "On the left breast, I think, Ernst. Just near the shoulder. Like a medal eh!"

Hartman laughed. "A star brand Excellency?"

Farid shook his head. "Too small Ernest. A letter 'F', I think. The large, cursive style." He walked over to Rachel and his podgy hand caressed her breast and the curve of her neck. "Then she really will know to whom she belongs!"

Then he returned to Hartman and together they moved the brazier a little nearer to Rachel, so a wall of heat hit her body.

Rachel began to suck in huge gulps of the stale air, her breath whistling through the improvised leather gag, her stomach sucking frantically in and out as her nervous panting became faster and more frenetic.

Hartman stepped closer to her then spread her legs wide, strapping them to ring-bolts in the floor. She gave a muffled grunt, as her weight came onto her arms, and she was stretched out, spreadeagled.

Hartman hissed into her ear. "If I were you, I would try to keep very still. You move too much and it will spoil the brand and it will have to be done again!" He pinched Rachel's left nipple savagely. "Somewhere else on your sluttish hide." He tweaked Rachel's nipple again. "Then you'll be of no value to us and you WILL be sent to a brothel where you will be used by the scum of the earth. You follow?"

Frantic now, Rachel nodded. The mere idea of being burned or scalded had always horrified her, but knowing she was to be marked, as if she was just an animal; that she would carry the mark for the rest of her life, sickened her to her stomach. She shook uncontrollably now, her muscles twitching, her heart racing, losing its pace as she shivered, waiting for the torture she knew was to come.

She tried to calm herself. This horror was inevitable. She must face it. She had to nerve herself to withstand the agony. It was the only way. There was nothing else she could do, but pray for the strength to see it through.

Hartman stepped over to the brazier and put on a thick leather glove before he took out one of the irons, silently inspecting the white-hot flamboyant letter 'F' at the end of the iron.

He looked at Rachel and grinned in eager anticipation. The slut was ready. She was shaking, looked as if she might piss herself with fright, but that wouldn't stop him marking her with Farid's brand. He pulled his lips into a cruel sneer. All women should be branded, to show they were the property of men, fit only to be slaves. The good looking sluts, like this one, were made just to give pleasure to men, in whatever way the men wanted. The others; the fat ugly bitches should do the work; the cooking and cleaning and all the rest of the hard labour. Either way, they should be branded. Well, here in Farid's palace that was just how things were. There was no other way of treating women. They were slaves and as long as they did whatever their Masters wanted them to do, they would be spared the worst of the whippings. And with a beauty like this, there could never be any other way.

He was going to enjoy branding this one; enjoy hearing her scream, when the iron touched her skin. That always gave him a charge. Also, as he looked at the helpless Rachel, he had to agree that the Sheik's emblem would look especially good on this lovely bitch.

For a gig-slave, or a galley-bitch, Sheik Farid's favourite spot for the mark was just mid-way between knee and hip. This slut, for the time being at least, was going to be used as a pleasure-slave, which meant, at times, being kept in her filth, to satisfy the tastes of some of the Sheik's guests, who liked to see Christian bitches treated like the pigs they were. So, she would be given the mark on her breast. Maybe another mark on the opposite side. She might even have a circular brand impressed around each nipple; where it really would hurt; where it would make her howl like a stuck pig; just so she knew her place, for once and for all.

Hartman shrugged mentally. That was up to Farid of course. For now it was just the simple 'F' brand on the breast.

Hartman stepped over to Rachel again and ran his gloved hand over her body, chuckling as she shied away from the iron each time it passed her face. He ignored her pain as his hands aggravated the welts and bruises on her body. He sighed slightly. This bitch was quality, although her flesh seemed to mark with the whip very easily. Even by Farid's cruel standards, it was doubtful if this little slut would have healed before the Sheik wanted to open her up. Farid might not be too pleased about that but then he liked clear flesh so he could mark it himself. Still, if Farid couldn't wait, he could always sell her on, to someone who didn't mind marked goods. She would fetch a decent price, even with whip marks all over her butt.

He leaned towards the chained girl and sniffed. She stank, but that was something she would have to get used to. Farid liked to work his Christian slaves and saw little point in allowing them to clean themselves, when they were only going to get dirty again. She was also sweating like a pig, which wasn't surprising considering she would know what was about to happen to her. Again, Hartman ran his hands over her body, tracing the swell of her shapely hips, running his palms inwards, then upwards, caressing the unshaven mound of her pubis, delighting in the feel of her soft pubic hairs against his palm.

Prolonging the agony of the branding was part of the game, although he had to agree, this one was a special! Skin like white silk; when it was dry that was. When this was over, he knew Farid would let him take the bitch away and lather her into a different kind of sweat. He took the goad from his belt, and stood there, smiling slightly, allowing the goad to swing in his hand.

The slavegirl was shaking, almost uncontrollably, obviously expecting a taste of the goad to go with the branding. Might have been a good idea, but it would probably render her senseless, making it futile to brand her without dousing her with water first. That helped the branding though. The water on the skin boiled instantly, scalding the flesh, but helping to keep the edges of the brand neat, after healing. In this case though, there was enough sweat on the girls skin to achieve the same effect.

Hartman's features split into a cruel leer as he approached Rachel again, waving the iron in front of her face. Once more he held the branding iron up for Rachel to see and grinned as she stiffened, screaming. There was no splather around the whip he had stuffed into her mouth now. Her mouth would be dry with fear.

Still grinning, he shook his head. "I reckon the iron isn't hot enough yet." He put the iron back into the coals, smiling to himself as Rachel sagged against the stonework. Then, her control gone, her bladder let go and her urine splashed over the floor, causing her to moan loudly in fear and disgust.

Hartman sniggered. "Can't you wait slut!" he walked over to her again and roughly took out the improvised gag, He looked at her closely. "I want to hear you scream bitch. I want to her you lift the roof with your screams, you understand!"

Shaking with fright, Rachel nodded mutely.

He pushed the handle of his whip beneath her chin and lifted her head. "So let me hear it when the iron goes in!"

Sobbing, Rachel nodded and mumbled a quavering. "Y-y-yes M-M-Master!"

Hartman pulled her head back, using her long hair, and grinned in satisfaction. The girl was learning it seemed. He gazed at her intently as he allowed the iron to touch her upper breast.

As if someone had pressed a button, the room was echoing to the tortured screams of Rachel as she suffered the agonies of the white-hot iron sizzling into the tender globe of her breast. The acrid stench of burned flesh rose around Hartman's head and he wrinkled his nose, slightly, as if savouring the smell, and immediately began to caress the screaming girl's body, making soft crooning noises. He was now sporting a fierce erection and suddenly his buttocks contracted and he gasped aloud as a spontaneous climax overcame him, his thick semen jetting upwards to arc away from him and splatter all over Rachel's belly and hips.

The thick, creamy liquid spurted from him for a full ten

seconds, until, finally, his passion spent, he bent over the tortured Rachel, his thick lips drooling, a look of absolute ecstasy in his eyes as Rachel's demented screaming bounced around the chamber.

Then, suddenly, the screaming stopped as Rachel collapsed into unconsciousness.

Hartman, shoved the iron back into the coals and examined the fresh brand, livid against the white flesh. Already the bodily fluids were flowing to the injury, orange blisters forming around the edges of the raw wound. They would soon heal and the brand would be perfect. Farid would have no cause to complain about this one.

Farid stepped across, carrying a bucket of water. "Here, Ernst!" he said. "Bring her round."

Hartman splashed the water over the unconscious girl's head and gloated over her as she came spluttering back to consciousness, and her private little world of pain.

Coughing, heaving for breath, trying to get the water out of her throat, Rachel recovered slowly, becoming aware of the burning wound on her breast. She suddenly felt physically sick as she realised they really had branded her. Oh God! Why! It was unbelievable they should do this to her; degrade her, debase her, treat her as an animal. Why? What difference would it make if...? Then she noticed the cold stickiness on her belly, where the dregs of Hartman's semen was slowly running off her and she vaguely remembered the filthy beast climaxing over her belly, just at the moment of her worst agonies, as if endorsing a waking nightmare. She was unable to stop herself suddenly vomiting at the thought of what the beast had been doing whilst she was suffering and she moaned to herself as the warm contents of her stomach, spilled from her mouth to run, unheeded, down her front.

Hartman ignored her plight. "You're back with us then, slut!"

Rachel tried to answer, but it was hopeless. "I spoke to you bitch!"

Rachel mumbled a slurred "I. I. I'm sorry M-Master!"

There was a sharp slap across the face, and Hartman said. "I ought to make you lick that mess up!" He shoved the goad under her chin and forced her head upwards. "But we have better things to amuse you. You have to learn a few tricks. For a start, you'll have to learn to bear your pain without all this yowling! Otherwise you will be of no use to Sheik Farid whatsoever!" He snickered. "It isn't over yet. You have to be ringed. Sheik Farid likes his girls to be ringed. Makes them a bit more interesting, see." He turned to the smiling Farid. "The spike please, Excellency."

Sheik Farid nodded and handed Hartman a long, wickedly sharp spike, which Hartman held up in front of Rachel's face, grinning at her. "Very sharp! It will slice through before you even know it!" He giggled, as horror distorted Rachel's face. "Then it's one nose-ring for one little cow."

Rachel began to shake and her mouth worked silently, as she tried to find words. Her fear constricted her throat and she merely let out a whimper as Hartman leaned towards her, reached out a hand towards her nose, and inserted a finger and thumb into her nostrils. He pinched her septum, hard, and her eyes watered. She felt her stomach go cold as she realised the enormity of what they were going to do to her. But before she could think about it, Hartman had pushed the spike through her septum.

There was very little pain at first. Then the tears ran from her eyes and she felt her warm blood dripping over her body, as her head swam. Rachel suddenly found her voice; once more her screams battered about the room, as she tried to bear the stinging pain. She wanted to faint away, but for some reason she couldn't. Maybe it was the knowledge that if she did, she would merely be revived again to suffer the agony. She sobbed in humiliation as she felt the cold, heavy ring inserted through the burning wound in her septum. Then, through tear-streaked vision, she had a brief glimpse of Hartman's fingers as he snapped the ring shut.

Rachel tried, ineffectually, to pull herself away from her torturer. She was moaning and trying to move her head, but it was a mere waste of time and effort.

"I told you, slut!" Hartman said. "Struggling only makes things worse!"

Gasping for breath, Rachel felt her heart jump in sheer terror then, as she felt her right nipple being pulled outwards from her breast. "Oh GOD NO!" She shrieked out as the needle sharp spike was pressed through the flesh behind her nipple, and yet another ring was fitted to her body. This time she couldn't hold on to her senses and she fainted. Her release was short-lived, for immediately she was revived with another douche of cold water.

Hartman wasted no time, and again Rachel shrieked out as her left nipple also was pierced and a further ring fitted and closed together. Her body was slicked with sweat and she wriggled ineffectually against her bonds as she screamed in torment. But there was more to come, and she howled her anger and agony as Hartman grabbed each of her ears in turn, to pierce the lobes and click further rings in place.

Then, the evil sadist took a thick fold of flesh, just below her navel, pulled it out and giggled into her tortured face, as he rested the spike against the fold of flesh.

Rachel screeched her agonies to the uncaring walls, as he squeezed and yet another hole was punched through her flesh. Then another ring; this one much larger, and thicker was fitted into place and closed, with a loud click.

Then Hartman turned to Farid. "Do you wish to fit an infibulator, Excellency?"

Rachel began to scream wildly, then struggling against the her chains as she realised what further degradation she was to endure. She was wasting her time and energy.

Hartman bent down to her sex-mound, pulling her labia apart, causing her to wail again.

Searing agony went through her and her hips moved upwards slightly against the chains, as a hole was punched through the tender flesh of each of her outer labia. Then Hartman held up the big link for her to see. It was rectangular, with rounded corners and was made of thick gauge stainless steel, with a sleeve-clip on one side. He twisted the infibulator around, in front of her face. "This will make sure you don't give free gangway to any bastard you just happen to fancy, slut!" He gave a cold smile and bent down to slip the ring in place, snapping it shut, so it all but closed her labia together.

Rachel was out of her head with pain, and she barely heard what he had said; only half-noticed him come across to her. Coming up close, Hartman smiled coldly. "All done slut!"

Farid came across and together the two men unchained the half-conscious Rachel and lowered her to the floor. Here, she was forced to her knees and her arms were twisted behind her back to be secured to the rear of her collar.

"On your feet!" Hartman snapped.

Stumbling, tottering, Rachel rose and stood shaking before them.

"Now," said Hartman, "out into the corridor turn left, and keep going." He nudged her buttocks with his foot. "And hurry, or it's the goad."

They didn't go far, before Hartman ordered her to stop, outside another metal door in the wall. The evil overseer opened the door and shoved Rachel through into a stone-walled cell, dimly lit and with a low ceiling. The floor was littered with foul smelling straw and Rachel groaned to herself as she realised she was to be left here again. Then there was another shove between her shoulder blades and she was sent sprawling into the stinking mess. The door slammed shut on her and there was the rattle of a bolt being closed. Then the sound of Hartman's receding footsteps, leaving her to her lonely misery.

15 - The Wall!

There was a loud, insistent buzzing in Rachel's head as she woke from her troubled sleep.

She blinked and tried to chase the sleep from her eyes. She shook her head sadly, as she realised she was still naked, lying on her side in the filthy straw. The wounds in her body where Hartman had branded and ringed her were burning and she winced as movement stretched her fresh brand, threatening to break the blisters that had formed. Careful of the injury, she moved slowly, and tried to sit up. Nothing clouted her head and cautiously she lifted her arms.

She stifled a sob, as she realised her arms were still manacled together, with a long bight of chain jingling between her wrists. She felt about her, and her spirits sank even lower when she realised that her cell was even smaller than she'd thought.

But there was nothing she could do about it, was there? She sighed deeply and, shivering slightly in the cool air, she began to pull herself upright. Then she groaned aloud as she felt the heavy collar about her neck and the cold steel of the chain that shackled her to a heavy iron ring in the wall.

Her thoughts were interrupted, suddenly, and the place was flooded with light as a door opened. She sucked in a nervous gasp, then immediately began to shiver, her stomach jumping about with nervous anticipation. Her breathing became spasmodic as she recognised the bulky figure, standing in the doorway.

It was Hartman. Using the exterior switch, he switched on the main, cell-light.

As her eyes adjusted to the light, Rachel could see that he was naked, but for knee-length spiked boots and a heavy, leather belt. The now familiar goad hung threateningly from his belt, and in his right hand, he held a bundle of thin dog-chain. He looked ridiculous. The huge roll of fat around his middle overhung the belt and huge thighs wobbled, pasty-white against the black leather of the boots. He also sported a fierce erection, but his huge firm prick was pushing into the roll of fat that overhung the belt.

He grinned at her, pulling his belly upwards a little, allowing his prick to stand up straighter. He caressed the huge shaft. "Don't worry slut," he said. "The belly gets in the way a bit, but, as you know, I can still spear you!" He giggled, and let the rolls of flesh go again. Then he came across to her, his heavy boots scraping ominously on the stone floor.

"Time for your first lesson!" He reached for her hair, to drag her towards him. He pulled her up short against her neck chain and held her head tight against his thigh, so she could smell his maleness as his desire pumped his erection even firmer. Then he did a surprising thing, allowing his hand to caress her matted hair and the nape of her neck.

Rachel shuddered, a mixture of revulsion and fear; yet the touch of this monster had been surprisingly pleasant. There was no real tenderness in the action of course. He was probably just assessing her as he would a piece of meat. Nevertheless, his touch had been soft and to her, having endured so much harsh treatment, it seemed like a speck of gold amongst sand; a casual gesture, but at least it hadn't been painful.

Then Hartman growled at her, and pushed her back to the floor, "Slut!" he shouted. "You're tempting me."

Again he grabbed her hair and pulled her head upwards, ignoring her squeals of protest as her scalp burned. He looked into her eyes, leering at her, then spat right in her face. He rubbed the globule of saliva all over her mouth and chin, grinning as she retched slightly. He pushed her away from him. "That'll do for a wash, today." He pointed to the floor. "Now on your belly and show me who's the Master!"

Rachel knew what was expected of her. She sank to the floor and rolled over onto her belly, trying to ignore the pain where the rings in her nipples pulled at her flesh. Grovelling in the filthy straw, she kissed his stinking feet. "Master!" she said, "what must I do?"

Hartman's arm lifted and the chains whistled through the air, to come crashing down across Rachel's exposed buttocks and lower back. She screamed, rolling herself into a protective huddle, cowering from him. All she did was present her buttocks again, this time a rounded, tight-stretched target for the chains, which sang through the air once more, smashing across her arse.

Rachel screeched out with pain and cowered from him. Hartman didn't hit her again, but he grabbed her hair and pulled her bodily to her feet, ignoring her wails. Pulling her face close to his, he bawled at her. "You're a slave, you little slut! You say nothing unless you're told to. And, unless we tell you otherwise, you say just. 'Yes Master', or 'No Master!' Understand?"

Rachel swallowed, looking at him fearfully. She trembled and quietly she muttered, "y-yes M-Master."

"Good!" He shoved her aside, this time with the outside of his right foot, sending her slithering in the filthy straw. "Now get on your knees!"

Rachel obeyed, swallowing her disgust as filth squelched

beneath her legs. She hung her head submissively. Then he came towards her, grabbed her hair, and pulled her head up. Then suddenly, his huge dick was being waved beneath her chin. She could feel the heat of the thing; smell his arousal as the massive prick began to pulse. He pushed the bloated end upwards against her chin, tilting her head back a little more, before pressing his knob against her mouth. The swollen head pressed against her lips and Rachel buried her disgust, knowing what she must do; anything to avoid a beating, or worse, that goad.

Her mouth opened and her manacled hands went to his hairy scrotum, to enfold his balls in a gentle caress. She opened her mouth wider still, moistened her lips and allowed the pulsating organ to slip into her soft mouth, the tip of her tongue teasing the end and sliding languorously, around the smooth glans.

Hartman grabbed her hair, jerking at it, pulling her face close into his body, shoving himself right to the back of her throat.

Rachel choked then, but knowing she had to, managed to relax her throat, so the awesome weapon slid deep into her gullet, as he slowly pumped back and forth. Each time he entered her mouth he would draw back, just enough so she could breathe through her nose between each thrust. Rachel quickly learned that she must time her breathing to the rhythm of his movements, or choke on the thick shaft.

Playing her part to the utmost, knowing she had to avoid more punishment, Rachel began to caress Hartman's thighs and buttocks with her hands, pulling his fat body even closer to her face, as she sucked and mouthed the huge cock.

Then, between each thrust, Hartman suddenly began to slash at her with the chains in his hand, not savagely, as he usually did, but with enough force just to sting her buttocks.

This surprised Rachel, for she realised that, paradoxically, she was beginning to enjoy sucking this ogre's massive cock. She began to run her tongue along the full length of the hot shaft, allowing her tongue to search for the tiny slit in the head of the thing, gently caressing his balls.

The kiss of the chains on her buttocks also enhanced Rachel's growing pleasure, causing her to squirm a little, whilst of course, increased Hartman's enjoyment.

Rachel groaned, trying to deny the sudden rush of her juices as the slow shafting of her mouth went on. But she couldn't deny the pleasure she began to feel. Again she felt the pleasure of submission, and her groans turned to genuine moans of pleasure, as she sucked and licked at the huge dick, swallowing the first weeps of his semen almost greedily.

Then Hartman's movements quickened as his shaft throbbed and became thick with his passion. He dropped the chains and clasped Rachel's head tightly into his groin, leaning backwards, shoving himself right home into her mouth and emitting a roar of pleasure as he allowed a fierce stream of hot, creamy spunk to spurt into Rachel's mouth.

Before she realised it, Rachel was swallowing greedily, delighting in the taste of the creamy warm semen as it slid down her gullet. She wrapped her arms around his hips, enfolding his podgy buttocks, pulling him close to her face, as her tongue and lips sucked at the pulsating cock. Eagerly almost, she drew every last drop of the salty liquid into her mouth and swallowed the stuff down.

With a last jerk of his hips, Hartman withdrew from her mouth, grinning as he watched her lick her lips clean. He jerked his hips once towards her mouth. "You know what comes now!"

She swallowed again, then leaned forwards and grabbed the softening dick, to begin licking the final traces of spunk from the end, cleaning the thing; pulling the foreskin back to get right around the swell of the glans, sucking the last dribbles from his pipe. She swallowed the cooling sperm then licked her lips, as though she had tasted the sweetest ambrosia.

He bent towards her face and then his fat lips were on hers, in a sloppy, wet kiss.

Rachel suppressed a shudder of revulsion then. Hartman was grotesque; a gargoyle almost. Fellating him was one thing, but to be kissed by those, wet slobbering lips, was another. She must have hid her distaste well, for Hartman straightened up and smiled down at her.

"You're getting to be too willing to interest me," he grinned. "You're starting to change into a real slave, aren't you?" He pushed her to one side. "I like a bit of resistance! Screaming! A bit of fear!" He looked at her. "But you've learned haven't you slut!"

"Yes Master!"

"You know it's best to submit?"

"Yes Master!" Rachel was well aware that to Hartman it didn't matter how she felt. She just knew what she must say to him. She lowered her head, realising sadly that he was speaking the truth. She wasn't fully their slave. Not yet, but she began to wonder if she could hold out much longer. She had the dreadful feeling that she would soon be their's completely. Finished! She would never be the same again! She really was beginning to think and act like a slave.

Hartman chuckled and picked up the bundle of chain once more. Then he unfastened the long chain from the collar, replacing it with the thin chain. Brandishing the whip he jerked once on the chain at her neck and said. "Crawl bitch! Out the door, turn left and keep going!" He slashed the chain into her buttocks once, ignoring her squeal of pain. "And get a move on! We don't have all day!"

Rachel obeyed, crawling over the rough floor, squealing

each time the thin chain-leash slashed into her arse, urging her onwards along the cold passageways.

In about five minutes, Rachel saw a heavy, metal-sheathed door in front of her. The door was half open and a soft, flickering glow was spilling out into the corridor. She could also hear the soft moaning of another girl. Rachel groaned to herself. What now! She was soon to find out.

"On your feet and through that door!" Hartman dragged her upright by her hair and pushed her towards the open door.

Rachel went into the gloomy space, and immediately began to sweat with the sudden warmth. The heat and the glow was provided by a glowing brazier in one corner, the hot coals shining; a clutch of steel rods sticking out; a mute threat. There was enough light to see one of the girls she had been brought in with, hanging by her wrists from a chain fixed to the ceiling, somewhere in the gloom above.

The girl's head was slumped against her chest, and her knees were buckled, her feet trailing on the floor. She was barely conscious and Rachel began felt her heart fill with pity, as she realised what had been done to the girl. Even in the low light, Rachel could see the Star-shaped brand, on the girl's right breast, about three inches below the shoulder. The brand was blistered and still seeping and the flesh around it was puckered, pulling tight around the raw wound, marring her otherwise flawless skin. Just as they had done to her, they had marked this lovely girl as though she was just a beast.

There was a movement in the shadows to her right and Sheik Farid emerged from the darkness. Like Hartman, he had a bundle of chain in his hand, and, his eyes gleaming sadistically, he walked towards the suspended girl, to stand before her half-conscious form. The Sheik waved Hartman over. "Bring the white slut here Ernst."

Hartman kicked Rachel in the buttocks. "Over to the Sheik

and kneel before him!" he snapped.

Rachel obeyed, hardly able to breathe; dry fear blocked her throat as she realised they were going to brand her. Again! Her heart began to race as she tried to shut out the thoughts of going through that agony once more. Oh God! No! Please no! Not again! Her mouth dry, her breasts heaving with terror, she stopped in front of the Sheik and lowered herself to her knees. Trying ineffectually to swallow, she hung her head in submission.

The Sheik laughed. "Her training is progressing well, Ernst. She is turning into an excellent slave. Worth money, eh, Ernst?"

"Oh yes, she'll be in demand Excellency. Should earn you a good sum of money."

The Sheik nodded, then looked down at Rachel. "You can stop your trembling," he laughed. "I brand a slave but once!"

Turning to Hartman, he went on. "Get her ready Ernst." He touched the slavegirl hanging before him. "Alongside this other white slut. We'll see how they can crawl as a matched pair."

Hartman's face split with a huge grin. "This I am looking forward to Excellency." Fearfully, Rachel wondered; her mind contorted with a mixture of relief and apprehension. She wasn't to be branded again, but still she suspected what was to come. Frantically, she tried to shut out the reality. Whatever it was, it was going to involve pain. She hadn't missed Hartman's slight movement towards his goad.

Hartman caught hold of Rachel's hair, and pulled her head up to face the Sheik. "Thank your Master slut!"

Puzzled, Rachel hesitated, but only for a moment. The goad touched her between the buttocks and she shrieked out as a surge of pain stretched her into a bow of agony. Quickly she blurted out. "Thank you Master!" yet having no idea why she was doing it.

The Sheik merely grinned. "You can thank me again when you have performed for us." He turned to Hartman. "Now Ernst, Hobble the slut please."

Rachel yelled out as Hartman dragged her to her feet by the hair, and shoved her brutally over to a green painted door in the other side of the room. There he slammed her to her knees again and in moments had fastened leg irons to her ankles, so her feet were separated by a mere eighteen inches of chain. Then he took the chromed dog-chain and wrapped it about her waist, nipping it in tightly above the generous flare of her hips.

He passed the end up to the ring at the front of her collar, threaded it through and pulled it back down again, securing it to the centre of the chain between Rachel's ankles. Once more he pulled the chain upwards, tucking it beneath the loop around Rachel's waist. She gasped in pain as her pulled the chain tightly down towards her love-mound, and bent her body forwards, before taking the chain through her thighs, positioning the links so they dug deep into her labia, forcing her sex-lips apart, threatening to tear the infibulation ring from her sex.

Grinning at her discomfort, Hartman took the chain back between her legs, and pulled it tight into the crease of her buttocks, before padlocking it to the chain, behind her waist.

Now Rachel was on her knees, gasping and sobbing at the continual discomfort of the chain digging deep into her soft, sensitive flesh. Her head was low, her nose touching the floor and her buttocks were stuck up high, the smooth curve of them a tempting target for Hartman's goad.

He chuckled and Rachel stiffened with apprehension as she felt the tip of the goad touching her tortured anus. Then she screamed out, and arched herself backwards with he pain as the jolt of power smashed though her body. This movement also caused the chains to dig even deeper into her tender parts and she screamed again, even after Hartman had removed the goad.

"Stand up, slut!"

Rachel tried to stand, but the pressure of the chain from her neck and the restriction of the leg irons, prevented her from doing more than just get into a crouch.

"I-I c-can't."

The goad touched her ear. "You can't what?" He pushed Rachel's head to one side. "Slut!"

"I can't stand up!"

The goad was switched on, oh so briefly, but for long enough to send Rachel sprawling, dragging another tortured yell from her.

"Can't stand up WHAT!"

Rachel realised what he meant. "I can't stand up, Master."

"Well now!" he said, his voice loaded with sarcasm and contempt. "Isn't that a shame?" His chuckle deepened. "That's what the hobble is for, idiot! From now on you crawl. Everywhere."

He bent down and grabbed the bight of chain between her wrists, pulling it backwards to clip it to the waist chain, just above Rachel's navel. "Now crawl, slut, all around the room!"

Head down, her matted hair brushing the floor, Rachel began an awkward crawl. The chain between her wrists was just long enough to allow her to move her arms forwards a few inches. She soon found that if she co-ordinated her arm and leg movements, it was easier to get along, but even so the rough stone beneath her was soon digging into her palms and knees, so that she began to suffer more pain.

Then the goad was inserted between her buttocks again and a small tingle of electricity sent her into a faster crawl. Again the goad touched her, this time pushing slightly against her tortured anus. It was a stronger burst of power and she yelped like a dog as once more she increased her pace. Soon she was obliged to raise her buttocks and crawl on all fours, the chain between her thighs stretching and digging deeper and deeper into her genitals, digging into the crease between her sweating buttocks.

The sweat was beginning to run from her and, between her thighs and buttocks, lathering up into a foamy mess, just as if she was a racehorse. Soon she was grunting with the effort, trying to hold in screams of pain, knowing it would just mean the goad if she yelled out. Another touch of the goad sent her into a near trot as she made her painful way around the room.

Finally, Hartman tired of his sport and he allowed her to stop. "Stay on you knees," he warned her. "Keep still and wait!"

Breathing heavily, Rachel obeyed, fearfully waiting for whatever they were going to do next.

But Hartman just left her, and went over to the Sheik. Together then, they took the other slavegirl down from the ring above, and pushed her to her knees, ignoring her wails of protest. In moments the hapless girl had been trussed, in the same manner as Rachel. The Sheik grabbed hold of her hair and dragged her bodily across to Rachel, shoving her down on her belly. "Now!" he snapped. "On your knees you white slut!"

Sobbing, the girl obeyed, giving Rachel a brief glance as she did so. All that did was to earn both of them a slash across the buttocks from the Sheik's dog-whip. "Slavegirls don't communicate unless they are told to. Understand you white bitches?"

They both nodded. "Yes Master!"

The Sheik chuckled and turned to Hartman. "They are both learning, Ernst. You are to be complimented on your methods, my friend."

The fat overseer grinned broadly, lifting the goad at his belt. "Me and Mr. Goad both Excellency!"

"Ah! Indeed, Ernst." The Sheik looked down contemptuously at the two crouched slaves, then with a strange sigh, almost one of contentment, lifted his dog-whip and brought it crashing down across the two naked, white backs. Both girls screeched and reared up in agony, their hands automatically going to their hurt. The movements just earned them another blow, this time across their breasts. Almost as one, they wailed out and dropped forwards again, but this stretched and presented their buttocks to the whip. In seconds they were huddled together on the floor, their screams reverberating about the room as the whip slashed into their unprotected flesh, in a protracted beating.

The Sheik didn't stop until he was breathing heavily. For a few moments he gazed at the prostrate girls in disdain, then, gathered saliva to spit on the two beaten girls, he glanced at Hartman. "These Christian sluts can't stand the whip, my friend." He shook his head and snapped his fingers. "Muzzle them please. Nose clips too. That might deaden their yelping."

Hartman gave a growl of pleasure and went to a chest beside the door. He took out two leather muzzles, and two divers' nose-clips. Then he came across to the girls. In moments he had them both muzzled, and Rachel tried to close her mouth. She couldn't. There was no tube in this muzzle, but the hole in the centre was surrounded by a hard rubber ring which was lodged behind her teeth forcing her mouth into a wide, stretched 'O'. The hole in the muzzle was also covered with fine wire gauze and a grinning Hartman casually applied the nose-clips to the girls.

Immediately they began to began to gasp, trying to suck air through the fine mesh. It was difficult though and soon their breath was whistling through the gauze, bubbling as their saliva began to run. Soon their saliva was dripping from the gauze covered holes in the muzzles, as they gurgled noisily, trying to breathe and swallow.

The Sheik looked down and nodded his satisfaction. "They

should find it quite difficult to crawl now, Ernst." He gave the girls one more contemptuous glance, then said: "My friend, I am going to eat. I'll leave these bitches to your tender care." He chuckled. "See they are well treated eh!"

Hartman chuckled. "I'll treat them to plenty of goad, Excellency!"

"I am sure you will, Ernst!" He pointed to the other girl, so recently branded. "When she has had enough, send her to my chambers." He bent close to the girl and caressed her shapely flank. "I shall look forward to opening her up." Still laughing the Sheik turned away and walked out in to the corridor to vanish into the gloom.

Alone with Hartman, the two girls began to shiver with fright. Hartman just grinned at them and then, with a piece of chain, connected the trussed slavegirls by their collars. He stood up and nudged each of them with his foot. "Now crawl sluts! Out of the room and turn left!" Then the goad was in his hand, and grinning he touched it to the cleft between Rachel's offered buttocks.

The shock blasted through Rachel's body and she reared up, her body arching back, her eyes bulging with the pain. Another surge from the goad, and she dropped back to all fours again, her lungs heaving for air as she tried to breathe through the fine mesh. She gurgled her agony through the muzzle, and began to shake in sheer panic, waiting for the next blast of pain to shatter her soul. But there was nothing and with her saliva dripping, beginning to sheen her firm breasts, she began to crawl forwards.

The chain linking her to her sister in bondage tightened, and the other girl was forced to move forwards, her breasts also shiny with a film of saliva. Each slave had to try not to cause further discomfort through pulling on the chains, and it was slowly and carefully that they went through the door and turned left, as they had been ordered.

However, their progress clearly didn't satisfy Hartman, for he growled at them. "Faster you sluts! Faster." He kicked Rachel in the buttocks, shoved the goad between the other girl's sweating thighs, forcing the cheeks of her arse apart. The goad dragged a screech of pain from her and both girls pitched forwards, grunting in pain as they slammed into the earthen floor. Hartman kept close behind them, the blunt end of his goad never further than an inch or so from their buttocks.

"And stay in formation!" he warned them.

The tormented girls got back onto all-fours, and, miserably, they moved on, trying to speed up, to avoid the goad. But as they turned into the corridor, the level started to rise. The floor was still just hard earth, but now it was wet and slippery. Both girls began to slide about as they tried to gain purchase in the slimy mud. Time after time they slipped, to fall flat on their fronts, their soft flesh becoming smeared with the cold, grainy mud.. The slope was became even steeper, and their progress became slower and slower. Three times more, they slipped backwards, crying out into their muzzles as the tight body chains cut into their sensitive parts and their limbs flailed ineffectively, trying to get purchase.

Hartman was becoming impatient. "Dig your fingers in and stop worrying about your finger-nails, you stupid prissy bitches!" Then, he gave Rachel's companion another dose of the goad, ramming the stick hard between her shoulder-blades. She wailed into her muzzle, and fell flat on her face once more, dragging Rachel with her, as both girls began to slide back down the slope.

Desperately, Rachel tried to stop herself being pulled backwards, her fingers clawing into the mud, digging her toes in too, but still she slid backwards. Then it was her turn for the goad once more, and the evil stick did its work, at the base of her neck, causing her to scrabble forwards in an attempt to escape the torment. This pulled the other girl forwards, and both of them, splathering into their muzzles, managed to scrabble back onto all-fours.

And so it went on, the torture continuing for about seventy yards as they were herded up the steep slope. Finally the tormented captives gained level ground and, sobbing with the effort and the pain, they crawled forwards into the gloom, their lovely bodies covered in streaks of the filthy mud, their hair hanging in thick, filthy hanks.

Sucking in huge breaths of air, Rachel finally raised her head a little, ready to continue the crawl. That was when she discovered there was nowhere to go. In front of them there was just a blank wall of dripping wet clay. The wretched pair of slavegirls had been halted with their noses pressed up against the clay and they paused, heads down in misery.

Hartman, his spiked shoes helping him keep upright, looked down at them in contempt, then grabbing both girls by the hair, he pulled their heads up and in the weak glow from pointed to a row of manacles, dangling from the clay at their eye-level.

"Put your arms out!"

Even had they wanted to resist, both girls were now virtually exhausted,. Resistance was futile, and in any case they were so exhausted, it was impossible. Shivering with pain and terror from their recent ordeal the girls obeyed mutely, stretching their arms in front of them.

It was an easy task for Hartman to shackle their wrists to short lengths of chain and he straightened up. "Welcome to The Wall, sluts!" he said, pointing upwards to a metal box about three feet above the girls' heads. "This is where you're in for a real shock!" There was a large, electrical power switch, on the box and it was all too clear what torture they were now going to face. Both girls began to wail into their muzzles, shaking their heads frantically, trying to plead with him.

It was futile.

Giggling, Hartman grabbed the rubberised handle and pulled the switch closed.

Immediately. Rachel and her companion began to shriek into their muzzles as they were thrown around in a demented, involuntary dance, as the high voltage scoured their nerves. At last, shattered, gasping and sobbing into their muzzles, they were allowed to rest, their saliva literally running from their muzzles.

Their rest wasn't to last, for Hartman merely grabbed both girls by their hair, yanked their heads back and snarled. "Keep your heads up, you bitches." Sneering at them, he unshackled their wrists, and, using their hair, he dragged both of them around to face down the slope again.

"Now we go all the way back down, turn round and start again." He shook both girls, yanking their heads from side to side, almost tearing their hair from the roots. "And this time, we get up here faster and together. Then you might not get any more shock treatment." He giggled. "We keep doing it until I'm satisfied! So it's up to yourselves."

He placed a hand against each girl's buttocks and with a contemptuous sneer, pushed them both forwards, onto the muddy slope.

The two girls yelled out, trying to stop themselves. But they were already over the edge and they slithered downwards, until their sliding suddenly turned into a roiling helter-skelter down the slope, as they rolled over and over, screaming into their muzzles each time the chains dug into their flesh, or their wind-milling limbs crashed into the walls and the wet earth beneath their bodies.

Finally they came to rest at the bottom, a tangle of arms and legs, their soft skin bloodied, bruised and smeared with the slimy clay. Hartman, with his spiked shoes, merely followed them down casually, until he stood over them. Rachel was lying on her side, struggling to get back to all-fours, trying to help her companion do the same.

But the other girl was unconscious and with a growl of displeasure, Hartman leaned over the two girls. Angrily then, he unclipped the unconscious girl from Rachel and stooped, lifting the girl over his shoulder. He walked back into the room, and Rachel winced as she heard the inert form of the girl crash to the floor, where Hartman had obviously just dropped her.

Then Rachel was worrying about herself again, as Hartman came back to her. For a moment he stood looking down at her, laughing he shoved the goad between Rachel's thighs, the metal tip finding her swollen, throbbing labia. A surge of power shocked through her and she screamed into the muzzle. She barely heard her tormentor as he growled. "Turn round and start back up again."

Rachel groaned and slowly obeyed. She knew they were beating her. There would be no escape. She had no option but to face the terrible ordeal of the slope once again. And she knew it would continue, until Hartman was satisfied that she was really trying or that she could simply, go no further. She resolved to try even harder. Maybe that way she would avoid the goad. She was deluding herself, for there was one more sudden touch from the goad, between her buttocks. A momentary shock; just enough to send a slight judder through her body. Rachel shivered with fright as Hartman said: "Get it right this time bitch, or I chase you back down with the goad!"

There was another slight nudge from the goad, this time not switched on. Sobbing, Rachel started the tortuous ordeal all over again.

Another day!

Another awful day to face.

What would they decide to do with her today?

The awful thought played around her mind as slowly, Rachel opened her eyes and blinked in the dim light. She groaned as she realised nothing had changed. Of course it hadn't. It probably never would. She still wore the stiff, unyielding leather muzzle and her arms were still pulled high up her back, secured by the wrists to the rear of her leather collar.

The stink of the muzzle was nauseous, the taste of the tube in her mouth was bitter, and she needed a drink. She was of course still naked, and was lying on her side, in filthy straw, in a small, stone-walled cell.

Shivering slightly in the cool air, she began to pull herself upright. Then her heart sank as she felt the steel collar about her neck; the brush of cold steel across her breasts, as the chain that shackled her to a heavy iron ring in the wall swung against her. Again she moaned into the stiff leather of the muzzle. She was so thirsty, and so hungry. What were they trying to do? Starve her? God, she had never been fat, but at this rate she would be wasting away. She screamed into the muzzle then, but shook her head, defeated. What was the point? Even if these beasts heard her, would they pay any attention?

She sucked in a gulp of air, her breath rasping through the saliva that welled inside the muzzle, around her mouth. She could swallow, with difficulty, but once her saliva had slid out from around the tube in her mouth she could not get rid of the constant wetness around her lips. The slimy excess was oozing from beneath the muzzle, running slowly down her front, adding to her discomfort. It was making the muzzle smell, but even so, it didn't mask the stink of the room she was in and the filthy straw on the floor. As she woke fully she looked about the gloomy room and shivering, in dread, pulled herself to a sitting position, the chain at her neck rattling as she moved.

She pulled her knees up to her naked body and dropped her head to her knees, choking slightly as the movement pulled the collar tighter into her neck. She adjusted her position to something approaching comfort then sighed into the muzzle as she reflected that maybe she was beginning to accept the hopelessness of her position. In the back of her mind, much a she hated the idea, she knew she would never escape the clutches of these awful people.

A shiver coursed through her. What on Earth had ever made her think she would like to be dominated by men? By anyone, for Heaven's sake. Her mind filled with sadness. The plain truth was simple. Fantasising in the privacy of her own room was one thing. Actually being enslaved was something else. No need to pinch herself any more, to see if she was dreaming. This was all too real and she was cursing her stupidity in leading on the sadistic Charles Stone. If only she had known -

Angry with herself, she shook her head. Churning all that over wouldn't change a thing. She just had to wait her chance then escape. Surely, one day, there would be a chance. They couldn't watch her every movement every moment. Could they?

Yet another pathetic groan escaped her, and was turned into a gurgle by the awful muzzle. Who was she trying to fool? Ever since she had been taken from the Club, she had been kept naked and in chains. The only time she was alone was when she was asleep; and even then she couldn't be sure. As for actually trying to escape, already she had learned; for the slightest transgression she got the whip, or the goad. A tremor shook her body! That awful goad! The agony of it. Just one press of the switch and she had to endure the mind-numbing torture of an electric shock, pulling her body into a bow of sheer pain.

Then, suddenly, she frowned as she experienced a slight, nervous tremor in her belly; as if she were a child, anticipating a long awaited birthday and a strange, warmth invaded her vagina.

She shook her head then, in self denial almost. No! That was mere fantasy. She just wasn't like that. There was no way she looked forward to being punished. All she wanted was to get back to her old life; her own room and -

Her thoughts were shattered as the door suddenly slammed open and the huge figure of Hartman eclipsed the light from the doorway.

Rachel cowered even further into the corner; shivered as she heard his throaty laugh, a laugh full of cruelty and evil. Cowed and submissive now, Rachel's began to shake with fright as the sadist stepped towards her. "Awake at last then, slut!" He laughed, switching on the overhead light, and Rachel could see that he was also naked, but for a wide leather belt about his waist. Hanging from the belt, the leather quirt lay threateningly along his thigh. He had a fierce erection, his huge penis standing up firm, thick and long against his belly. He leaned over her and unfastened the muzzle. "Come on slut!" He growled at her. "You've work to do!"

Rachel was swallowing and, working her jaw to ease the cramps, now that the muzzle had been removed. Then, she cowered as she heard Hartman growl at her.

"No time for that slut! Supplicate yourself to me!"

Rachel remembered how she must behave. She must debase herself before this pervert. She didn't want to, but she knew the caress of that quirt. She had felt its sting and she knew she couldn't take much more. Fully immersing herself into her new role, she sank to the floor and rolled over onto her belly, grovelling before him, kissing his feet. Then she got to her knees. Leant right back, her buttocks against her calves. She threw her head backwards and murmured. "Master," she said. "What must I do?"

The whip slashed into her offered breasts and she screamed.

Hartman grabbed her hair and pulled her bodily to her feet, ignoring her wails of pain. Pulling her face close to his, he bawled at her. "YOU KNOW THE RULES COW! YOU ANSWER WITH JUST, YES MASTER OR NO MASTER! UNDERSTAND SLUT!" He pushed her to the floor again, and administered another slash of the quirt, again across her exposed breasts.

Rachel yelled in pain and automatically her hands went to the hurt and she doubled over, trying to ease the searing burn of agony. Still massaging her breasts, she looked up at him fearfully. She had forgotten. Hadn't she? No! No one had said anything about that! Or maybe they had and she hadn't understood. So much had happened to her; the abduction, the almost unbelievable experience of actually being auctioned off, just like an animal at market. There had been the countless whippings and the dreadful bondage. No wonder she was confused.

She cleared the bewilderment from her mind, realising she had been asked a question. As the burning in her nipples eased, she said, "Yes Master!"

"Good!" Hartman sneered. "Now slut! On your knees!"

Rachel obeyed, swallowing her disgust as filth squelched beneath her legs, and hung her head submissively. Then she felt the hugeness of Hartman's penis, its gristly length pulsing member beneath her chin; felt the heat of the massive thing; smelt the male scent of it, as he pushed the bloated end upwards against her chin, tilting her head back a little, before pressing the knob against her mouth.

The huge knob touched her lips and, she gagged as it forced her lips against her teeth. She knew exactly what was expected of her and, anyway, she saw the movement of his hand towards the quirt. She HAD to please him. She MUST! Feeling debased and sluttish, she lifted her hands and enfolded his balls. Softly, she caressed the hairy scrotum, as she opened her mouth wide, to admit the swollen tip, sliding her tongue around the glans.

Hartman grabbed her ears and pulled her face close into his groin, shoving his dick right to the back of her throat.

She gagged a little, but managed to relax her throat so the member slid deep into her gullet as he slowly pumped back and forth, withdrawing just enough so she could breathe through her nose between each thrust.

Knowing what she must do, Rachel began to caress his thighs and buttocks with her hands, pulling his body even closer to her face, sucking at the huge knob as he pulled backwards.

Then, between each thrust, Hartman began to slash at her with the quirt. Not hard, but delivering each blow accurately and with just enough force to sting her back and buttocks, causing her to squirm. This clearly enhanced Hartman's pleasure and his other hand began to roam over Rachel's breasts and neck, caressing her soft skin, leaving her to concentrate on pleasuring him.

Suddenly, it seemed so natural to her, that she was able to ignore the sting of the quirt and now she put her arms around his buttocks, to pull his hips towards her face, forcing the huge weapon into her own mouth. Rachel had always enjoyed oral sex, that she had to admit. She was also suddenly aware that only since her abduction, had she really learned how to perform in this way; to use her tongue and lips to pleasure a man properly. That had changed, and she knew she was also learning to let Nature take its course. She was a slave, even though she didn't like the fact, but still, in this one respect she was beginning to feel that maybe fellatio was one way a woman could enjoy her natural submission, and that it was a means of pleasing her man.

Hartman wasn't 'her man', but all the same Rachel was beginning to enjoy this, and she groaned as she felt his foot invade her crotch and he began to rub between her labia, his toes forcing into her.

She tried so hard to deny the sudden rush of her juices, not wanting him to know she was beginning to yield. Because she was, she really was. She knew. The slow rape of her mouth went on. But she couldn't deny the pleasure she began to feel. There was something in the act of submission which thrilled her and her groans turned to genuine moans of pleasure, as she sucked and licked at the huge penis, almost greedily, swallowing the first weeps of his semen.

Then his hips began to jerk spasmodically and his thrusting became more urgent. His huge shaft swelled even more as his passion mounted, Grunting in animal pleasure he grunted, dropped the quirt, and clasped Rachel's head tightly into his groin.

"OH CHRIST!" he yelled out. "You sexy little bitch! Come on! Suck me dry you little slut! Milk me girl! Milk me!" One more protracted groan came from him and suddenly a fierce stream of hot, creamy spunk spurted into Rachel's throat. The glutinous warm liquid slid down her gullet and she wrapped her arms around his hips, enfolding his firm buttocks, pulling him close to her face, embracing his firm flesh, as her tongue and lips sucked at the pulsating cock, drawing every last drop of his seed into her mouth, to swallow it down.

With a last jerk of his hips, Hartman withdrew from her mouth, grinning, as he watched her lick her lips clean. He lifted his softening penis in front of her face. "Clean me properly slut!"

"Yes Master!" Rachel leaned forwards and grabbed the

softening member, to begin licking the final traces of his love-cream from the end, cleaning him, pulling his foreskin back to get right around the swell of the glans, sucking the last dribbles from his pipe, swallowing the cooling semen as though it was ambrosia.

He bent towards her face and then kissed her lips softly. "You're getting to be too willing for me." He chuckled. "But Christ can you give a blow-job." He caressed her cheek with the back of his hand. "Sheik Abbas was right. You're going to be real easy to train on." Again he grinned at her. "It's starting for you isn't it? You're beginning to understand!"

"Yes Master!" Rachel stifled a sob, realising he was speaking a half-truth. She would never fully accept captivity; that she was a slavegirl, but she couldn't deny the pleasure she felt at submitting to these people. If she was brutally honest with herself, the only thing she regretted was losing her freedom. Well, that and the constant physical abuse. She certainly didn't want to be beaten all the time. Yet she knew the answer to that problem. She just had to learn to obey. Learn to debase herself as these people demanded and please them. Slowly, it dawned on her. She was finished! She would never be the same again! She was even beginning to like being a slavegirl.

Hartman chuckled then and stood up to go across to the rack on the wall, where he collected a long thin chain. Coming back to her, he unfastened the long chain from the collar, replacing it with the thin chain. Next he replaced the muzzle, and rammed the tube to the back of her throat. Rachel groaned as again, her arms were shackled high up her back and clipped to the rear of her collar. Brandishing the whip he jerked once on the chain at her neck.

"Crawl bitch! Out the door, turn left and keep going!" He slashed the chain into her buttocks once, ignoring her muffled cries. "And get a move on! We don't have all day!"

Rachel obeyed, crawling over the rough floor, squealing into the muzzle, each time the thin chain-leash slashed into the crease between her buttocks, urging her onwards along the cold passageways.

In about five minutes, Rachel recognised the heavy door of the Round-Room and she groaned to herself. What now!

"On your feet slut and into the Discipline Room!" Hartman dragged her upright by her hair and pushed her towards the open door.

Rachel went into the brightly-lit room to see another of the girls who had been abducted with her, hanging from the beams, suspended only by her wrists. The Sheik was standing before her, dressed, as usual in his caftan, He was also holding a large plastic bucket full of a glutinous green liquid. Rachel frowned as even through the muzzle, she caught the strong smell of shower-gel.

Grinning up at the suspended slavegirl, the Sheik dug his hand into the bucket and crooning to the suspended girl, he began to smear her body with the gel.

The girl began to groan, but the Sheik merely laughed, rubbing the gel into her flesh, massaging it into her soft, white skin. Fearfully, Rachel wondered; half-suspecting what was to come. Desperately she tried to shut reality out of her mind. Hartman sneered at Rachel. "Stop bitch!"

Rachel halted, still trembling as she watched the Sheik smearing the girl's lovely flesh with the gel, massaging the slave, allowing his hands to wander all over the girl's generous curves and sliding his fingers in and out of her vagina.

Finally, the Sheik stepped back and chuckled. Then he took the chain and lowered the hapless beauty to the floor. He pressed down on her head.

"Kneel slut!"

The slavegirl obeyed, her body glistening with the gel.

Clearly the Sheik was not satisfied, for the whip slashed into the girl's back and she screamed out her agony. The Sheik looked down impassively. "Perhaps you will now see just how much we think you're worth!" he said. "Now, lick the soap off the floor!"

The girl shook her head. "No! I couldn't do that! Please! Don't make -!" The whip slashed into her flesh and she rolled about in the mess, screaming as the lash cut into her body.

"Obey me!" the Sheik roared,. "or I'll whip you to shreds!"

Finally the slavegirl stopped sobbing and miserably scrambled to her knees again, obviously realising the Sheik was serious. She bent to obey and began licking at the mess on the floor. It took her some time but somehow she managed to swallow the soap, without vomiting. She knelt before the Sheik, head down, waiting for the next command.

The Sheik lifted her head then pointed to a low wooden bench, fastened to the floor, in the centre of the room. "Crawl over to that bench! Prostrate yourself across it, with your arse presented to me."

The wretched girl frowned, and the Sheik growled his anger. "Move yourself, slut!" He lifted his quirt, and the leather whistled down across the girls buttocks, the impact causing gel to splatter about, wrenching a scream from the girl. She scrabbled away from him, and moved as quickly as she could to obey. Panting with fright, she laid her upper body over the bench and pushed her buttocks up towards the Sheik.

Kadar chuckled with satisfaction then, motioned to Rachel. "Over here you Christian bitch!" he barked. "It's time to show this slut how slavegirls behave."

Rachel began to tremble. Would she have to lick soap off the floor too? Oh God! Please no! She shuddered, knowing she had to obey.

Hartman was becoming impatient. "Move bitch!" he

snapped at her, kicking her in the buttocks, pushing her towards the Sheik, who had gone to a rack on the wall. The Sheik took down a huge, U-shaped, double-ended, plastic dick; a long, thick dildo. He pointed to the floor in front of him. "Here slut. Kneel before me!"

With widening eyes, as she looked at the monstrous dildo, Rachel obeyed, crawling over to him and knelt, to lower her head submissively.

"Head up slut!"

Rachel looked up and the Sheik grinned as he unfastened the muzzle, dropping it to the floor.

Rachel sucked in a grateful breath, but knew she must stay silent. She lowered her head in submission.

The Sheik chuckled. "She's learning Ernst! Learning well!" He put his fingers beneath Rachel's chin and lifted her head up. The dildo clearly had a malleable core, because the Sheik straightened the thing out, and placed one massive end against her lips.

Obedient now, Rachel opened her mouth and allowed the Sheik to slip the plastic dick to the back of her throat. Then he smeared more of the gel over the thick shaft before pushing Rachel towards the slavegirl.

"Now! Go over to the slut and shaft her with the dildo, in your mouth!"

Trembling with fear, Rachel tried to shut out of her mind, what she had to do. She nodded obediently, and crawled over to the kneeling girl who was now on all fours, and went behind her.

Hartman slashed the whip into the new girl's buttocks. "Wriggle those buttocks slut! Show me how you enjoy this!"

Moaning, the girl obeyed, moving her hips from side to side as Rachel approached.

Hartman stopped Rachel and grabbed her hair, pulling her

head upwards. "And make sure it goes right up her slash; see that she enjoys it." He grinned at her. "You know what will happen if you don't!"

Rachel nodded frantically, as Hartman released her. Then, closing her eyes, and her mind to what she had to do, she nudged the dildo against the offered swell of the girl's swollen labia.

The slavegirl whimpered as the dildo slid into her vagina, until Rachel's face was pressed against the slippery globes of the girl's buttocks. Then, with some difficulty, Rachel began to move the dildo in and out, gripping it with her teeth, and allowing her hands to caress the slippery thighs, her fingers seeking the girl's vagina, to slip in beside the dildo.

Soon the girl was squirming, moaning with mixed pain and pleasure as Rachel's hands and the monstrous dildo did their work in her vagina. The girl's juices were soon beginning to run; to mix with the gel and Rachel also was beginning to lose herself. Suddenly, in her passionate frenzy, she spat out the dildo to grab it with one hand, to shove it even deeper into the girl's body.

In moments, the room was filled with the moans of the two girls, as Rachel pummelled her fellow slavegirl with the dildo. Then, gasping her pleasure, Rachel bent the dildo into a U shape again and straddled the girl's buttocks, allowing the free end of the dildo to slip fully up her own vagina, grinding down on it, her hips sliding around on the smooth, slippery flesh of the slavegirl as she impaled herself on the thick plastic shaft.

Soon the other girl, lost in her own passion, pulled away to turn to face Rachel then slipped the free end of the dildo back into her vagina, grabbing Rachel's body, as together they fucked on the double-ended dildo, They rolled about the floor in passion, screaming and writhing, kissing; caressing uncaring of the gel which began to froth up with the friction of their writhing bodies.

The crack of a whip rang out. "STOP!"

Obediently the girls stopped and rolled apart as the Sheik came across and removed the dildo. He bent over Rachel. "Now suck each other's vaginas and clean each other with your tongues!"

The new slave moaned and then reached for Rachel's body, her head sliding between Rachel's thighs. Eagerly, her tongue searched for Rachel's slit and, in moments, the two girls were locked in a passionate embrace, as they licked and sucked each other to a shuddering climax.

They fell apart, breathless and Hartman motioned to Rachel. "Now, slut! Lick her body clean and don't stop until you're told!"

Rachel stiffened with horror then. She looked up pleadingly. "Please Master. It will make me want to -"

The whip slashed into her shoulders and Hartman snarled. "I know what it will make you do. That's the idea you stupid bitch!" He laughed into both girls' faces. "We have to clean you out, before you perform for your first guest!" He slashed her buttocks with the whip again. "Now get on with it or you'll feel the goad as well as the whip."

Groaning in her misery, feeling debased and degraded, Rachel bent to the other girl's body and tentatively, began to lick the soap of her skin. It tasted vile, and very soon her stomach was aching, as the she slowly cleaned the girl of the gel. At the same time, the girl was cleaning Rachel's body too and together they rolled about the floor, gradually losing themselves in the fascination of the other's body.

Then their moans turned to wails of agony, as both men began to slash into their bodies with their whips, following the terrified, screaming girls about the floor, as they rolled about, trying to evade the lash.

The leather blind-hood was tight about her face. Only her nose was free, having been slipped through the rubber lined hole in the hood. Below this there was another, larger hole, with a steel ring surround. The ring had jammed behind her teeth, forcing her mouth into a large 'O', and she was constantly gurgling and dribbling saliva over her naked front, as she tried to swallow.

So, Rachel could see nothing.

Neither could she hear anything but the roaring, white noise that filled her mind once again. All she knew was that she was being herded to somewhere they had called 'The Slave-ring' someone, presumably Hartman, flicking at her naked buttocks as she stumbled and staggered along.

She could barely keep on her feet, her arms having been taken behind her and secured across the small of her back with thin chain, which had been used to bind her forearms together, exposing the swell of her shapely buttocks to the whip.

She was shivering, and but for the ring in the hood, her teeth would have been chattering. It was cool down here in the depths of Sheik Farid's Pleasure Palace, but it wasn't that causing her to shiver and shake. Nor was it the constant punishment from the whip. Pain and discomfort, of the mild sort she was experiencing at the moment, she was beginning to get used to.

No, she was trembling because of her fear of the unknown. They were taking her to the 'Slave-ring', and the way they had described its terrors to her, and the suffering she had been promised, was filling her mind with dread. That she could see and hear nothing was just another ploy to heighten her fear. She knew that. Oh yes she knew! And it was really working. She was terrified; scared out of her skin.

Then she wailed as the whip suddenly railed into her buttocks, cutting a line of fire across her arse-cheeks. Then the chain attached to the top of the hood was suddenly pulled up sharply, stopping her, almost yanking her head from her shoulders. She tottered, but managed to prevent herself falling over backwards, until someone grabbed her shoulders to steady her.

Then, abruptly, the noise stopped, leaving behind just the ringing in her ears. Still she could hear very little, but slowly her hearing was returning to something like normal.

What she could hear she didn't like very much.

There was the low mumble and murmur of a crowd of people. Nothing definite, but she knew she was right. She trembled again and her spirits sank ever lower as she guessed, whatever was going to happen to her, would be witnessed by a crowd of leering, jeering perverts, just like when she had been sold off to Sheik Farid.

Her legs began to wobble and her knees felt like rubber as her imagination went wild, wondering what exactly she would have to do; what new horrors lay in store for her.

Her thoughts were shattered as she heard Hartman's voice in her ear. "We're here!" he hissed. "The Slave-Ring!" A hoarse chuckle. "Sheik Farid wants a quiet word with you."

Then, she could smell the sweaty, obese Farid beside her. Her Master's cruel tones grated in her ear. "Now my little slut." He said. "We both know how you tried to escape from the compound at Sarinka, yes?"

Rachel nodded miserably. Then she yelped with pain as Farid's huge fat hand landed on her buttocks in a stinging slap. "You answer me slut! At all times. Hood or no hood. DO YOU UNDERSTAND?"

Rachel in her private misery wondered what the hell was the point, but obediently she gurgled what she hoped sounded like a "Yes Master!"

"Better!" Farid grated in her ear again. "Now slut," he went on, "you may have the notion that you can escape from Sheik Farid?"

Rachel shook her head emphatically, and gurgled a negative reply.

Farid's hoarse chuckle sounded again. "Well, that is good." He took a handful of the flesh just above the flare of her right hip and twisted the looser flesh, savagely.

Squealing in pain, Rachel tried to pull away from the vicious grasp, but was unable to do so. Eventually, she remembered and stopped crying out, bearing the pain as best she could. Only then did the fat sadist release her flesh.

"That was painful, was it not my little slut?"

Another gurgle from Rachel.

Farid treated her to a full waft of his rancid breath as he spoke. "You are going to find out what pain is all about. You will wish you had never tried to escape from Sheik Abbas, and you will certainly never try to escape from me!" With that, he quickly unfastened her arms, then deftly unfastened the hood, to drag it from her head.

For a moment, Rachel, still shocked and panting, blinked as her vision returned to normal. They were near the end of a stone corridor, and a few feet ahead of her there was a semicircle of light; bright light, and it was from here that the noise of the crowd was coming. She turned to the two men, in panic, wondering what was happening.

Her reply was a terrific shove in the back from Hartman and she staggered forwards to lurch through the entrance, to go sprawling into the thin coating of sand that covered the hard stone floor.

Immediately she was all but deafened as the murmur of the crowd became a wild swell of shouting, as though with Rachel's sudden appearance they had finally been rewarded for an impatient wait.

Above the noise, Rachel heard Hartman's shout. "On you feet bitch! Show yourself to the crowd you stupid slut!"

Shivering with fright, she looked around, wild-eyed with apprehension and bewilderment. She was in another large domed room, and in the centre there were two thick poles set in the stone about five feet apart. At the top of each pole there was a pulley-wheel, and threaded through each pulley there was a heavy hempen rope. At the other side of the poles the ropes vanished beneath a large curtain and on Rachel's side they were pulled out straight along the ground.

She swallowed, clapped her hands to her ears to shut out the swelling, yelling, calls of derision coming from the audience.

She began to scream, and turned towards the entrance, knowing she had to run to get away from all this noise and the leering lustful glances of the crowd, staring at her nakedness. Then she stopped screaming as she realised the doors had swung closed and she was alone in the semi-circular arena, feeling so lonely and vulnerable. She sank to her knees and crouched, covering her breasts with her hands.

Then a small door in the larger ones opened, and two plump sweating men stepped through in the circle. They were stripped to the waist and each had a coiled whip attached to the belt of their dirty, tattered jeans.

The crowd began to bay again as the two men turned, to give a brief theatrical bow. With evil grins distorting their already ugly features they waddled over towards Rachel. They each grabbed one of her arms, and effortlessly they jerked her upright again.

The bearded man on her right snarled in her ear. "The folks here want a show, and you're gonna help us give them one." Both men yanked Rachel's arms down. "So get your hands away from your tits! slavegirls don't cover up unless they're told to!"

"Oh God!" Rachel started to plead "Let me go. Please. I'll be a slave I'll do anything you say, but please don't do anything to me in front of all -"

The man's hand crashed into her face, the slap sounding even above the crowd noise. But it was soon drowned out as instantly the crowd seemed to go wild, yelling, shouting out encouragement to the men.

"Let's see something, fellas!"

"Give the slut what for!"

"Come on, let's see her squirm!"

"We want to hear her scream!"

Rachel was beside herself with terror now. She tried to shut it all out of her mind but it was hopeless. She couldn't avoid visualising what was going to be done to her. But then, these perverted people had so many things they could do to hurt her, so many warped ideas to torture her. She really had no idea what the might be going to do. One thing was for sure. The two men were not carrying whips for decoration, and somehow Rachel also knew that whatever was going to happen, the two poles standing in the arena would have something to do with it.

She realised that she badly wanted to use the toilet, and knew that to 'disgrace' herself here would not only be to her utter embarrassment, but would earn her even more punishment. Without any real hope of being accommodated she turned to the bearded man. "Please Master! I have to go to -"

Her words were cut off as the man swung his arm back and his meaty hand smashed into her right buttock. "You want a piss, slut?" He grabbed her hair and shook her head. "Is that it?"

Rachel hung her head, her cheeks burning with shame. She nodded slightly. "Yes Master."

He shook her head. "Well ask. PROPERLY. SO WE CAN HEAR YOU, YOU STUPID BITCH!"

Rachel swallowed and a nervous tremor in her voice said loudly: "I want to go the bathroom, Master!"

The man roared with laughter and then smashed his hand into her buttocks again. "I don't understand you slut!" He shook her once more. "ASK PROPERLY!"

Rachel frowned, "I-I-I I d-don't understand Master!"

He hissed in her ear. "WE don't understand either. We don't use prissy-sissy words here. If you want a piss, ask!"

Rachel swallowed her pride, hung her head and murmured. "I want a p-piss M-Master!"

"I can't hear you. Neither can the audience." His hand twisted in her hair and pulled her head back.

Rachel piped up louder, still blushing, "I want a p-piss M-Master!"

The other man laughed then and shouted to the crowd, "She'll just have to wait a few minutes, won't she?"

There was an appreciative cheer from the crowd and the bearded man, shouted, "She wants a piss folks!" He laughed. "So we'll give her something to make her piss!"

Again there was an appreciative shout from the crowd, as they settled down to watch the entertainment.

Rachel felt her body begin to shake again and she knew her face was burning with shame and degradation, but it was clear there was no time for that, for the men pushed her towards the poles. Then without warning they each grabbed a handful of her hair, and sliced a hand into the backs of her knees.

Rachel yelled out in pain and surprise as she was swept from her feet, so her bottom smashed onto the hard floor, jarring her spine.

Before she had time to even think about it, she was pushed backwards. The breath whooshed out of her and the world started to spin as the back of her head jarred on the sand.

Again the crowd started to yell, urging the men on, and before Rachel was even half-aware, she was pulled up again, into a suiting position. The man on her right, growled into her ear and pointed to the manacles, on the ends of the two ropes.

Rachel knew it was pointless to resist them and, sighing to herself, she reached forwards picked up the anklets and clipped them onto her ankles. Oh God! Not only were they going to torture her, they wanted her to get herself ready for it! What the hell was wrong with these perverts? But she knew in a way. It was all part of the treatment, just another way of asserting their utter control over her. She had no option but to obey, and they meant to see that she never forgot it.

Then the two men bent to her again and her arms were wrenched behind her back, her wrists handcuffed, and her forearms pulled up between her shoulder blades. She heard the click of the shackles as her wrists were fastened to the rear of her collar. And once more she started to shake violently and she knew she wanted to pee, she wanted to pee so very badly. She doubted that she could hold onto it. But she knew she had to and she clenched her thighs together, trying to prevent it happening.

The two sadists stood up then and turned to the crowd once more. "Are we ready folks?" the bearded one asked.

An instantaneous roar, YES!

"So we begin!" he shouted. Then a louder call, "Lift the curtain!"

The curtain started to raise, like a theatre drape, and Rachel started to goggle as she looked at the sight before her.

About ten yards in front of her on the other side of the poles, two naked slavegirls were kneeling with their backs to her. They each wore a wide leather waist band, and emerging from between each pair of creamy, white buttocks there was a wicked looking piece of thin chain. Although Rachel couldn't see exactly how the chains were arranged, it seemed that they were secured to the front of the belts, and had been taken back through the girls' thighs, then up to the rear of the belts, where the links were threaded through large rings in the small of the girls' backs. Then each chain had been secured to the other end of the ropes which Rachel had just fastened to her own ankle

The bearded man knelt to Rachel's ear and chuckled. "Now do you see?"

Indeed, Rachel did see! Now she was panting and shaking violently, as panic surged through her. She started to shake her head in disbelief. "No! Please no! You can't do this to me."

The bearded man giggled at her. "Don't waste your breath sweetie-slut! You're going to need it to scream once we get going."

With that both men walked over to the two kneeling slaves, themselves now clearly shaking in their fear. The bearded man snapped out: "On all four sluts!"

The chains clinked as immediately the two girl obeyed, their tight buttocks becoming stretched even more. The men took the whips from their belts, and again they acknowledged the crowd who were now beginning to shout and scream in lustful abandon. Then, in concert, the two men began to slash into the offered buttocks of the two unfortunate slaves. Their screams were muffled, by their muzzles, but Rachel could still hear the cries of their agony. Then she stopped worrying about them as they started to crawl forwards, the whips continually battering into their flesh, urging them onwards towards the blank wall ahead. Rachel began to scream than as she was pulled along, her legs beginning to stretch wide apart as the slack of the ropes was taken up and they started to shorten, inexorably pulling her feet upwards and outwards towards the sheaves of the pulley.

The pain was intense as her sex suddenly gaped and her hips felt as though they were going to be pulled out of joint.

Still the men sliced their whips into the naked beauties, who were now screaming into their muzzles, their cries sounding louder as the leather continued to cut into their defenceless bodies, adding their noise to Rachel's cries, and to the continual baying of the crowd.

Rachel thought she would go mad with the cacophony and the pain, But it wouldn't stop. Struggling for purchase in the sand, they scrabbled their hands into the stone flags beneath as they strained to lift Rachel clear of the floor. Their agony must have been just as bad as Rachel's, as the strain caused the chains to dig into their soft genitals, deeper with each yard they gained and with each extra inch they lifted their screaming burden.

Straining at their load the two slavegirls tried desperately to evade the whips slamming into their sweating bodies, each contact sending sprays of perspiration into the air.

Then Rachel was suddenly hanging between the poles, her legs stretched wider than she could ever have imagined possible. Now she was sweating, her perspiration pouring from her; the sweat of fear dripping from every pore, so much so it was running down her inverted body in rivulets. She was panting, screaming, praying for the strength to withstand what she knew was coming.

The bearded man gave the two straining, screaming girls one final slash with the whip, then stepped in front of them, to secure a chain, from their necks to rings in the floor just in front of them. He grinned at the two shaking, battered girls. "Just in case you think of easing back for her sake!"

Then both men walked back towards Rachel and cracked their whips into the air, much to the delight and amusement of the crowd.

The two men took up position one each side of the poles, and Rachel began to babble to herself, crying out her misery, as she caught an inverted view of the bearded one standing behind her. He came forwards and then bent his head into the wide open vee of her thighs, to kiss her offered sex. His huge tongue rasped along the stretched slit of her gaping labia and he allowed his saliva to drool all over her parts. Then, straightening up, he grinned into Rachel's inverted face.

"We need the lubrication slut. Makes the whip sting even more!" Another throaty chuckle and he smeared the slime into Rachel's sex, before stepping back again.

The other man was out of Rachel's view, on the other side of the poles. For that reason the surprise of the first blow was all the more effective. She heard the leather whistle through the air, then a burning sear of pain, such as she had never experienced sent waves of pain through her body. She let go an ear-piercing shriek, which sounded even above all the noise in the arena...

The crowd went wild then and their lunatic baying increased, as the supple leather struck, again, this time from the bearded man. His blow sent another mind shattering burst of pain coursing through Rachel's soul

The leather was jerked away again and then there was the whoosh of air as the other man delivered his second blow, again wrenching an awful shriek from Rachel. Then another lash from the bearded man at her head and Rachel suddenly passed in to what seemed like a different world. There was no sound, but that of the whips, no feeling but the raging seat of her agony each time the leather struck home.

Slowly, her mind was becoming demented as she twisted and struggled, her lithe, young body twisting under the lash; writhing trying to soak up the punishment. But it was all to no avail, Time after time, the leather whips thundered home, until her ravaged, flesh began to go numb, the shattered nerves giving up the struggle to send messages to her brain.

Then there was one final indignity as her bladder suddenly let go and her own warm stinging urine ran freely, to course over her as she finally gave into the pain.

Blackness closed in and she slipped away from reality. Not unconscious, but strangely detached, as though reality was somewhere near, but out of reach. She was still aware of the sounds about her, but they were inconsequential to her. Now, there was but one thought in her tortured, mind.

Never again would she try to escape.

18 - Master Toshio!

Rachel fought the waves of dizziness as she slowly came to her senses.

She had spent the last few hours in a strange world of her own. As if her mind had closed down to the awful reality of her position. Now, full awareness pushed away the dream world she had occupied and she started to feel the pain once more.

The first thing she felt was the cutting agony of the thin chains wrapped tightly about her body, pulled tight into the vee of her thighs, and cutting into her genitals; threatening to almost cut her in two. She struggled, but only for a moment, as she realised the extent of pain this caused.

She sagged, realising that she had been chained so that she was virtually immobile. Her body was bent forwards, over a steel rail which was digging into her stomach, making it difficult to breathe. She groaned, and realised she was gagged with a chain-gag that had been forced into her mouth, pulled right back into the angle of her jaw, and taken around the back of her head to be secured tightly in place.

Her head ached and her saliva dripped unheeded to the floor as she splathered around the chain-gag. Her buttocks were tilted up and the pain in her head was made worse by the fact that it was being forced downwards. She tried to move again Hopeless. She opened her eyes to see that she was in a large stone-walled room, and that she was secured to what looked like a crush barrier.

Her legs were stretched painfully wide and her ankles were manacled to the stone floor, with her arms stretched out and downwards, to be shackled with lengths of china to the floor in front of her. Around her neck there was a wide, studded, leather collar and from this leather collar a semi-slack chain depended towards the floor.

There didn't seem to be anyone else in the room, and she began to tremble, wondering why she had been brought here and secured in this horrendous fashion. Oh God! Was there to be no end to this torture, she thought, as her stomach churned and her legs began to tremble violently. She coughed, tried to swallow, only half-succeeding, then sagged in defeat again, wondering what terrors lay in store for her.

Then she jumped in nervous shock as she heard the Sheik's voice coming from behind her. "She's with us Ernst! Raise the bar and stretch that body a little. Let's see how supple she really is."

There was the sudden whine of a motor and almost immediately Rachel felt a blast of pain as the bar began to press deeper into her stomach. She started to gasp, to struggle to breathe. More saliva dripped from her mouth, and she tried to struggle against the steady pull as the bar continued to rise, pressing painfully into her belly, causing her buttocks to peak upwards. The shackle at her ankles and wrists began to cut into the sparse flesh and she screamed through the chain-gag, as she felt her joints threatening to pop. Just as she knew she could stand no more, the Sheik spoke.

"Enough Ernst! That position is just fine!"

Rachel screamed into the gag as a whip whistled through the air to land with a sharp crack across the cheeks of her arse, and she felt the fire as her skin began to redden. Three more terrible blasts of pain across her tight buttocks, then two more, this time lashing into the backs of her thighs.

She sagged against her bonds, sobbing as the burning pain set her legs quivering. God! Just how much more did these perverts think she could take? But then, she reminded herself. They didn't care. She was a mere piece of flesh to them. A slavegirl was a slavegirl, and it didn't matter how much she could or couldn't take. If they felt they wanted to whip her, they would whip her. It was as simple as that!

The Sheik's voice cut across her thoughts. "The grease Ernst!"

"Got it!"

"Good!" The Sheik chuckled sadistically.

Rachel felt her heart miss, as she wondered what they were going to do. She wasn't kept waiting, and she gasped as one of them suddenly smeared grease all over her buttocks, concentrating on getting a thick glob of the stuff between her cheeks, smearing it all over her anus. Now she knew what was going to happen and she whimpered into the gag, trying to turn so she could see them, to beg them to leave her alone. But she knew it was futile, and finally she stopped whimpering, accepting what was to happen, bracing herself for the terrible onslaught she was about to suffer. She was going to be buggered, and there was absolutely nothing she could do about it.

Then Hartman was in front of her and grinning into her

terrified face. He had a black, conical object in his hand, shiny, like plastic. It was about twelve inches long and the tip was fashioned into a blunt point. All the way along the length there were flanges, each one bigger than the one before it. At the wider end there was a large flange with four straps attached. Hartman shook the frightening thing in her face.

Rachel's heart leapt. She had never seen a butt-plug, but she had heard of them. There was no doubt that this was a but plug! It looked enormous and she would never be able to stand the agony of this thing spearing her flesh.

Rachel knew, though, that these monsters didn't care about such niceties. This awful thing was going to be pushed inside her, she would scream, and struggle, but it would make no difference. Almost involuntarily, she began to shake her head and to gurgle into the chain-gag, pleading with him.

All that she got was a hard slap across the face. "Shut it bitch!"

Rachel lapsed into silence. Then a gasp as Hartman lifted her head by her hair. "Now kiss the plug!" He pressed the cold plastic against her contorted lips and, as best the gag would allow, Rachel obeyed and kissed the monstrous thing.

Hartman grinned in satisfaction, and disappeared behind her again.

Almost at once she felt the first thrust of the plug as it nudged against the lips of her anus. She screamed out as it slowly invaded her body, then her screams turned to high pitched shrieks as the first flange began to widen her anus. She began to cry out, feeling her throat becoming hoarse. There was to be no respite, for as soon as the first flange had breached her anal lips, her muscles caused the normal reaction and her anus closed over the next section of the shaft. Still the thing was being pressed into her, and more agony as the next flange began to push insistently against her tender flesh. Again her back passage opened as the second flange slipped into her, to be sucked in by the natural muscle reaction of her anus.

Her screams were rending the air and despite the secure chains she was writhing and struggling against this new torture.

The Sheik's voice cut across her screams. "Enough Ernst! We must stretch her, not rip her apart. We'll leave it at two for now. Tomorrow, we give her another one."

Then Hartman's voice. "That's just half of it!" He giggled, and Rachel heard him whisper into her ear. "The other half will come soon enough!"

He disappeared again, and Rachel felt the straps being fixed around her hips and thighs, keeping the butt-plug in place. Then, suddenly, and to her utter relief, the chain-gag was released. But the relief was short-lived for the gag was immediately replaced by the familiar muzzle, and she retched as the tube inside was forced down her throat.

The Sheik came around to the front now and he smiled cruelly down at Rachel. "It's feeding time, slut!" He turned to Hartman. "The swill Ernst! And the funnel"

Rachel groaned then as Hartman was in front of her and was grinning evilly into her face. He grabbed her matted hair and jerked her head upwards. He was still grinning as he held up the funnel and its piece of red rubber tubing.

"Time to eat! Come on! Open up!"

It took both men to hold her head still and feed the rubber tube into her stomach. Then, trembling, gurgling and groaning, she was forced to suffer, while the Sheik grabbed her head and pinched her nose. Hartman began to pour the filthy swill into her stomach.

It was quicker than it had been on the boat and in moments Rachel felt her stomach distended by about half a gallon of the evil mess, distending her belly painfully against the bar across her middle. She retched as the tube was withdrawn and once again she cringed as she suffered the degradation she had first felt, when being force-fed on the boat.

Finally Hartman was satisfied and he grinned into her tear-streaked features. "Have to feed you like this slut. You will stay shackled here for a few days while you are stretched." He grinned. "And don't worry. We'll be here when it's necessary to take the plug out." He giggled. "From time to time." He leant towards her and sniggered. "When you got to go, well, you got to go!" he turned away and went behind her again.

Rachel tried to keep the food down, but inevitably she began to retch. Then she screamed into the muzzle as a line of fire traced across the backs of her thighs as the whip slashed home. "Keep it down slut!" Hartman warned, "or we just scoop it up and funnel it back into you!" He cackled and then turned away, leaving her to her misery.

The huge room was much like the Discipline Room of Sheik Abbas. It was roughly dome shaped, and apart from the concrete floor, it was completely sheathed in stainless steel, so that inside it was like being in an upturned, bowl. Fixed to the floor near the circular hatchway, there was a long wooden rack, festooned with coils of rope, lengths of dog-chain, collars, whips, manacles, leather hoods and other cruel bondage devices.

In the centre of the floor there was a round patch of brown floor tiles, about twenty feet across. In the middle of this tiled circle there was a large, old-fashioned, leather birching-stool, complete with heavy adjustable leather straps.

Shivering with the cool air on her flesh, Rachel was kneeling in the centre of the circle, close to the birching-stool, sobbing to herself. She was hardly aware of what she was doing here, or even where she was. There was the pain and discomfort of the huge butt-plug, now pushed even further into her anus; the soreness of the scourging she had suffered after swallowing all that shower-gel; the fresh welts on her body, bringing horrific memories of the whippings and the stinging burn on her left breast, where they had pressed the white-hot iron into her flesh. Another shiver convulsed her; revulsion at the memory of the branding, the humiliation at being treated like an animal.

Rachel sobbed then, recalling how, just an hour or so before, she had been unshackled and taken to a freezing room, virtually an open drain. They had left the butt-plug in place, even pushing it in a little further. Then they had bound her hand and foot and, for what had seemed like eternity, they had played a fierce jet of cold water over her, the force of the water pushing her helpless body all over the room. Then they had taken her for a bath. Or what they had called a bath. It had merely been another sadistic ordeal.

They had used this room. Shackling her knees and calves to the floor, and securing her wrists to one of the rings fixed at intervals around the wall, once more the monsters had hosed her down, this time with hot water. Then they had smeared her body with glutinous, soft soap, and Jeyes fluid, scrubbing at her tender flesh with hard-bristled brushes, just as they would an animal.

After another hosing down they had left her shivering, to dry off. Later they had returned to completely cover her body with a liberal dusting of talcum powder. Then two slavegirls had entered the room, unshackled her wrists and had begun to wash and blow-dry her long blonde hair, brushing it out into its normal, soft silken state.

Then, carrying his dog-whip, the repulsive Hartman had entered the room. Playfully almost, he had chased the two slavegirls from the room, laughing aloud as he flicked his whip around their jiggling buttocks. With delighted squeals the two girls had run from the room, casting tempting, saucy glances behind them at their sadistic Master, as they had fled.

Immediately they had gone, giggling and chattering down the corridor and out of earshot, Hartman's playful manner had deserted him. He had stepped across to Rachel and wrenched her hands behind her back to fasten them together with more chain.

Next he had forced her arms high up her back and clipped her wrist chain to the makeshift chain collar. Finally, he had smeared Vaseline over the recent brand, and then released her legs. Effortlessly he had lifted her to carry her to the centre of the room, where he had dropped her on her knees. He had leaned towards her ear and hissed. "You wait here slut. Head down and stay still, until you are told otherwise." He pulled her head back and grinned into her face. "You better please the guest too, or it's more of the whip and the goad.

He hadn't waited for a reply but had just pushed her head back down to her chest, and left her in her chained nakedness, to wait for her first initiation into pleasing a guest of Sheik Farid.

Now, trembling with the fear of the unknown, Rachel was beginning to accept the truth of her situation. She was a slave to these people, she was in the severest bondage and she knew that escape was impossible, at least for the present. Knowing the slightest wrong move, would result in a savage whipping or another encounter with Hartman's goad she had to suffer it all. Obey or be tortured. These people had no right to abuse her, but there was nothing she could do about it.

They considered her as their slave; their animal. It was clear that, to them, whatever a slave wanted, thought, or felt didn't matter. She was in the control of people who had far different values to her own and she was in strange country.

Exactly where, she didn't know, except that it must be somewhere in the Middle East. That really it didn't matter. All she could do was wait for another chance to escape. Next time she might be luckier. Her mind clouded. She didn't really believe that. Her one aborted escape attempt had shown her that getting away would require a near miracle. There was no one to help; and even if she got clear of this awful place, she would be naked, penniless and at the mercy of fate and whoever she happened to meet.

She trembled, recalling the torture that had ensued after her first aborted attempt at escape. For the moment, then, Rachel had come to terms with her situation. She must behave like a slave and obey them. So now she waited, in submissive silence, her head lowered, her long blonde hair brushing the cold tiles beneath her knees, wincing as the pain from the terrible, butt-plug kept reminding her of its presence.

Suddenly Rachel's heart jumped as someone came into the room. She heard footsteps approaching her, but dared not move her head to look. Eventually a pair of jack-booted legs appeared beside her, and then a million needles lanced her scalp, and the butt-plug seared her anus again, as someone grabbed her hair, and lifted her head up, to stare down at her terror-stricken face.

Her first guest!

The man was small, with a fat, florid face and a wispy, grey moustache. He appeared to be Japanese; dressed in the uniform of a wartime officer, his attire complete, right down the terrifying ceremonial Samurai sword hanging at his belt. In his free hand he held a coiled leather whip, and his tiny black eyes gleamed in his heavy cheeks. His uneven, yellow teeth showed in a cruel smile and his breath rasped as he spoke.

"I am Master Toshio!" He chuckled. "I am not Japanese by the way, although I always wanted to be. Especially if it could have been during the war years eh!?" He shook Rachel's head, dragging squeals of pain and shock from her. He leaned over the terrified girl, treating her to a wave of stale garlic breath. "I am an expert in torturing sluts like you. In fact compared to me, my wartime heroes were just playing at it." He twisted Rachel's hair tighter in his fist. "As you are just about to discover!"

He placed the whip on the floor, and, still holding her head back, he started to run his hand all over her body, his blunt fingers searching between her rounded buttocks. Then he released the chains, holding the butt-plug in place, and with a savage wrench, pulled the awesome thing from her body.

Rachel screeched out as the thing came free, its serrations, ripping into the tender flesh of her anal passage.

Toshio ignored her wailing as he cast the butt-plug aside and immediately his fingers were seeking her anus and her vagina, his thumb sliding into her rear passage and his fingers parting her labia from behind. He grunted in satisfaction. "Ah! You'll make a good shag!" Another chuckle. "But first I have other plans for you!"

Then a sudden gasp was wrenched from Rachel, as his hand twisted tighter into her hair, yanking her head upwards, so she was looking into her Master's cruel features. He sneered at her.

"Open my trousers. With your teeth!"

Trying to bear the pain in her scalp, Rachel swallowed, and leaned her head towards his groin, her teeth seeking the large metal ring on his fly-zipper. Swallowing her fear, Rachel clamped the ring between her teeth and began to pull downwards. Now she could smell the man's arousal, feel the heat through his underpants, as his trousers opened at the front, allowing his penis to lift and jerk as his erection began to grow.

He had loosed her hair now, and he leaned over her to unfasten her hands. He held her wrists tightly, then pushed her upper body downwards. "Kiss my feet!" he said. "Then undress me! Slowly, as a lover should!"

Rachel shivered in fear, knowing she had to obey. She bent towards his feet and kissed the cold, shiny leather. Then she tried to remove the boots. The whip seared across her shoulders. "Not like that you stupid bitch!" He grabbed her hair again and twisted her around so her back was to him. Then he shoved her head downwards, and rammed his shin against her buttocks, the supple leather of the boot sliding into the crease between the globes of flesh. "Now," he shouted, "grab the boot you stupid slut! And pull!"

Rachel obeyed, screaming out as the whip lashed her back again, Then she grunted as his other foot was pressed against the base of her spine, shoving her away from him. The boot slid off, suddenly, so she was pitched forwards to sprawl across the floor. The whip burned her shoulders again and he yelled at her "Back on your knees cow! Remove the other boot!"

The performance was repeated. This time the man's stockinged foot was placed against her spine, the sole of his foot spreading her buttocks, pressing against her genitals. forcing open her labia from behind.

The evil sadist wriggled his foot about slightly, chuckling as Rachel grunted. Then he shoved her forwards.

Rachel was ready this time and as the boot slid off the man's foot, she was able to remain kneeling upright in front of him. She dropped the boot to one side then turned towards him, knowing what she must do. Slowly and deliberately she allowed her hands to caress his legs, feeling her way beneath his trousers, rolling her palms about his stumpy legs. She was smiling at him now, as she began to tease down his trousers with her teeth, murmuring to herself in mock passion as her fingers tackled the belt-buckle. She pulled the trousers down and then shuddered, pulling his legs to her body, as he stepped out of the trousers, kicking them aside.

Now Rachel was at the waistband of his underpants, and she pulled them over his hips, to allow them to slip down.

Toshio's penis, was now at full erection and it sprang upwards as it was freed of the undergarment. The smell of his maleness was pungent and Rachel could feel the warmth of the huge member beside her cheek. She slipped her hands around his waist, and allowed her fingers to tease the podgy flesh beneath his upper clothing.

By now the man was breathing heavily. His erection was beginning to pulse, and Rachel pressed the hot gristly thing to her cheek.

Frantic now, the stunted Toshio tore at his uniform tunic, unfastening the belt himself, dropping the thing, sword and all, to virtually rip his jacket off.

Rachel was now able to straighten up, slowly, pressing her naked front against his legs, allowing his rock-hard penis to slide between her breasts as she rose, even squeezing her bosom together, clamping on the massive, hot weapon.

He seemed to like that, as a gasp of pleasure escaped him, and he uttered a sibilant. "Yeeess, Yeeeess! You gorgeous little slut! Yeeess!"

Rachel shuddered then, feeling strangely pleased with herself, not even worrying about being called a slut! Because that's what she was behaving like, wasn't it? She knew she had to, but strangely, although she was supposed to be the slave, she felt a sudden power over this ridiculous little man as she got slowly to her feet. Now she was pulling his shirt and vest up and groaning his pleasure. He lifted his arms as she pulled the garments over his head, to cast them aside. His arms went around her slender body, and soon they were pressed close together in their nudity.

The man's pasty flesh was surprisingly smooth, and the warmth from his body had a musky smell to it. At least, Rachel reflected, he was clean, and she offered a silent prayer of thanks for that small mercy.

Rachel was a good four inches taller than the man and an expression of displeasure crossed his features as his arms lifted and he pressed downwards on her shoulders. When their eyes were level, he scowled at her. "You keep your head lower than mine at all times slut! You understand?"

Rachel swallowed and nodded. "Yes Master."

Then Toshio smiled. "That little performance was quite good!" He wagged a finger in her face. "Not perfect, but good enough for a novice slavegirl!" He pressed downwards again. "Now it's time to assume your proper position. On your knees! Now!" he snapped.

Rachel dropped her gaze and lowered herself to her knees. Then she squealed out as the whip slashed into her shoulders. "Speak to me then you stupid bitch!"

She looked up "Master?" She frowned. "I, I don't know what -"

The whip stung her shoulders again. "Just say 'Yes Master', or 'No Master', when I tell you to do anything or ask a question. Is that simple enough?"

"Y-y-yes Master!" Rachel mumbled, her head lowered in submission.

He grabbed her hair again and wrenched her head backwards.

"I can't hear you, slut!"

Grimacing with the pain, Rachel managed a tortured "Yes Master!"

He pushed her head down and loosed her. "Good." He shoved his hips towards her face. "You know what comes now?"

Rachel smothered a sob. "Y-yes Master!" Slowly she

reached for the still-erect penis and softly she caressed the length of the pulsing, silky-smooth member. It was a gorgeous length of maleness, she had to admit, and like the rest of his body, it was clean. Almost without hesitation, her lips opened and she allowed her saliva to wet the huge member, as she began to lick up and down the length of it. Her tongue teased itself beneath the foreskin, and she forced the tip of her tongue in to the slit, whilst pulling the skin gently back.

He was groaning now, as his hands grabbed her hair, and slowly he started to push into her mouth, seeking to force the thick shaft down Rachel's throat.

Rachel allowed herself to relax so the huge penis slid easily into her throat, and she began to move her head backwards and forwards, in time with his thrusts, breathing through her nose as he withdrew, Slowly, the stunted man approached his climax, and soon he was thrusting ever more urgently into her mouth. Then he grabbed her hair, pulling her head into his groin as he surged into the moist tunnel of her mouth, slamming the end of his prick against the soft flesh at the back of her throat.

The penis grew thicker, swelling, the blood-heat almost burning her mouth. Then the thing began to pulsate as his seed was suddenly jetting into her mouth.

She tried to swallow, but he withdrew from her mouth, pushing her backwards to the floor.

He was grunting, groaning and gasping as he allowed spurt after spurt of his seed to splatter across Rachel's naked recumbent form, pushing his hips forwards so some of the hot creamy spunk splashed her face, to run down her cheeks, and to puddle in the well of her neck and shoulders.

Finally the gushing became a dribble, and he knelt astride her shoulders. Pushing the softening prick towards her mouth. It was awkward, and she had to strain her head forwards, but finally she managed to get her lips around the shrinking penis, so she could suck the final seeps of his love cream, cleaning him up with her tongue.

He sat back, and with a contemptuous sneer on his face, he deliberately scooped up the cooling sperm from Rachel's body with his hand, He held his hand up. "Open wide bitch!" he said.

Rachel pushed aside the thought of what the cold semen would be like and swallowed her disgust. Obediently, she opened her mouth and, holding back the urge to vomit, she allowed the thickening sperm to drip into her mouth. Trying not to throw up, she swallowed the stuff, then, suddenly realised that it wasn't so bad after all. In fact, she recognised the old feeling. Her masochistic tendencies were rising again, as she began to thrill at the act of submitting to this stunted little man.

Finally, Toshio got up and grabbed Rachel's hair. He dragged her to her knees and looked down at her. "How long have you been a slave?"

Rachel shook her head, still gazing at the floor. "I don't know Master."

"Come on, slut! Answer me. Is it weeks? Months? Or what?" He prodded her none too gently, with his foot. "Speak up!"

Again Rachel mumbled. "I don't know Master. I've lost track." She gazed up at him, a pleading expression on her face. "Please Master you must believe me."

He nodded. "All right! I know how it is." He drew in a deep breath. "So that means, you have some tricks to learn doesn't it?"

"Yes Master!" Rachel said, gazing back at the floor.

The man moved away towards the birching stool, where he stood quietly looking at Rachel, kneeling docilely before him. "What do you think of my performance so far slut?"

Rachel looked up at him and frowned. "Please Master. What must I say?"

"Just tell me the truth."

She took a deep breath. "Master is clean and it was nice having you in my mouth!" She cringed at her words, but she knew it must be what he wanted to hear.

The sadistic maniac seemed to ignore her and he whistled the vicious looking whip through the air a couple of times for effect.

Flinching, Rachel jerked her head upwards in alarm, the sudden movement causing her shapely breasts to push forwards provocatively, Toshio sneered at Rachel.

"Well?"

"Master?"

"You heard slut! What do you think of my performance?"

Rachel trembled and looked about her. "I just told Master!" she said.

The man sniggered and using Rachel's frightened submissive tones, mimicked. "I Just told Master!" He cracked the whip into the air again. "Well." he continued, "you've every reason to be satisfied!" He giggled. "I have never had any complaints from elsewhere." He lowered the whip and pulled her head upright, to gaze into her eyes. Softly he said: "You're scared and you don't know what to expect do you?"

"No Master, I don't."

The whip whistled through the air again, this time slashing into Rachel's upper thigh, curling viciously about her legs and cutting into her buttocks. Screaming, she fell to the floor and tried to roll away. A waste of time. The burning, vicious slashes kept finding new targets lashing into her and she rolled her shapely body into a ball wailing and screeching each time the whip seared across her buttocks, thighs and shoulders, the fiery end curling into her waist and belly. Every time she tried to get up the whip would cut her flesh again, forcing her back to the floor. Screaming and shrieking Rachel, rolled about in a huddled ball as she tried to ride the vicious blows that tore into her body.

Then the demented attack ceased and Toshio snarled at her. "Now you know! You little bitch!" He grabbed Rachel's long hair and jerked her to her knees bending her head backwards. "Now on your feet, slut. Lie across the birching stool and show me those buttocks of yours."

Trembling uncontrollably, each step aggravating the agony of her burning, lacerated skin, her pain-laced genitals, Rachel struggled to her feet and approached the stool awkwardly, barely able to keep her balance. Wobbling slightly she lowered her body over the stool, catching her breath as the cool leather made contact with her burning front. She closed her eyes now, and held her breath, waiting again for the agonising kiss of the whip. Nothing came! Instead she felt the man spread her legs and fasten her ankles to the stool. Then he was in front of her, his hands reaching for her arms to stretch them forwards, where he secured them to more straps in the side of the stool. Then he stood back and Rachel began to shake in terror, as she heard the whip whistle through the air.

But no blow came, and she let her breath out in a rush as she heard the whip drop to the floor. She heard him breathing heavily then, just standing behind her, chuckling as she began to shake in fearful anticipation. Then his hands came in front of her face and she gave a sad groan, as a muzzle was applied to her face. She winced and moaned again, as he buckled it tight behind her neck.

Another soft chuckle, then he said. "It's opening time slut!"

Rachel felt his hand resting in the crease of her buttocks, and then stiffened in shock as one of his fingers wriggled into her anus. She whimpered, and started to shake her head, but the finger slowly forced deeper into her traumatised anal orifice. The finger was withdrawn and she sighed in relief; but in short-lived relief. Suddenly there was the feel of some cool grease being applied to the tight lips of her anus. It did nothing to ease her pain, and she drew in a breath, trying to will the agony away. Then she felt his huge, hot prick, nudging at her and she began to wail.

Trembling, sobbing, Rachel waited for the lunge of his monstrous weapon, but instead she felt Toshio's hand at the back of her neck. Squeezing her neck in his strong grip, he pushed her face deep into the leather of the stool. He released her neck. "Stay still slut!" he hissed.

Rachel obeyed, but still could not resist trembling in fearful anticipation as his hands began to roam over her defenceless body.

Toshio was chuckling as he caressed her and quietly, he went out of her range of vision to go behind her trembling, helpless form. He slapped her buttocks with his hand and laughed as she flinched. Grabbing a large handful of flesh inside her soft thighs, he said: "You really have got a beautiful arse!"

Yet again Rachel trembled and tried to plead with him. "Please Master, don't hurt me any more!" Then she howled out in anguish, as the whip cut into her buttocks again and she wriggled her buttocks, trying to ease the pain.

Toshio leaned over and, grabbing Rachel's hair, he lifted her upwards against the restraint of the leather straps, causing her joints to crack, as they stretched. "Keep your mouth shut and don't wriggle your arse until I tell you to. Understand?"

"Y-y-y Yes M..M..Master." Rachel's tears ran freely as Toshio lowered her back to the cool leather surface. Her mind filled with loathing as she realised that Toshio was going to have sex with her, and he was going to take her like an animal. And worse! She knew he was going to bugger her! That would change her for ever. Even if she escaped from here, she would always feel dirty and used, after that!

Oblivious of Rachel's discomfort, grunting and moaning with naked lust, Toshio allowed his hands to wander over Rachel's defenceless buttocks and thighs. His hand slid into the crease between her buttocks and then he lunged his finger into Rachel's back-passage.

This new invasion was as forceful as it was unexpected and she wailed as the wounds inside her were aggravated as his fingers worked inside her passage. She writhed and squirmed, trying to wrench herself away from the pain, but it was useless.

Toshio, fondling her leg just beneath the swell of her right buttock, dug his fingers in and, viciously, squeezed a good handful of the tender flesh. Ignoring her pitiful wails, he took his finger from her anus and then pulled her buttocks wide apart. Then Rachel's heart almost stopped as she felt grease being applied to the cleft between her buttocks. Immediately, she felt Toshio's huge penis pushing against the tender ring of her anus. Horrified, Rachel, realised now the moment had come. Screaming, she tried to pull away from him. "Please!" She cried. "No! Please! Not that!"

"You still haven't learnt have you?" Toshio leaned over the terrified Rachel. "Now listen to me, slut! You will take whatever I give you." He cracked the whip again for effect. "Or I will flay the skin off your back." He slapped her haunches hard. "Now, how do you want it to be?"

Rachel knew she was finished. This monster was going to do THAT to her and she would never be the same again. She had to face it.

There was nothing she could do to prevent Toshio doing as he wished. She was at his mercy. If she didn't obey him. Then she really would be lashed. And as for struggling, trying to actually stop him... She shuddered. What would be the point? That would probably give him even more enjoyment of her body. Far better perhaps to submit. Sooner or later, she would find a way to escape. In the meantime...? She trembled again. Oh God! What was wrong with these monsters?. Were there no depths to which they wouldn't sink? She knew what she had to say. In a soft, defeated voice she whispered "yes Master!"

Toshio chuckled. "Now you see sense!" He shrugged. "You'll soon realise that we can make you do anything and make you enjoy it too." He worked the grease all around the insides of Rachel's buttocks, and well into her stinging, anus. Then he got down on his knees behind her. "Now get ready!"

Viciously, he pulled the globes of her buttocks apart and again he nudged his member against her anal ring. "Keep still!" he warned again. "This might hurt me as much as it does you." He giggled then and made one vicious lunge at her soft flesh. He yelled his pleasure, as his member sank into her abused body.

Rachel screamed out as even the grease failed to ease the pain, as her virgin flesh gave way, tore open, despite the stretching it had received from the plug. She sobbed as she felt the massive organ surging into her.

Toshio paid no heed whatsoever to her discomfort and he laughed aloud as he ground into her defenceless body.

Rachel felt her internal flesh distending and she shrieked out her agony, until she became too hoarse to shout any more. She began to cry as the evil sadist Toshio lunged into her body again and again, his upper legs slapping against her tight buttocks. He began to roar out as his passion mounted and his member swelled even more.

Rachel let out another agonised shriek as Toshio grabbed her hips, pulling her against him, stretching the leather straps to their limit. He rammed himself right home into her body his fingers digging deep into the flesh of her hips, as he held her wriggling posterior hard against his loins. His member pulsed, sank even deeper into Rachel's body, filling her, invading her soul almost. Then Rachel screamed out in agony as she felt the enormous penis swell until finally, Toshio yelled out his passion and climaxed. Yet another scream was wrenched from the helpless Rachel as her shattered body was filled with a hot jet of his seed.

Still the awesome member pulsed its load into her, surged upwards into her body, Toshio's final thrusting pushing deep into her and she screamed, frantically trying to move her hips away from him. It was hopeless and all she did was force herself into the tight embrace of the leather bindings around her limbs, the leather searing her flesh. Her insides seemed to be bursting. She vented one awful shriek, as the agony seared her mind, then the pain went. Suddenly, she sagged in her bonds, a great sadness overcoming her as she heard Toshio's breath rasping in her ear.

"That was very good," he was saying, so matter-of-fact. "You are becoming a true slavegirl now." A deep chuckle, as he moved away from her. She heard him go from the room, leaving her, like a chattel. A toy for which he no longer had any use.

Rachel knew she was finished, never to be the same again. She felt used; dirty. Even if she got away from these monsters, who would want her now? Quietly she began to sob into the leather of the birching-stool.

It seemed only moments after Master Toshio left, that Hartman came into the room. Without a word, he unfastened her from the birching stool and pushed her unceremoniously to the floor, grinning as she sprawled onto her belly. He looked down at her in contempt. "On your knees slave! Show me your buttocks." Weary now, with all resistance gone from her, Rachel obeyed, lowering her head, turning away from him, and pushing up her buttocks. Then a scream was dragged from her and she arched her back in pain, as the butt-plug was savagely re-inserted into her ravaged anus.

Hartman seemed oblivious to her suffering. He fastened the plug in place, tightening the chains around her hips. Next, he slipped a leather half-hood, over her head and tightened the straps. The hood was provided with slits, so she could just see and groaned as she saw him taking a ball-gag from the hold-all.

"Open you mouth, slut!" he snarled.

Rachel obeyed, and he rammed the ball into her mouth, tightening the gag behind her neck. Then he wrenched her arms behind her back and clipped on a pair of handcuffs. He chuckled as he looked at his bound slave, then reached upwards to a length of heavy chain. The chain had been doubled up out of the way and with a sadistic grin on his face, he unhooked the end and lowered it to its full length. As if she were a bag of feathers, Hartman lifted her and slipped the hook through the chain at her wrists. Then he let her go.

Rachel fell just a short distance, but all of her weight came onto her shoulder joints and she screams through the ball-gag, as she reached the limit of the chain, leaving her suspended about a foot or so from the floor. Screaming through the gag, she was now swinging slowly about, and Hartman waited patiently, until she quietened. Finally Rachel had stopped crying out and with her face contorted in pain, she was gasping, her saliva dripping from the gaga, as she tried to bear her torture.

But, Hartman wasn't finished yet. He walked across to the rack near the door and took down a thigh spreader. Sauntering over to the suspended Rachel, he fitted the bar between her feet, clenching the bracelets tightly to her ankles. Then he stepped back to gaze at Rachel's fully exposed genitals.

Then Rachel's heart leapt with fright, as she heard the door clatter open and footsteps approaching her. An idea! She could feign unconsciousness. They might leave her be.

She tried to make it look good, letting out a moan, then allowing her head to fall forwards. Through half-closed eyes, she saw the Sheik coming close. She knew it hadn't worked. Even if it had fooled them, it wouldn't have mattered. They were going to torture her, and that was it.

The Sheik grinned up at her. "Give her a taste of the whip Ernst!"

Hartman stood back, and took his dog-whip from his belt.

The whipping began and Rachel babbled into her gag, screaming and struggling, her breasts jiggling about, as the thin leather cut into her exposed flesh. Soon the room was full of her futile screams as her defenceless body was comprehensively worked over by the evil Hartman. Time after time the leather raised red and blue welts on her skin and only when her screams had been reduced to hoarse gasps, did Hartman cease the onslaught.

He tucked his whip back into his belt and stepped over to her, lowering her abused body a little. He grabbed her hair and lifted her head to look into her wracked face. He removed the ball-gag from her mouth. "Now slut!" he said. "Are you ready to serve as a slavegirl should, or do I start all over again?"

Rachel's heart sank as she finally realised she was finished.

She could stand no more. It was time to face up to her fate. She knew that escape was impossible, and that she was here for the rest of her life, or until they decided to let her go. Which was highly unlikely. So, she had to submit, fully, and become their slave. She didn't like the idea, but it was better than suffering this continual punishment and abuse. There would be enough of that anyway. These monsters liked torturing their slavegirls, but it was never so bad as when she was being punished for disobedience. So long as she obeyed, they would perhaps spare her the worst of their sadistic ways. She nodded, and through her pain, murmured her answer softly.

"I'm ready Master! I'm ready! You know I'm ready!"

"What are you ready for bitch!"

Rachel was submissive now and she hung her head, as she whispered. "I am ready to serve as your slavegirl Master!"

"And what does that mean slut!"

"That I will do anything Master!"

"Willingly!"

"Willingly Master!" Rachel knew she had submitted herself completely now. Strangely she felt relieved. Perhaps her masochistic tendencies had finally surfaced properly and a hidden desire to be a slave really had been awakened. At least, would help her through the trials to come. She nodded, "I am your slavegirl Master! I will obey. Always!"

Hartman chuckled. "I think she's ready Excellency!" He caressed her legs again, allowing his hands to wander over the swell of her tortured buttocks. "She's been awkward, but she was worth it, Excellency." He stroked her buttocks again. "That's better now, isn't it slut!"

Rachel nodded, submissively. "Yes Master!"

Hartman then lowered her completely to the floor, and quickly unshackled her legs. He lowered her so her feet touched the floor, then released the hook from her wrists. He held onto her shoulders as she tottered a little, then he said. "Kneel, slave!"

Rachel dropped to her knees, gasping as the butt-plug seared her with a burn of pain.

Hartman grinned. "I think we can take the plug out now." He bent, and undid the straps. Then, slowly he withdrew the evil plug, which Rachel realised had been pushed further into her by her struggles under the whip. Maybe it was the overall agony she was feeling from that lashing, but strangely the removal of the plug caused little pain. She merely winced as the thing was drawn clear.

Hartman pushed her head downwards. "Present those buttocks," he commanded.

Rachel obeyed, her stomach churning, her mind full of panic, panic she knew she dare not show.

The Sheik stepped forwards and stroked her waist and buttocks. "So! I have another brothel-slave to add to my flock. At last you are ready to give pleasure to your Masters and Mistresses! Is that right little slave?"

Again Rachel nodded. "Yes Master, it is right!"

The Sheik patted her buttocks gently. "Then welcome to your new life!" He lifted Rachel's head a little. "And just one last word of warning. For you, there will be no escape. You understand that my little white-slut?"

Rachel nodded. She knew the truth of it now. She lowered her head. "I understand Master!" she said.

The Sheik grinned triumphantly and turned to Hartman. "Ernst, She is ours! Take her to the recovery suite and unchain her. When her bruises have healed and she is fit enough, she can take her place in the Pleasure Palace."

Hartman chuckled sadistically. "At once Excellency." He bent to Rachel, grabbed her arms and lifted her gently to her feet, He turned her to face the door and nudged her forwards. "Walk on, slave."

Rachel knew now, knew that she really was theirs; a submissive slavegirl who belonged to them completely. They could do with her as they wished and she knew she would suffer at their hands. Much as she knew she ought to feel sad, Rachel, had to admit to a pleasurable tremor of anticipation, that caused her stomach to flutter. She didn't know why this was so, but she accepted it, as a true slavegirl should. So, with her head bowed, as befitted her lowly status, she obeyed Hartman and walked towards the door and the start of her new life of slavery.

End

Here is the opening of our book for next month, NAKED TRUTH II, The Whip Hand, by "Nicole Dere"

Vee turned in the darkness at the bottom of the stairs. She could see the eyes glinting in the black face, the flash of his teeth at his smile. Her heart was pounding with excitement, and with fear. You're mad! her brain screamed. Absolutely mad! He's a boy, for God's sake! Sixteen years old, seventeen at the most. One of your own students!

But already that other, wickeder part of her brain was chuckling that it was too late. Behind his bulk, the front door was shut, securely locked against the outside world. And that hulking shape was far from boyish. That was what had started the whole thing, the sudden vivid reminder of that other towering shape, the rebel sergeant who had plucked her naked form up so easily the night of her capture, in that far off African land, and who had later so potently possessed her body in the narrowness of that stifling tent.

At least, that's what had started things for her, what had led to this seminal moment in this blackness at the foot of her stairs. Though, in her defence, she had to argue that it would never have been, but for the chance encounter with Wayne Grainger, and the breathtaking insolence of his approach to her. She could spread the blame farther - her desolation, the loneliness of this poky little flat, her feeling of being so cut off from every human contact and emotion, and at Christmas, too. The one time of the year when even the most feeble familial ties and relationships were strengthened, however temporarily. And there was no one, no one at all, she could turn to, or be with, in this freezing festive season.

It didn't help to tell herself that was what she had wanted, planned for herself, glad only to escape into anonymous isolation after the glare of world media attention had focused so mercilessly upon her. She recalled the shock of seeing those photos of her, and of the Danish girl, Katya, both naked, staring forlornly into the lens, and the others, in the glossy magazines and the newspapers which Keith, her husband - ex-husband, she reminded herself bitterly - had hoarded away in his sick jealousy.

Those unrelenting newshounds had almost ferreted out the truth, that her marriage was on the rocks before her captivity in the rebel's hand's, but even so, after the trauma of her months of capture, she had clung tot he hope that her relationship with Keith could somehow be saved. When it all fell apart so catastrophically soon afterwards, she had fled back to England like a fugitive, afraid that she would never escape the terrifying publicity. But her brother David had been right. A change of name, of hairstyle, burial in the anonymity of London and the humdrum existence of a schoolteacher, had worked all too well. Until the ache of loneliness and the need for some kind of human contact other than the cautious, guarded role she was forced to play at work, had driven her to this desperate madness.

The heavy hand on her shoulder brought her back with a jolt. "You gonna keep us 'ere in the dark all night then, Miss?" Wayne's voice rumbled with laughter.

She knew that the 'Miss' was far from a term of respect. Quite the opposite. He was mocking the status which had been so comprehensively shattered in the last eventful hour or two since they had met in the launderette. She had been breathless, rigid with shock, at the sight of that great dark hand closing over the delicate little scrap of her underwear, crushing it as he picked it up from her bag, rubbed it savouringly across his smiling lips, so that those other, secret lips of her own, hidden smotheringly under the layers of winter clothing, had twitched and spasmed in helpless thrill. And somehow, fiendishly, he had known about it. It had led inevitably to that same hand cradling in her back, steering her out into the garishly lit, steambreathed night, and, in the awful, sneaking intimacy of the under table groping in the coffee bar, those thick fingers outlining the groove of her beating, moist sex through the thickness of her woollen tights, the hugging dampness of the body shaper.

She turned, climbed ahead of him up to the flat. The lamp light was discreet, even cosy, hiding the bareness of the rented bolt hole. She hurried across and turned the gas fire on full, though Wayne blew out his cheeks as comment on the heat thrown out by the central heating, which had never been off since the start of the holiday three days ago. "Jesus! You really have come from Africa, incha?" He tossed his fleece jacket onto the sofa, stood there grinning at her.

She blushed fiercely, could not meet his direct, mocking gaze. "What we talked about", she stumbled, her voice husky and small. "I don't want any of it to get out. To anyone. It's a secret. I'm sure you can understand. I don't want to have to run away again."

"My lips are sealed, Miss. As long as you promise to be nice to me, that is. And speakin' of lips. How's about a little Christmas kiss, eh? Just to get the ball rollin', as it were." He moved easily towards her, and she glanced up at him, wide eyed.

"Don't you think - " she stammered, her blood hammering. "I mean - is it a good idea? I'm your teacher. Older -"

"Old enough to be my mother?" he cut in aggressively. "No fuckin' way! How old are you? Twenty four? Five?"

"Twenty six." Her voice shook. She tried a pathetic little smile. "A lot older than you. Ten years."

He shook his head fiercely, closed in on her. He pulled the woollen hat from the back of her head, unwound her scarf, dragged off her beavy coat. He let them fall on the rug. "Forget that shit. Come here!" He grabbed her, pulled her against him. His head bent, his mouth seeking hers, with frank sexual hunger. She was limp. She did not struggle or reciprocate his urgency, but when his lips closed over hers, she felt her blood racing, and eventually, with a smothered whimper, she opened her mouth, and the kiss became mutual, a blaze of raw passion. His tongue drove into her, and she clung, shaking in his tight embrace.

She was panting, half weeping, when he released her mouth. His arms still clasped her to him. "You're all clothes!" he growled. "I want to see you. See what you really look like." He put his big hands on the hem of her sweater, pulled it over her breasts, her shoulders, then her head. The short, fair hair was tousled when he pulled the heavy cloth clear. The thin straps of the body bisected the fragile hollows of her shoulder bones, its thin cotton clung to the rising shape of her slight breasts, whose erect nipples thrust against the cloth. The pale divide showed above the dipping piping of the garment's edge.

All the while, she stood submissively still, trembling, offering no resistance or assistance. His hands fumbled with clumsy haste at her thick skirt, finally succeeded in unhooking it, drawing down the zip, and pulling it down off her hips. It fell with a soft whisper to catch at her ankle boots. The thick black tights came up to just below her breasts. "You are fuckin' wrapped up. It's like pass the parcel, this is!"

She stared down at the woolly kinks of his hair as he knelt and lifted her legs, to ease her skirt clear of her ankles. He unlaced the heavy boots, slipped them off. The great fingers reached up, hooked into the high waistband of the tights, rolled them down, dragged them slowly down her thighs, her calves, and she lifted her feet obediently, one after the other, so that he could remove them altogether. Her voice caught on a sob. "My luh - legs! They're skinny!"

He came slowly upright, his hands moving over the curve of her behind, only half concealed in the body shaper. "I like my gals skinny," he said. The fingers plucked at the shoulder straps, pulled them down to where they clung to her upper arms. She could feel her excitement, weakening her now with its need, feel the wetness, the swelling of her crotch, her vagina spasming with her excitement, and suddenly she was both afraid and titillated by her need.

"Wait!" she cried out shrilly. "I want to see you, too." Her fingers went to his chest, where the buttons of his shirt lay, but he thrust her hands roughly aside, and peeled off his upper garment hastily. The muscled sheen of his torso took her breath. She timidly laid her hands on the dark, satin flesh, quivered at the intensity of the contact. Suddenly, she sank to her knees in front of him, and her fingers tore at the flies of his jeans, clawing, fighting, and again his hands were there, undoing himself with difficulty, so that she could tug down the clinging garment until it hung hung about his knees. He wore tiny striped trunks underneath, filled with the huge swell of his genitals. She could see the rounded head of his prick, the dark patch of wetness at its helm. She smelt the yeasty male tang of him, her throat already working as she reached out, gently now, fearfully, and eased the elastic down, to bare his manhood.

She saw the tight, small scrub of pubis, then the long, writhing column of his prick uncoiled, like a live creature, the helm already poking clear of the thick ruff of foreskin. The split was agleam with moisture. It leapt to meet her, the shaft springing forth, jutting proudly. And it was hot under the reverent touch of her fingers.

"What - ?"

She cried at his protest, stilling him. "No! Please!" she

begged. Her fingers were stroking, stirring, sliding up and down the hard column, whose giant head bobbed in front of her eyes. Frightened, transfused with her own pounding excitement, she bent forward, let its slimy wetness touch her brow, before smearing it worshipfully across her features, into the depths of her eyes sockets, along the sides of her nose, rubbing it across her closed lips, larding herself in the cloying thickness of his issue, anointing herself in the fluid abundantly seeping from it. Then her tongue poked out, flickered in a paroxysm of ecstatic fear across the slit of that pale dome, tasted the sweetness of his emission before her lips stretched wide, and she strained her jaw to take its massive beat inside her warm, suckling mouth.

Her head turned slightly sideways as she drove herself down, jaws agape, working furiously, until she gagged at its filling shape choking her. She bobbed up, her lips sliding to the dome, then she plunged down again, swallowing him as far as she could, dizzy at the savage swelling thrust of him into her. His hands were twisted in her dishevelled hair, tearing at her scalp in his frenzy. Swearing pungently, he dragged her mouth clear of him.

The breath was buffeted from her at the force with which he drove her back, and then fell on her on the rug. She felt his fingers scrabbling, scratching her tender flesh cruelly as he tried to claw the wet scrap of cloth from her loins. She dove between them, her own fingers frantic as she unsnapped the three pop studs to release the garment, which flew up about her waist, and she was as naked as he. She felt that great prick jab and slide all along her soaking, eager slit, and she fought for him, grabbed him, guided his stabbing strength into her madly welcoming sheath. Their pubic bones clashed at their coming together with a grunt which merged simultaneously from their riveted mouths.

She lifted her legs high, her feet waving in the air around his plunging shoulders. She cried with the pain of his burning thrusts, yet her belly leapt upwards to meet them, to impale herself on his driving invasion, helpless against her clamorous hunger, after all these months and endless months of solitary denial. Her head was back, tossing wildly on the hardness of the worn rug, her long throat exposed, its muscles rippling at the cries drawn from her as the orgasm surged up through her, to every part of her jerking frame, died, came again, and again, a roller coaster of consummation that left her sobbingly exhausted.

She whimpered at her renewed awareness of agony, the lancing nightmare now as he bucked, drove, grunted, battering her, before, at last, she felt the deep spurt of his coming, and that fearsome hardness eased, died a little, and they collapsed together, sweating, quivering, clinging in the lost aftermath of their mutual tempest.

She came through from the bathroom, stood in the doorway, staring at his relaxed, naked frame bathed in the rosy glow of the fire. His prick looked dark, vulnerable, small and curled on his thigh. "You'd better go," she croaked. "It's after two. Your folks. They'll be worried."

"They'll all be pissed." He held out his arms. Wearily, she walked across to him, very conscious of his gaze on her nakedness as she moved.

"God! I can hardly move. I'm sore just about everywhere." And that was no exaggeration, she thought. She lowered herself carefully beside him, and he folded her into his arms, so that she half lay on top of him, her head on his smooth shoulder. His hand moved between her thighs and she caught at his wrist, held him from laying it on her vulva. "Please! Not there! It's swollen up like a football. I haven't - done this for so long I've forgotten what it's like."

"I can't believe that." He shook his head in what seemed like genuine wonder. "You - you're fucking gorgeous."

She giggled. 'Thank you, kind sir." Her voice was serious as she resumed. "I mean it, though." She felt herself blushing. "Not since - before I left my husband. A long time before."

"He must be bloody mental."

And so must I be, she acknowledged tiredly, lying here literally shagged out with a school kid. Could I go to gaol for it? she wondered, not really alarmed at her speculation. No. There's nothing kiddish about this hunky specimen of young manhood in my arms. And, oh God, how much I needed him - it - after all these endless, sterile months of trying to satisfy myself each nights. And most mornings, too, and with nothing but the most temporary of reliefs. Well, maybe I've got it out of my system for a good while. Or have I?

She knew clearly that it would not be so. That she had stirred up a whole new hornet's nest of troubles for herself by her crazy action. Wayne was no little pupil, to be patted on his curly head and sent back to his seat with a winning smile. "Thank you, Wayne. There's a good boy. That was very nice. Now go and sit down and behave yourself."

She felt ashamed at the realisation that she did, indeed, just want him out of the flat. Out of her life altogether, until the next time she felt the overwhelming urge for a fuck. It wouldn't be like that. It never was. His next words proved it. "It's Christmas Eve tomorrer. Sorry. Today. I'll come round tea time. I've got a present for you." He gave a broad smirk..

TITLES IN PRINT

Silver Moon

ISBN 1-897809-08-5 Barbary Pasha *Allan Aldiss*
ISBN 1-897809-14-X Barbary Enslavement *Allan Aldiss*
ISBN 1-897809-16-6 Rorigs Dawn *Ray Arneson*
ISBN 1-897809-17-4 Bikers Girl on the Run *Lia Anderssen*
ISBN 1-897809-20-4 Caravan of Slaves *Janey Jones*
ISBN 1-897809-23-9 Slave to the System *Rosetta Stone*
ISBN 1-897809-25-5 Barbary Revenge *Allan Aldiss*
ISBN 1-897809-27-1 White Slavers *Jack Norman*
ISBN 1-897809-29-8 The Drivers *Henry Morgan*
ISBN 1-897809-31-X Slave to the State *Rosetta Stone*
ISBN 1-897809-36-0 Island of Slavegirls *Mark Slade*
ISBN 1-897809-37-9 Bush Slave *Lia Anderssen*
ISBN 1-897809-38-7 Desert Discipline *Mark Stewart*
ISBN 1-897809-40-9 Voyage of Shame *Nicole Dere*
ISBN 1-897809-41-7 Plantation Punishment *Rick Adams*
ISBN 1-897809-42-5 Naked Plunder *J.T. Pearce*
ISBN 1-897809-43-3 Selling Stephanie *Rosetta Stone*
ISBN 1-897809-44-1 SM Double value (Olivia/Lucy) *Graham/Slade**
ISBN 1-897809-46-8 Eliska *von Metchingen*
ISBN 1-897809-47-6 Hacienda, *Allan Aldiss*
ISBN 1-897809-48-4 Angel of Lust, *Lia Anderssen**
ISBN 1-897809-50-6 Naked Truth, *Nicole Dere**
ISBN 1-897809-51-4 I Confess!, *Dr Gerald Rochelle**
ISBN 1-897809-52-2 Barbary Slavedriver, *Allan Aldiss**
ISBN 1-897809-53-0 A Toy for Jay, *J.T. Pearce**
ISBN 1-897809-54-9 The Confessions of Amy Mansfield, *R. Hurst**
ISBN 1-897809-55-7 Gentleman's Club, *John Angus**
ISBN 1-897809-57-3 Sinfinder General *Johnathan Tate**
ISBN 1-897809-59-X Slaves for the Sheik *Allan Aldiss**
ISBN 1-897809-60-3 Church of Chains *Sean O'Kane**

Silver Mink

ISBN 1-897809-13-1 Amelia *Josephine Oliver*
ISBN 1-897809-15-8 The Darker Side *Larry Stern*
ISBN 1-897809-19-0 The Training of Annie Corran *Terry Smith*
ISBN 1-897809-21-2 Sonia *RD Hall*
ISBN 1-897809-22-0 The Captive *Amber Jameson*
ISBN 1-897809-24-7 Dear Master *Terry Smith*
ISBN 1-897809-26-3 Sisters in Servitude *Nicole Dere*
ISBN 1-897809-28-X Cradle of Pain *Krys Antarakis*
ISBN 1-897809-32-8 The Contract *Sarah Fisher*
ISBN 1-897809-33-6 Virgin for Sale *Nicole Dere*
ISBN 1-897809-39-5 Training Jenny *Rosetta Stone*
ISBN 1-897898-45-X Dominating Obsession *Terry Smith*
ISBN 1-897809-49-2 The Penitent *Charles Arnold**
ISBN 1-897809-56-5 Please Save Me! *Dr. Gerald Rochelle**
ISBN 1-897809-58-1 Private Tuition *Jay Merson**

*UK £4.99 except *£5.99 --USA $8.95 except *$9.95*